Down & Dirty: Hawk

Dirty Angels MC®
Book 3

Jeanne St. James

Editor: Proofreading by the Page
Photographer/Cover Artist: Golden Czermak at FuriousFotog
Cover Model: Mav Willett

www.jeannestjames.com

Sign up for my newsletter for insider information, author news, and new releases:
www.jeannestjames.com/newslettersignup

Dirty Angels MC, Blue Avengers MC & Blood Fury MC are registered trademarks of Jeanne St James, Double-J Romance, Inc.

Keep an eye on her website at http://www.jeannestjames.com/ or sign up for her newsletter to learn about her upcoming releases: http://www.jeannestjames.com/newslettersignup

Author Links: Instagram * Facebook * Goodreads Author Page * Newsletter * Jeanne's Review & Book Crew * BookBub * TikTok * YouTube

Chapter One

Hawk grunted.

About fucking time.

As the annoying high-pitched buzz sounded, the magnetic door lock released and the reinforced steel door clanged open, he glanced up and saw a guard pushing through the door.

He'd been sitting here long enough, waiting in this sparse room that only housed a bolted-down, dented and scratched metal table and two chairs that sat unevenly on the concrete floor.

Not that he had anywhere else to go. He was stuck here until the club's attorney showed up and did his legal hocus-pocus to get him the fuck out of county jail.

All he knew was that he did not look good in an orange poly-cotton blend. He preferred denim and leather. He'd rather not be wearing a *one-size-does-not-fit-all* jumpsuit at all. It wouldn't take much flexing for him to split the seams with the one he currently wore.

Like the Hulk.

He grinned.

But that grin was quickly lost as the person following the guard into the room did not look anything like his lawyer.

Not unless the Dirty Angels MC's attorney had a sex change operation, lost at least fifty pounds—which included a gut—and slapped in colored contacts. Not to mention, found some sense of style.

Hawk closed his dropped jaw before he started to drool like a fool. Because, for fuck's sake, slobbering all over himself wouldn't be very badass biker. Not. At. All.

He drew himself up straighter in the uncomfortable metal chair and puffed out his chest until the top snap of the jumpsuit popped open.

Then he let his gaze slowly run down that fine piece of ass from top to toe.

Oh, fuck me, he thought as he took in the woman's long, wavy dark brown hair, her plump *suck-my-cock* lips, her bouncing tits that wanted to bust out of the blood-red blouse that fit her like an *if-you-can't-acquit* glove, her narrow waist, her *not-so-narrow* hips, which were encased in a black skirt that only came down mid-thigh—thighs that would fit perfectly around his ears—those long-ass, lickable calves, slim ankles, and... *fuck... higher-than-hell* heels.

She could walk all over him as long as she wore those fucking shoes.

He heard the clearing of a throat and reluctantly lifted his gaze to flashing, but amused, deep blue eyes.

He hadn't even realized the guard was gone and the door had been closed. They were alone.

With a hard-on that wouldn't quit, he now couldn't wait to get back to his cramped cell to rub one out. He didn't even care if his cellmate watched. Fuck that strung-out weasel dick.

"Where's Pudwhacker?"

And when that vision opened her mouth to speak... Yeah, he just about creamed in his county-issued tighty whities. "I was assigned to your club by Mr. Pannebaker."

"Why?" came out sounding more like a grunt than a question.

"Because I'm good—"

In bed? I'll be the judge of that.

"And he's busy," she finished.

The woman yanked the chair away from the table and the metal legs screeched along the filthy, pitted concrete floor. She smiled when he winced at the sound.

"You gonna be able to sit down in that skirt?"

She proved it when she slid that ass, which he had yet to get an eyeful of, onto the seat.

He was jealous of that scrap of metal. No doubt. She should be sitting on his face instead.

"Sure thing, Mr..." She flipped open his file, ran a long blood-red fingernail—one that matched her blouse—along a document inside and then tapped it. "Mr. Dougherty."

"You wear that for all your clients? Or am I special?"

She plastered on an *I'm-only-here-because-I-have-to-be* smile. "All my clients are special, Mr. Dougherty."

"I'm sure," he muttered. "Bet everyone who pays those fuckin' high hourly fees feels special." He reached around and rubbed his ass. "Feelin' *real* special right 'bout now."

She tilted her head and considered him. "You wouldn't have to pay anything if you hadn't been arrested."

Well, that was true. But sometimes statements had to be made and he, as well as his club brothers, had to be the ones to make them.

"Shit happens."

"That it does. So here we are. Can we get started, Mr. Dougherty?"

"Hawk."

She pursed her lips for a moment. And in that moment his balls tightened painfully. Damn, didn't he want to shoot his load all over her face.

Suddenly, she dropped her torso beneath the table and then popped back up. Hawk watched as her tits also bounced back, testing the top button of her deep V-neck blouse.

He blinked. Since when were threads so damn strong?

Then his breath rushed out of him loudly when she slipped on a pair of glasses.

Holy fuck. She just became every man's sexy librarian wet dream.

I've been a naughty boy, Ms. Librarian.

She placed some sort of flat computer that didn't have a keyboard on the table. What Ivy would call a tablet or some such shit. Not that he cared. He didn't fuck with those types of things. He barely knew the basics when he used the computer at his bar and even then, he let his computer whiz of a cousin do the rest.

He didn't have time for that shit.

She dropped her gaze to the folder. "So, I went over your charges—"

"Read my last name without your glasses."

Her head rose and those deep blue eyes blinked at him. "What?"

"Read my name without your glasses, now you need 'em?"

She stared at him. "I forget to put them on sometimes since they're just for reading. Your name was a bit blurry, but I could make it out. Does it matter if I'm wearing my glasses or not?"

Fuck yeah it does. Especially if you're naked.

And in my bed.

"Gotta name?"

Her mouth opened and closed once before she said, "Sorry, I should've introduced myself. I'm Kiki Clark."

His brows shot up his forehead. "Kiki?"

"Yes, sir," she said on a dramatic sigh.

Hawk muttered, "What the fuck."

She shrugged. "Ask my parents."

"So, you ain't lyin'."

"I never lie."

His brows shot up once again. He had a hard time believing that coming from an attorney.

"Okay, maybe sometimes. But only when it's important. Like when someone's freedom hangs in the balance."

Well, damn. "You lie to judges," he stated.

Without even the slightest hesitation and a fleeting smile, she answered, "I plead the fifth."

Hawk leaned back in his chair and barked out a laugh. "Yeah, you're just like a real super hero rightin' wrongs." He shook his head. "Damn, wanna get in your skirt."

"I'll dry clean it for you first if you would like to wear it. Might be a bit tight on you, though." She lifted a shoulder slightly. "No loss for me, since I've never been fond of it anyway."

"Fuckin' goddamn," he whispered.

She arched a brow. "Does that mean good?"

"Fuck yes. For me, anyhow. But I'll make sure it's good for you, too."

"I'm relieved," she said, sarcasm dripping from her voice. "I've already had too many selfish pricks in my bed."

"I'm not a selfish prick."

"So you say."

He studied her, wondering how many notches she had on her bed post. "How many is 'too many?'"

"You first, Mr. Dougherty. How many women have *you* had in your bed? I've heard rumors about those biker parties."

"If you're talkin' about at the same time... then a few. Wanna be one?"

She adjusted herself in her chair, then pushed her glasses higher on her nose. "How about we just agree to keep our relationship on a professional level. Me as the lawyer and you as the defendant."

Hawk gave her a half-assed grin. "Doubt that's gonna happen."

She made a noise. "It'll happen."

"You say so, babe."

Now she gave him a *Do-I-really-have-to-tolerate-this-asshole?* smile. "I certainly do, *pumpkin.*"

Hawk snorted and his grin widened. He liked a challenge. And she was pushing all his buttons. In the right way.

She again arched a perfectly shaped eyebrow at him. "Now, can we get down to business?"

He wasn't ready to get down to business. Or at least the business she was here for. He liked playing with her. And she didn't seem to mind it, either. He liked that. No, he fucking *loved* that. "Right here on the table?"

She shook her head and sighed, then ran her gaze over his head before switching gears without a warning. "Did it hurt to get your head tattooed?"

It hurt like a bitch. "Tickled."

Now both of her brows rose. "You're ticklish?"

"Wanna find out?"

"Another time, but thanks. The guards might frown upon it if we get into a tickle fight."

Hawk's grin widened. They'd probably be jealous, if anything. "Not scared of bikers, are you?"

"Should I be?"

"Depends how bad they wanna fuck you."

"You want to fuck me..." She glanced down at her file. "Hawk? Is that your real name?"

"Yeah. On both accounts."

"*Ah.* Okay. I'll take your uncontrollable desire into consideration before I step into a dark room alone with you."

Once again, Hawk sat back in his chair, crossed his arms over his chest, and smiled. She was a feisty one. Classy. Curvy. A lot of hair to pull. Smart and a smart ass mouth, as well.

Right up his alley.

Yeah, he liked a good challenge.

He might have to taste her between her legs to see if she was sweet as well as spicy.

"Gotta get outta here. Got a bar to run."

"Right." She peeked back at her paperwork before meeting his gaze directly. Head on. Nope. No fear at all in those eyes. "The Iron Horse Roadhouse. Maybe you should have thought about that before you kicked that biker's ass."

"Just defendin' myself."

She leaned forward, giving Hawk a better view of her tits. "So, let me get this straight, the man that you knocked out and badly injured put his hands on you first?"

Shit.

"He put his paws on DAMC property."

When she noticed where his eyes had focused, she sat back. "Him specifically? Or someone in his club?"

Hawk shrugged, then stretched his neck out toward the left and then toward the right, cracking his spine, before answering, "Don't matter. All the same."

"Not in the eyes of the law."

"Justice is blind," Hawk grumbled, thinking about the ten years the former club president, Zak, spent in prison for a crime the Shadow Warriors set him up for.

Fuckers. They deserved everything they got and then some.

"I can't disagree with you on that. That's why I got into criminal defense."

Speaking of defense... "Where's my brother?"

"The other Mr. Dougherty has been released."

What the fuck? "How'd he get sprung an' my ass is still sittin' in here?"

Kiki lifted a shoulder, one he wanted to sink his teeth into as he was making her come. "He didn't waste my time trying to get down my pants. Or up my skirt."

Right. He was sure Diesel would take a shot at that if given half the chance. "Doubt that's the reason."

"And you would be correct. Though this can't be proven, I have a feeling your brother's size alone intimidated the witnesses. No one saw him do anything but hold the front door open to the pub to let the rest of your crew in."

Lucky fucking bastard.

"What did these so-called witnesses see me do?"

"They saw enough that you would be held responsible for the damage."

"So, has nothin' to do with crackin' some Shadow Warriors' heads. Just the damage to that bar?"

"Sort of, but not exactly."

"That's clear as fuckin' piss."

"I agree."

Hawk grunted. "Club'll pay for the damage."

"Already done."

He cocked an eyebrow. "So what's the hold up?"

"I have to go before the District Justice and plea for leniency. He

7

seems determined to make an example of at least one of you. You came into his jurisdiction and wreaked havoc, Mr... Hawk. Judges tend to frown upon that. They tend not to like motorcycle gangs—"

"Club," he corrected her.

"What?"

"Club," he barked. "DAMC's a fuckin' club, a brotherhood, not a gang."

"Okay, well," she pushed her glasses up her nose once more. "Club, then. Judges tend not to like *clubs* going to war in their area. Can you see where he's coming from?"

"You know this DJ?"

"Yes."

He narrowed his eyes as he watched her face carefully. "Good?"

"Very well, yes."

Hawk leaned forward over the table until they were almost face to face. "You fuck 'im?"

He couldn't miss the uncomfortable swallow and the flash of shock that crossed her expression. Finally, he got a reaction from her. But it quickly disappeared as a blank mask slipped over her face.

"I'm not going to answer that. That's simply ridiculous."

"You gonna wear a skirt like that when you plead my innocence?"

When she sighed with impatience, Hawk's gaze became glued to the rise and fall of her chest.

"I'm not pleading your innocence. I'm shooting for a reduced sentence."

"Then you plan on fuckin' me an' not in a good way."

"I'm going to do my best to get you out of here and back to your *club* and your *brotherhood* as an 'upstanding business owner who made an unwise decision that won't be repeated.'"

"An unwise decision." Hawk snorted. "In self-defense."

"No. I'm not going to insult the judge that way. You've learned from your time here and you've learned from your mistake. You're taking this as a life lesson and will be a better citizen because of it."

Damn, she was good. She almost convinced him with that bullshit. "Sure, babe. Sounds like a plan. Long as it works."

8

"It'll work if you keep your mouth shut in the courtroom and you don't stare down the judge in defiance. You let me do all the talking, while you're as quiet as a church mouse and looking as harmless as one, too."

"Mice can do a lotta fuckin' damage."

Hawk bit back a laugh when she slapped a hand to her forehead and her eyes bugged out behind those sexy little glasses. "Fuck my life," she said under her breath.

Damn, that was hot. "Love a classy lady with a dirty fuckin' mouth. Wanna wrap my fist in all that hair when you're suckin' my cock with it."

She opened her mouth, blinked, sucked in a deep breath and then sighed loudly before saying, "You really know how to sweet talk a lady."

"Don't want you to be a lady. Want you to be a hellcat. Not prissy. Sweatin', screamin', bitin', scratchin', fuckin'. Comin' so hard you see spots."

"Well, all righty then. Let me pull up my calendar so we can schedule that." She held up a finger as she tapped an app on her computer/tablet/electronic thingy. "Date?"

"First night I'm outta this joint."

"Location?"

"On the floor, against the wall, on a table, in my bed."

"Well, that's a lot of typing." *Tap, tap, tap.* "Okay, let me make sure I got this down correctly... *Suckin', scratchin', bitin', sweatin', fuckin',* and..." She glanced up from her tablet.

"Screamin'. Forgot screamin'."

"Ah." She nodded, tapping the screen. "*Screamin'.*" She lifted a brow his direction. "Anything in particular?"

"My name."

"Got it. Screaming *H-A-W-K*. All that against the wall, on the bed, the floor and hanging from a ceiling fan. Right?"

He smirked. "That'll do for starters."

"Right. I can't wait."

"Me neither." She might be taking all of this like a big joke, but she was going to find out just how serious he was.

She focused her pretty blues on him. "Can you promise me one thing?"

"What's that, babe?"

"It's going to be the best fuck I've ever had?"

Fucking goddamn. "Have a feelin' it's gonna be the best fuck I ever had."

She tapped her finger against her bottom lip—which he had the urge to bite—then tilted her head. "Okay, I lied. I need another promise."

His lips twitched. "Shoot."

"If I get you out of here, you're not going to punch anyone else."

He studied her a couple beats. "Can't promise that, babe."

"Why?"

"Got enemies."

Her eyes narrowed. "Who?"

He zipped his lips shut.

"Who?" she prodded. "Those bikers you beat up in that bar?"

Hawk leaned forward, no longer amused at the direction the conversation was going. "Know you're new to this. Know you're here to help me, help all the brothers when we're in a jam. Know it. Appreciate it. But you'll learn... Club business, babe, ain't a woman's business. When you're needed, you'll get the info we can give you an' no more. Got me?"

Kiki abruptly shoved her chair back with a squeal and stood. "Sorry, but no, I don't *got* you. You want me to stick my neck out for you and your boys—"

"Brothers," he cut in.

She ignored him and continued, "Then you need to be open and honest with me or you can hang out to dry for all I care. *Got me?*"

Hawk smiled, leaned back in his chair and ran his gaze over her once more. Yep, he was going to get a piece of that hellcat. "Damn, woman, can't wait for that appointment."

"We have to get you out of here first."

"You do that."

She stepped closer to the table to look down at him. "Are you going to be checking out my ass when I leave?"

"Fuck yeah."

With a nod, she spun around, strutted her way to the door and pressed the buzzer.

Hawk didn't miss the guard checking out her ass, either.

Son of a bitch.

Chapter Two

KIKI SAT behind the table about to not only face an unhappy judge but she was being seared by the heat of the large biker sitting next to her, who just stared at her.

Well, she did tell him not to stare at the judge. So, it *was* all her fault.

She really should rethink her career. She should switch to real estate law like her ex. Elder law, family law. Something, *anything* other than defending a badass biker and his "brothers."

She bit back a groan. If she knew this was where she would end up, she certainly wouldn't have joined Pannebaker's firm. Even though it was one of the best criminal defense firms in the area.

She should be wondering how a motorcycle club consisting of a bunch of derelicts could afford Pannebaker's hourly rate. Though, they had no problem paying for the damage done to that pub in South Side. The club's treasurer, Ace, simply scribbled out a check for six figures. He didn't even tell the owners to hold it before cashing. No. He said it was good and could be deposited right away.

Imagine that. But all that money could come from illegal activities. Though, Pannebaker assured her she wouldn't be representing an outlaw club, that they were on the up and up.

Kiki let out a snort. Right.

"You okay?" came the deep voice next to her.

She refused to turn her head toward him when he was this close. His heavy denim-clad thigh brushed against her stockings. No suit for this guy's courtroom appearance. No. He insisted on wearing his whole biker get-up sans the vest with filthy patches she insisted he *not* wear.

She cleared her throat. "Perfect. Remember to keep your mouth shut and at least appear sorry for your actions," she whispered.

"Not sorry."

She ground her molars and then unlocked her jaw. "Act like it."

Fingers brushed along her knee and then the skin at the edge of her skirt. She sucked in a sharp breath.

"Get outta here today an' then we'll have our appointment later."

Oh good lord. He actually took her serious when she made that so-called appointment. She had to clear that misconception up and do it quickly.

"I was only kidding about the appointment," she whispered fiercely. She gritted her teeth against the shiver that wanted to run through her as his fingers climbed her thigh.

She should be very afraid of this man and not for the obvious reasons.

"I wasn't," he said way too softly.

Apparently.

Before she could smack his hand away, the District Justice entered the room and they all stood, including the hunk of tattooed muscle next to her, who was suddenly stuck to her side. Like Gorilla glue.

Kiki swallowed hard and her nipples pebbled under her blouse. Great. That wouldn't be too obvious.

"Ms. Clark," Judge Powers greeted her.

She shifted an inch to the right to give herself some breathing room. "Your Honor."

He sat and so did everyone else. Well, everyone except for Hawk.

"Sit down," she demanded under her breath, tugging at his faded Myrtle Beach Biker Week T-shirt.

With a smile, he sat, his body visibly shaking in silent laughter.

"So, what do we have here, Ms. Clark? A," the judge glanced down at his papers, "member of a motorcycle gang who decided to come into my district and make a mess."

"Club, Your Honor."

Judge Powers looked up. "What was that, Ms. Clark?"

"It's a club, Your Honor, not a gang. They're not engaged in any illegal activities." Holy crap, she hoped that was true.

"A club," he repeated like he was taste-testing the word. "You mean a club like the Boy Scouts?"

"Very similar, sir."

The judge let out a bark of a laugh then his eyes swung to her client, then back to Hawk's father, Ace, and his brother, Diesel, who sat in the seats directly behind them.

"What badge do they get for beating up a member of another *club*?"

"Your Honor, Mr. Dougherty has seen the error of—"

Powers raised his hand, palm out toward her. "Save it, Ms. Clark. I wasn't born yesterday."

"But—"

Powers interrupted her again. "Here's the deal, Ms. Clark. You want to defend such upstanding gentlemen? That's fine. But maybe you should be responsible for them. Or at least," he wagged a finger at Hawk, "this one."

Oh shit. "Your Honor..."

"No, Ms. Clark. You can be his babysitter for the next three months."

Oh shit. "Your Honor, please!"

"Want me to make it six?"

Oh shit. Kiki sucked in a breath. "No, Your Honor."

And not just no. Hell no! She did not want to get stuck being responsible for a damn biker. Pannebaker couldn't pay her enough.

For crissakes, she'd quit.

Walk right out.

Powers leaned forward. "Here's the deal. Take it or leave it. I'm sentencing him thirty days for the reduced offense of simple assault."

Kiki couldn't miss Hawk's large frame straighten and go solid next to her.

She ignored him. "Thirty days, Your Honor... That's—"

Powers raised his palm again. "Let me finish, Ms. Clark."

Shit. "Yes, Your Honor."

"I'll release him on time served which is the ten days he already did, but and this is a big but, Ms. Clark, he needs to keep his nose clean for the next three months and he needs to do some sort of community service. I'll let you decide what that will be. But I do want a report. In addition, you'll be responsible to make sure he serves that community service. Then you're free of him. I suggest letting them pay you for your time."

Kiki opened her mouth to respond, but the judge wasn't done yet.

"Furthermore, he needs to stay out of my district. His whole *club* does. I don't want to see them again. He's lucky I'm not slapping an ankle monitor on him for the remainder of his thirty days." Powers lifted an eyebrow in Kiki's direction. "What do you say, Ms. Clark? Does your client want to walk free today or cuddle up with his cellmate for a few more weeks so they can read each other bedtime stories?"

She glanced at Hawk, who was looking down. Not at the table, no. But at her feet. The heels she was wearing to be more precise.

Oh good lord.

"Can we have a minute, Your Honor?"

"Sixty seconds. Go."

Kiki sank her butt into the chair and twisted toward her client.

"Those are so fuckin' hot," he said in a low, deep voice.

Jesus. His voice alone could make her panties soaked.

"No time for that. Do you want to take the deal? I'm not thrilled about—"

"Why? 'Cause you'll be stuck to me?"

"I won't be stuck *to* you. I have better things to do with my time—"

"Take it. Ain't goin' back to that hole. Anyhow, me an' you got an appointment I don't wanna miss." His dark brown eyes stared into hers. "You ain't missin' that appointment, either."

Right. "We'll discuss that later."

"No discussin' to be had."

"Times up, Ms. Clark."

Kiki pushed to her feet. "We'll accept that, Your Honor. He'll be glad to do community service. He has all kinds of progressive ideas on how to serve it."

The judge snorted then got serious. "Fine. Just see that it's done." Powers pointed a finger toward Hawk. "Stay out of my district."

When Hawk opened his mouth Kiki laid a hand on his shoulder and squeezed hard. "He will, sir. No problem."

"Right."

Then they all scrambled to their feet as the judge got up from his bench and disappeared through a side door.

A large presence behind her made her shiver. She looked over her shoulder to see Hawk's brother standing right behind her with their father, an older and slightly, but not by much, smaller man.

Diesel clasped hands with his brother and did a shoulder bump over the divider that separated them, then Hawk turned toward his father.

"Pop."

"Boy, you're lucky you ain't doin' more time than you did."

"Keeks got it covered."

Keeks. She sighed. She already hated the name that her hippie, yoga-loving parents had given her but him calling her *Keeks* made it so much worse. She'll have to thank them again the next time they returned to the States from one of their "soul-cleansing" retreats.

Ace's eyes landed on her. "I see that."

"We gotta date later."

Oh shit.

Ace's eyebrows rose. "Yeah?"

Diesel let out what sounded like a combination of a grunt and a caveman chuckle before muttering, "Lucky bastard."

As one of the sheriff's deputies approached them, Kiki cut in to interrupt the touching family reunion. "Okay, you need to go with the officer back to the jail. And I need to do paperwork. As soon as every-thing is processed, they'll release you."

"Diesel will pick you up," Ace said to his son.

Hawk shook his head. "No. Keeks is gonna pick me up."

I am? She stared at Hawk.

"Go on back to church or home. Wherever. She's got this covered."

I do?

He curled a heavy arm around her shoulders and pulled her against his side. "Right, babe?"

Oh shit. "I... uh..."

Ace snorted and shook his head, whacking his son on the back. "Got good taste, boy." Then he turned and walked away.

"Wait," she started, looking desperately at Diesel. "You're going to pick him up, right?"

"Nope." Then he also turned and walked away.

She twisted her neck toward Hawk who still held her like a vise. "Let me go," she whispered.

"Let's go," the deputy said to Hawk, who gave the uniformed officer a big smile.

"Gotta go. See you in a bit, babe." And with that, he dropped his head and planted a big, wet kiss on her lips before pressing his mouth to her ear. "Don't be late. Got a lot to do."

He gave her a wink as the deputy escorted him out of the small courtroom.

Kiki sank into her chair and dropped her head into her hands.

Jesus.

Just what in the hell had she gotten herself into?

SHE ASKED herself that again when she pushed through the double glass doors of the county jail, Hawk hot on her heels.

"Babe. Wait up."

Every time he called her babe she wanted to close her eyes and scream. But she was a woman on a mission, one she wanted to finish as quickly as possible. And closing her eyes when she was rushing down the concrete sidewalk in three-inch heels might end badly and delay getting the man out of her hair.

"Yo, babe."

"If you're talking to me, my name is Kiki," she threw out over her shoulder.

"Yeah, 'bout that..." Suddenly he caught up to her. Which was actually no surprise. He might be bulky but he was tall, too, and his long legs had eaten up the distance between them. "Babe, slow down, don't want you breakin' your pretty little neck in those fuckin' shoes of yours."

Kiki skidded to a halt and slammed her hands on her hips, her briefcase smacking hard against her thigh. When he stopped and turned to her in surprise, she stated, "Let's get something straight right now. You don't get to boss me around."

The corner of his lip twitched and Kiki had to fight stomping her foot in frustration.

"'Kay, babe. Got any more rules?"

"Yes, don't call me babe, damn it!"

He shrugged his heavy shoulders. Shoulders which were covered by a black leather vest decorated with those filthy, disgusting patches on both the front and back.

"Hate your name, babe. Sorry. It's the name of some stuck-up bitch."

She blinked. At least they agreed on something. "Then call me Ms. Clark."

Now the other side of his mouth twitched. "Only gonna do that if you're wearin' your glasses an' nothin' else."

All the oxygen left her lungs in a rush. She shook herself mentally at the image his words put into her head.

What the hell? She was *not* getting naked with this man. This biker who had tattoos all up and down his arms, even on his scalp. And probably the rest of his muscular body.

No, she wasn't.

"Babe."

She glanced up from his broad chest and met his amused gaze. Oh good lord. She was actually considering it. What was wrong with her?

"Don't have to imagine what I look like naked. You'll see for yourself soon enough."

Kiki closed her eyes and sucked in air slowly, counting to ten. And when she was finished, she realized she was no longer considering it. "Fine. Let's go."

She was doing it.

Fuck it.

She only saw his look of shock for a split second before she strode forward, leaving him frozen in place behind her.

She smiled and headed to the visitor's parking lot and to her car with determination.

When life hands you lemons...

And all that crap.

When she got to her car, she turned to wait for him, wondering how he was going to fold his bulk into her Corvette Z06.

"Fuck me," Hawk muttered, stopping feet from her little red Corvette and staring at it.

"Just so you know, your club will be helping me make the payments on that." She dug into her black leather briefcase, searching for her keyless remote.

"Then I drive."

Without looking up she said, "No."

As soon as her fingers snagged it, he pulled it from her fingers. "No woman drives me. Whenever me an' you are in a cage, I'm drivin'. Not an argument. Fact."

"Cage?"

"Yeah." He jerked his chin toward the Vette. "That ain't a cage to you, but one to me. But I'll suffer through drivin' that sweet thing, then I'll be drivin' into somethin' that's even sweeter."

She bit back a whimper and squeezed her thighs together. What was wrong with her? There had been plenty of times where men whistled or cat-called at her or said some perverted, stomach-churning things, but she'd never reacted like this.

Not once.

And now she had to get into close quarters with him. In her tight sports car. Why the hell did she ever buy that car?

He surprised her by opening the passenger door and offering his hand. She stared at his broad palm and long fingers. His tattoos stopped abruptly at both wrists like the cuff on a sleeve.

"Not gonna bite you."

She lifted her eyes to him.

"Okay, yeah I am. But not now." Then he laughed, which shot lightning down her spine and it landed right in her center, heating her belly.

She'd lost her damn mind. That was the only thing she could think of when she wondered why she was reacting to him like this.

She usually preferred men who wore suits and ties, polished shoes and expensive watches. Tailored dress shirts and pinstripes.

Not worn, holey jeans, a Harley T-shirt that looked like the sleeves had been ripped off, a leather vest and—her gaze dropped—heavy biker boots with all kinds of buckles and zippers on them.

Yes, she had lost her mind. Truly. Completely.

She sighed, placed her hand in his and let him help her into the car.

Chapter Three

KIKI CHEWED HER BOTTOM LIP. She had no idea where he was taking her. Normally she wouldn't be afraid to ask, and even though she was in no way shy, she wasn't sure if she really wanted to know.

Maybe it would be easier to swallow if it was a surprise.

Because, apparently, the man who had stuffed himself into her driver's seat took his "appointment" with her very seriously. What had started out as a joke for her just to get him to cooperate, now wasn't so much.

However, the longer they drove, the more curious Kiki became on what it would be like to just let loose with someone like Hawk. It wasn't like they traveled in the same circles, so no one would ever know. Plus, she was sick of men who were afraid to mess up their carefully styled and gelled hair during sex.

She was bored with the so-called "gentlemen" she'd dated after the separation from her husband. Their conversation was mediocre at best since they tended to talk more about themselves and boast about their many successes. Even worse, their skills in bed were just so-so. Once again, even in bed, they were more worried about themselves rather than making sure she was also satisfied.

Though, she couldn't imagine the man sitting next to her cared about anything other than getting himself off, either. She turned her head just enough to eyeball his bulk.

"Did you even graduate high school?"

Without taking his eyes off the road, they crinkled at the corners and he barked out a laugh. "That a requirement to get into bed with you?"

I don't know, is it? She never thought about any "requirements" for a man who she had a relationship with, sexual or otherwise. But she did have some standards. She did tend to gravitate toward a certain type of man.

However, the more she studied Hawk as he drove her car, the more she doubted he met any of those standards.

"To answer your question, babe, yeah, I did." He finally turned his head to meet her gaze. "Feel better?"

No. No, she didn't.

When he turned into a short, paved driveway in front of a house in a town called Shadow Valley, which sat just southwest of Pittsburgh, she blinked.

She leaned forward and looked closer at the small house through the windshield. It was well-taken care of with wood siding and painted shutters, a covered wood porch that ran the length of the front. It was a cute two-story cottage, or what some may call a bungalow, with dormers and everything. And surprise, surprise, it was in a really nice middle-class neighborhood.

What. The. Hell. "Are you lost?"

Pulling up next to the house in front of a detached, matching cottage-like, two-car garage, he put the car in park and shut off the engine.

He shoved the driver's door open and, with a curse and a groan, untwisted himself out of the low, cramped sports car. Then he leaned into the open doorway and gave her a look. "Stay put."

She did. He was probably just going to run inside to grab whatever from whomever owned this house and then off they'd go again to what he had called church, which was apparently the clubhouse where most of the members resided.

But she watched in shock as he moved around the long, low front end of the Vette and came to the passenger side to open the door. He leaned in really close—like she was glad he smelled like soap and not like he'd *just-done-a-ten-day-stint-in-County* close—and unlatched her seat belt before offering her his big, meaty hand.

She stared at it like she had no idea what it was.

He shook it at her. "C'mon. Let's get crackin'."

Her eyes traveled up his arm until she had to lean out a little bit to see his face, which clearly showed his impatience. "Why?"

"Whataya mean *why*?"

"Why am I getting out? Aren't we headed to your place?"

"So you wanna go back to my place?" His impatience quickly dissipated and he gave her a grin.

Uh oh.

"Well, I thought that was the plan..." Her voice drifted off when his whole face changed and his eyes darkened.

"Yeah, babe, it is. Didn't think you were all in. But now I see you are. Good to know." He offered his hand again and this time she tentatively took it.

Was she *all in*?

With a grip that could easily crush her hand, he helped her out of the car, and before letting her go, he pulled her against his chest and wrapped his beefy arms around her, embracing her tightly.

She automatically grabbed his biceps, her eyes dropping to his hard muscles as she squeezed them.

Yes, she may just be all in. At least for tonight. Tomorrow she'd scrub him off and go back to her life.

"So soft, babe," he murmured in her ear as he palmed her hips, his breath fanning the hair by it.

Her thighs quivered and she felt a traitorous rush of wetness. "And you're so... hard."

He tilted his hips, brushing his denim-clad crotch against her, proving his muscles weren't the only thing hard.

Her breath caught in her throat and her heart began to pound. "Aren't you anxious to get going?"

Because if he wasn't, she sure was. Or at least the lower half of her body was.

"We'll go in the house in a sec."

"No, I meant back to your place."

He leaned back and stared down into her face. "Babe, this *is* my place."

Wait. What?

"You don't live at this 'church' Pannebaker told me about?"

"Got a room to crash there. That's it. Got tired of that shit years ago. Bar does well, club coffers are full. Ain't hurtin'."

Whatever all that meant. But even so... "I wasn't expecting—"

He released her abruptly and stepped back. His eyes narrowed and he gave her a sharp nod. "Right. Bikers like me can't have nice things." He tilted his head toward her car. "Like your Vette."

"I didn't—"

"Like a house."

"I—"

"Like you."

"Me?" she asked, her voice *slightly* higher than normal.

"You," he repeated. "Though that's gonna change in a few."

"I wasn't expecting this." She glanced over her shoulder at the very normal looking house and then back at Hawk.

"Expected me to be slummin' it, huh? Some stained mattress with dirty sheets, or no sheets at all? Empty beer bottles an' cans? Cloud of pot smoke? Bunch of drunk bikers scratchin' their beer bellies an' belchin' with naked bitches runnin' 'round?"

Umm. She decided to keep her mouth shut, but that actually was what she had expected.

Her boss had been to their "church" a few times before and described it exactly like that.

"Maybe you're disappointed now you know you won't be gettin' as down an' dirty as you thought. That take away the thrill?"

"I... No. Sorry, I... *shit.*"

She really didn't expect this bad boy biker to live in this quaint little house in the 'burbs of Shadow Valley. She had a tough time picturing him outside mowing the grass or weeding the flowerbeds.

Without warning, she was against her car, his hands grasping both sides of her face as his head dropped and he took her mouth.

He didn't just kiss her. Hell no, he *took* her mouth. Like he was claiming it as his.

His tongue pushed between her lips, shoving them open so he could take the kiss deeper, harder, and she swore he explored every part of her mouth.

A sound bubbled up from her throat as he stole her breath.

Damn, the man could kiss.

Another surprise.

His fingers dug into her hair on both sides of her head, keeping her right where he wanted her. With him holding her head and his big body pinning her against the car, she couldn't escape even if she wanted to.

Though, the longer he kissed her, the more she realized she didn't want to go anywhere but inside.

Their tongues tangled and fought for control, hers pushing against his, trying to take over his mouth instead. But he wouldn't allow it and when he finally broke away, she was left breathless and every part of her body tingled. Her nipples ached for his mouth and she was pretty sure her panties were completely drenched.

His mouth remained a hair's breadth from hers, though, and she flicked her tongue over her lips as she stared into his deep, dark brown eyes. He seemed as shell-shocked as she did.

And that wasn't something that normally happened to her. She could safely assume that may have never happened to him.

He didn't seem shakable.

But he was. And that kiss did it to both of them.

How crazy was that?

"Oh good lord," she finally whispered.

His huge hand pulled out of her hair to cup her cheek. "Fuck me," he muttered as if in disbelief.

Her lips twitched. "After that kiss, I have to say yes."

He dropped his gaze to her mouth for a second before saying, "Wasn't a question, babe. But, after that, glad you're all in."

She lifted her hand to wipe away a smudge of her lipstick from his mouth with her thumb. "Do I have any lipstick left?"

"Nope."

"I was afraid of that. Can we go inside now?" *Before I melt into a big puddle in the middle of your driveway with your neighbors probably peeking from behind their curtains?*

"Fuck yeah," he said softly, then stepped back, snagged her hand and practically dragged her behind him over the concrete walkway to the front door. He dug a set of keys on a Harley keyring out of his jeans and plugged one into the door.

He pushed it open and guided her through, slamming the pretty door with the decorative stained glass panel shut with a *bang* and then turned the deadbolt.

Okay, then. This was really happening. She was going to actually have sex with this man, this... this biker.

Jesus, she truly lost her mind.

As she felt his large presence behind her, she thought *screw it.*

Then she told herself it's only one night. One night to let loose before going back to her neat little life of wearing suits, being a successful attorney and fighting for justice.

She jerked in surprise when her hair was brushed away from the back of her neck and his lips were there. Soft, warm, wet, and... *shit*... her knees started to buckle, until he wrapped an arm directly under her breasts to help hold her up.

Oh shit.

His lips brushed across her skin, then she felt the light scrape of his teeth. His other arm curled around her, though lower... much lower, and he pressed a palm against her lower belly, slowly sliding it down...

Down...

Oh shit, down...

When he cupped her through her skirt, she thought she might self-combust. She dropped her head to the side as he took gentle bites down her neck, only stopping when he reached her suit jacket. He used the arm under her breasts to reach up and cup one in his hand, then a wide thumb brushed back and forth over her pebbled nipple.

"This gotta go." He clearly meant the suit jacket.

Why yes, it did.

And, crazy enough, she was ready to shed all of her clothes and do him right in front of the door, right there on the floor.

He released her only long enough to pull her jacket off her shoulders and toss it on the floor.

Oh God, don't look where your three-hundred-dollar designer suit jacket just ended up. Don't look...

Don't—

Large fingers deftly pulled at the top buttons of her blouse until it hung partially open and his hand slid into the cup of her bra. His cock, solid as a steel rod, pressed into her lower back.

He growled into her ear, "Can't wait to drive my dick deep inside you," then he tweaked her nipple hard, pulling a gasp from her.

She throbbed, actually *throbbed* for this man. She needed to chalk that up to temporary insanity.

That seemed to be a reasonable defense.

As he slipped his hand under her breast and began to lift it out of her bra, he froze.

Then Kiki froze. Her gaze followed a twenty-something female walking through the living room right in front of them. She had her head down as she did something on a cell phone and had earbuds plugged into her ears.

Kiki grabbed the edges of her open blouse and yanked it closed, even though Hawk's hand was still firmly planted inside it.

A muttered, "Fuck," came from behind her.

The young, blonde, very, very, *very* pretty woman stopped dead in the center of the room, glanced up and froze, too. Then her eyebrows shot up her forehead before a slow smile crept over her face.

She popped out one earbud. "Hey, Hawk."

"Where's your fuckin' car?"

Oh boy, the man didn't sound very happy at all.

"The shop. Crash dropped me off." She ran her eyes over Kiki from head to high heels, only hesitating slightly on where Hawk's hand disappeared. "Didn't know you were getting out today. Would've made you dinner."

She makes him dinner and walks around like she owns the place?

Kiki tugged desperately at Hawk's wrist and with a sigh, he released her breast and removed his hand from her blouse.

She was too old for him to be her father. But too young to be anything else.

All of her youth was definitely on display with her slender legs that went on for days out of her teal short shorts and perky breasts that were barely contained in a snug pink camisole that had a drawing of an antique motorcycle on the front.

She gave Kiki a half-assed wave. "Jazz."

Kiki opened her mouth but it wasn't until the second try that she could spit out, "Kiki."

"Really?"

Then Hawk moved, bumping against her back with his chest and pushing her forward, deeper into the room. "Yeah, really. Get in your room an' keep those things in your ears for the rest of the night."

Jazz frowned and looked like she wanted to argue.

"Jazz," came out of Hawk's mouth in an unmistakable warning.

"Shit. Okay. Can I grab a pop and some snacks first?"

"Yeah, get your shit an' get gone."

After throwing a final eyeball at Kiki, Jazz wore a knowing smile as she headed into the open, modern kitchen right off the living room. "Shouldn't panic if the house shakes, right?"

Hawk's deep chuckle surprised Kiki. "Nope." He snagged Kiki's hand as he pushed past her to drag her up the staircase that sat to the left of the entrance. "Don't disturb us, got me?" he yelled over his shoulder.

"Got you," came from the kitchen area.

"Rather she not be here, but gotta do what ya gotta do," he said, climbing the steps.

Gotta do what ya gotta do.

Kiki lowered her voice. "You still want to..."

"Fuck yeah, babe. Been locked up forever."

"Ten days."

"Like I said, forever."

Kiki rolled her eyes as they hit the upstairs landing. "You can't go ten days without sex?"

"Not willingly. Can you?"

"Not willingly," she answered truthfully. Then he threw his head back and laughed.

Kiki stopped at the top of the stairs and stared. The upper level had a completely open floorplan similar to a suite. A *neatly made* California King sat against one wall. Dressers, chairs, and a desk filled up the rest of the area. One wall was lined with closets. She couldn't imagine a biker needing that much space for holey jeans and ripped T-shirts. And from what she could see, there was an en suite bathroom at the back of the room.

But no bedroom door. Nothing to stop anyone coming up the steps and intruding.

She didn't like that.

"She ain't gonna bug us."

She turned to face Hawk, who was shedding his leather vest and tossing it over a recliner that faced a large flat-screen TV that hung on the wall in one corner of the room.

"She'll hear us."

"She ain't gonna listen."

"How do you know?"

"Told her not to."

Well, there you go. He told her not to listen, so she won't. That was laughable.

"Okay, let's get rid of the elephant in the room."

He frowned as he sat in the recliner to unbuckle and unzip his boots. "Whataya mean?"

"Who is she?"

"Jazz."

Kiki closed her eyes and took a breath before reopening them. "I heard that. *Who* is she?"

"My house mouse."

His *what*?

She opened her mouth and then shut it with a groan.

"My house mouse," he repeated like his words explained everything but to Kiki they meant nothing. Then he shrugged before yanking off his boots, tucking his socks inside them and putting them to the side of the recliner.

Hawk pushed to his feet and approached her. Surprisingly, she held her ground until he was so close they were almost touching, but not quite. It didn't mean she couldn't feel his searing heat.

Because she could. She swallowed.

"Ain't a sweet butt, no worries."

And that cleared everything up even more perfectly.

"Umm..."

"Babe, don't be jealous."

Jealous? She shook her head, trying to rid herself of the disbelief that filled it. "You want to explain all that in English this time?"

"Jazz's a house mouse. Lives here. Takes care of me an' the house. Cooks. Cleans. Woman shit."

"And what's a sweet butt?"

"A bitch who spreads her legs for us brothers whenever we want it."

"*Aaaaah*. Okay. That's clear as piss," she said, repeating the phrase he used at the jail the day she first met him.

He grinned.

"Let me get this straight... You have women who will just... sleep with you whenever you want?"

"Not sleep. Fuck. Gotta keep it simple or they get clingy."

"And you partake of this yourself." It was more of a statement of incredulity than an actual question since she was still processing this information.

He cocked an eyebrow. "Babe."

"I'll take that as a yes. So, tell me... What's the difference between a house mouse and these..." She waved a hand. "Other women?"

"Told you what she does. Ain't repeatin' myself."

"So, no sex?"

"Didn't say that." He ran a finger down the open buttons of her blouse then pushed one side away from her breast, exposing her bra.

"You have sex with Jazz."

"Didn't say that, either." He pushed the other half of her blouse away from her other breast. "Gotta get that off you before I tear it off an' snap the buttons."

She grabbed his hands in hers and tried to pull them away before he succeeded in distracting her. To say she was unsuccessful was an understatement. He slid his hands around to her back and undid the clasp. She caught the bra as it fell forward. Though, since she still wore her blouse, it wouldn't have dropped to the floor anyway. But still...

"Hawk."

"Yeah, babe?"

"How old is she?"

He shrugged as he attempted to peel her blouse off her shoulders. She swatted at his hands but he ignored her. "Twenty... somethin'. Twenty-two, maybe. Don't give a shit. Just care she gets shit done 'round here."

"Do you think it's appropriate that a college age girl lives with a single thirty-something year old man?"

"Yep. An' if I touched her, that grumpy old fuck Grizz would have my hide."

But did he *want* to touch her? "Who's Grizz?"

"Jazz's grandfather. Fellow brother. Old as dirt. Wouldn't disrespect him like that."

"Why isn't she his house mouse?"

"He's got one. But 'cause he's got so many grandkids he tries to farm 'em out when possible to help pay for their schoolin'."

"So, she *is* in college?"

"Babe, you gotta stop talkin'. Do I need to stick somethin' in your mouth to get that done?"

"But—"

"Babe, I'll say this once an' that's it." He leaned into her, pressing his mouth to her ear. "Like *women*. Not girls. Like *you*. She's like a niece. Ain't climbin' in her bed. But you soon need to get in mine. Got me?"

All the breath rushed out of her as his deep voice resounded through her.

"Now... can we get naked?"

She tried to fight the smile, but it was impossible. Instead, she kept it contained as much as she could. "Yes, please."

"That's it, babe. Like your spunk, believe me. But right now, need to fuck you."

Yes, you do, floated through her mind.

Chapter Four

HAWK IMPATIENTLY SHOVED her shirt over her shoulders and down her arms until it fell free to the floor. Tugging at her loose bra straps, he tossed that aside, then stepped back and stared.

Fuck.

He should've grabbed her briefcase from the car and made her put on her glasses.

Next time.

He only recently met her but both times they've been together she was dressed as an uptight female attorney would be. Right now, just wearing her tight skirt, stockings and *fuck-me* heels, she didn't look so uptight. She looked downright dick hardening, smoking hot.

He yanked at his erection, adjusting it to a more comfortable position in his jeans before circling her. Brushing her hair to the side, he studied her long, elegant neck. There was something about it that turned him the fuck on.

He was going to leave his mark on that perfect skin, too. And that mark was going to say: "Hawk was here. Back the fuck off. This is mine."

When he ran a knuckle down her spine she visibly shivered. He could imagine that made her nipples pop out into hard peaks.

His mouth will be on them soon enough. Right now, he had to

finish unwrapping the *hot-as-fuck* package that stood in front of him. He wanted his mouth on every inch of her body.

And that surprised the hell out of him.

Sex was sex. Normally, a woman was just a hole to bust a nut into, to get off, to drain his sac. Like his brother Diesel, he didn't want to be tied down, have some woman clinging to him like she owned him, nagging his ass and wearing him down.

No fucking way. He liked his freedom and he was his own man. The back of his bike could remain empty forever for all he cared. He didn't need some bitch dictating to him, rolling her eyes at him, bringing drama into his life.

That's why either the sweet butts or Dawg's girls, the strippers at Heaven's Angels Gentlemen's Club, were good in a pinch. Pop a nut, pull up your pants and show them the door.

This one, though...

Fuck...

He was actually having second thoughts about bringing her into his home, which is something he never did. Ever.

She wasn't his normal fare. Not at all.

And that fucking kiss in the driveway... For fuck's sake, it knocked the shit out of him. He had to be the one to pull free before he fell head first down that deep, dark abyss. A place where he'd have to claw his way back out of.

But now... she stood there, half dressed, tempting him. A tightness pulled at his chest.

Just a taste, he promised himself. Just a taste, and then she'll run out the door after she gets what she wants from him, anyway. She'll go home to her upper-class condo, or whatever, in her car that cost more than his house and wash him off her so she could continue on with her life like she hadn't slummed it for a split second.

He had to remind himself that she won't be hanging around, getting possessive and clingy. Nope. She was only here to scratch an itch, get some strange, and then get gone.

He could live with that.

That was what he preferred, anyway.

Yeah it was.

He snagged the tiny zipper at the back of her skirt between his thick fingers but couldn't get a good grip on it. He grunted with impatience and then her hands were behind her back, slapping his out of the way, grabbing the narrow zipper tab with ease and lowering it until the skirt loosened around her hips. However, it fit so snugly it didn't drop.

He decided to help it along and shoved it down. When it fell to the floor, he said, "Step out."

She lifted one high-heeled foot, then the other and kicked the skirt out of the way.

His gaze roamed over her stockings and, fuck him, if he didn't want to rub his dick all over them.

He contemplated on what to do with all that slippery material that encased her legs, whether to fuck her with them on, as well as her high heels, or to remove them so he could feel her skin against his.

That thought stopped him dead. Sometimes he didn't do more than drop his jeans enough to get his dick out when he fucked one of the women who hung around church and offered themselves up like a Thanksgiving dinner plate.

Nope. But tonight he planned on some real skin to skin contact. He wanted her completely naked. And he wanted to be also. He needed to feel every line of her curves, every crease, every drop of sweat. He wanted to savor both the salty and the sweet taste of this woman.

He wanted the full experience.

A flash of panic swept through him. Was this how Zak felt when he first laid eyes on Sophie?

If so, he may very well be fucked.

He squeezed that thought out of his noggin, shoved his hands into the waistband of her stockings and pulled until they tore. He continued to shred them down her legs until he was kneeling at her feet, running his hands over her ankles.

He pulled off one of her heels, then the other, throwing them over his shoulder.

Then it hit him, neither were saying a word. But he couldn't miss her rapid, heavy breathing.

It wasn't like he was having an easy time of it, either. His chest was rising and falling like he'd run a mile.

His head was about to explode. And not just the one attached to his neck, either.

He rose to his full height and circled her once more, his eyes not leaving one inch of her untouched.

She only wore black lace panties that matched her bra. They needed to go, too. But first...

He dropped to his knees in front of her, grabbed her hips and shoved his face against the front of her panties. He nuzzled her mound with his nose and inhaled her scent deeply. His dick kicked in his jeans wanting to be released, wanting some relief. But he needed to taste her first.

Pressing his mouth against her, the fabric became damp and clung to her pussy. He traced his tongue along the elastic that circled her thighs before tucking his fingers into the waistband and slowly tugging them down her hips and...

Fuck him.

That pussy not only smelled sweet, but when he licked along the small strip of hair and down her crease, he realized she tasted sweet, too. Suddenly, he couldn't rip her panties down fast enough. They dropped to the floor and he grabbed her inner thighs making room for him to get his tongue in deeper. She almost lost her balance with his hurried actions and grabbed his shoulders to keep from falling.

He buried his face, slid two fingers along her pussy to open her up and sucked at her clit. Somehow through his foggy brain, he heard her say something or make a noise, whatever. He didn't care. But he needed to get closer. Her standing wasn't letting him do what he really wanted to do. Which was bury his face completely in her cunt. He growled in frustration and pulled away, gazing up her body.

Her head was tipped down and she was watching him, her unfocused eyes said it all. She was ready for him, she wanted him. No fucking doubt about it.

Even if it was only for the next hour or so. She was his for as long as she was in his house, in his room, in his bed.

So, he needed to take his time.

"Gotta get you on your back, babe, so I can eat your pussy good."

"Okay," escaped her on a breath.

With a grin, he pushed to his feet. Before dragging her over to the bed, she stopped him with a hand on his arm. He looked down at her fingers wrapped around his forearm before looking back up to her face.

"Wait. You need to get undressed, too."

That he did.

Then before he could do it himself, she was yanking his T-shirt out of his jeans and ripping it up his torso and over his head. She balled it up and threw it, then hesitated as she stared at his chest.

Yeah. Reality might be hitting her about now as she studied all of his tattoos. Her palm pressed against his pectoral muscle and she met his eyes. "That's a lot of ink."

"Yeah, babe, it is. It bother you?"

She shook her head as her gaze ran over his skin. "No... Do they all mean something?"

"Yeah. Most of 'em."

"Maybe one day you can tell me the story behind each one."

Hawk's nostrils flared as he sucked in a breath.

Maybe one day...

Fuck. She might be a clinger. Though, for some strange reason, he felt no dread at the thought.

So he pushed it aside. He certainly wasn't a *needs-to-explore-his-feel-ings* type of guy.

They were there to fuck and that's what they were going to do. All that other shit he could deal with later after he drained his balls dry.

"Gonna finish or do I gotta do it myself?"

She smiled and took a step back. She lifted her chin at him. "Go on. I want to watch."

Fuck him. She wanted to watch him strip down. His cock kicked again against his zipper, which he quickly yanked down after unbuckling his belt and unfastening the top button.

He shoved his jeans down his thighs and he noticed her gaze followed his movements. Then her eye shot back to his in surprise.

"You don't wear underwear?"

"Nope."

"Damn," she whispered as she stared as his erection which was long and hard, now bobbing free.

And, fuck him, when she licked her lips, he just about shot his load.

He finished removing his jeans and then quickly grabbed her arm to propel her over to his bed.

"Babe, so much I want to do to you right now. Don't even know where to start."

She climbed onto the bed and all the way to the headboard, settled on her ass, bent her knees while spreading her legs and said, "Start where you left off."

He stared at what she just offered up to him. "Yeah. Think that's a good idea."

He followed her onto the bed to settle between her legs. He watched her run her fingers up and down her slit, teasing him.

After a moment, she opened her fingers to a V, showing him how shiny and pink her center was. "*Bon appetit.*"

"Fuck me," he muttered and couldn't help but grin before he buried his face against her.

And he enjoyed his meal. He stroked his tongue along her folds, fucked her with it, flicked at her clit, sucked it, and then finally, he shoved two fingers deep inside her.

Her hips jerked and she cried out. Curling them forward, he worked her until he felt it. She came so hard there was no mistaking it. He couldn't wait to feel her convulse like that around his dick.

Even before she came down from her orgasm, he had hands wrapped around her ankles and was pulling her down the bed, shoving her knees up and driving deep.

Then he had to stop, close his eyes, and take a breath. The soft liquid heat surrounding his dick was just about his undoing.

It took him a moment before he realized she was wiggling like a wild cat underneath him. He thought it was because she was impatient for him to start moving, to start fucking her hard and deep to bring on another one of those intense orgasms.

But the words she kept repeating finally sank into his mushy brain. "Hawk... condom..."

Fuck.

His heart skipped a beat. How could he forget shit like that?

"You need a condom."

Problem was he didn't keep any at the house and he already used the one he kept in his wallet before getting thrown in jail.

He opened his eyes and searched her face. "You on the pill?"

Her mouth opened, shut, then opened again. "What does that—"

"You on the pill?" he asked again, more forcefully this time.

"Yes, but—"

"We're good."

Before she could complain any further, he began to move, driving hard into her, rocking her body, her tits swaying. He sucked one of her nipples into his mouth, scraping the tip with his teeth.

Underneath him, she arched against him, tilting her hips to take his onslaught.

"Hawk..."

He lifted his head for a split second. "Yeah, babe, say my name." Then dropped it to snag the other nipple with his mouth, sucking it as hard as he could.

"Hawk..."

Damn, his name on her lips made him want to thrust deeper, but he was hitting the end of her already. When she tightened her inner muscles around him, his pace hiccupped.

Holy fuck.

Now he was afraid this was going to end sooner than he planned. As his balls tightened, he slowed, closed his eyes and told himself he needed to keep his shit together. He couldn't blow his load this quickly. Couldn't do that and have her want to come back for more.

He released her nipple and blew out a breath. "For fuck's sake," he grumbled. He slowed to a stop and pressed his forehead to hers, mumbling, "Just need a sec."

"Hawk..." Her saying his name with that husky voice of hers just made it even more difficult to keep himself under control.

"Fuck, babe. Gotta say, your shit is sweet. So fuckin' sweet. Gotta understand I'm strugglin' here a bit. Gotta say I love you sayin' my name when I'm fuckin' you, but need to quit for now. Just 'til..."

Her nails clawed at his ass as she totally disregarded everything he just said. "Hawk, fuck me."

"'Kay, but—"

"Just do it!"

Goddamn.

She wanted him to just do it, then it was going to get done. He ground his hips hard against her, and she hissed out a "yes."

"Want me to just do it you're gonna hafta keep up."

"I'll keep up. Go!" She slapped his ass. Hard.

He jerked at the stinging pain.

Jesus.

He wasn't sure if her being bossy was turning him on or not. What the hell... he was just going to go for it. If she didn't come then that was her problem now, he was trying to take care of her needs first, but—

"Let's go!"

Damn.

He let go, giving it to her like she wanted, and the woman became a hellcat underneath him. Clawing at his ass, his back, sinking her teeth into his shoulder. Screaming at him to fuck her harder and faster.

And damn if she didn't come two more times, one right after the other. Each time her body rippled around him like a rock thrown into a pond. And that just drove him right to that dangerous edge.

He was *right there.* He grunted as he slammed her hard, her body moving up the bed with every thrust.

Finally, he wrapped his arm around her shoulders to keep her in place, curled his body over hers and made her come one more time before he threw in the towel. He couldn't hold back any more and not combust.

With a shout, he emptied deep inside her and then struggled to keep from collapsing on top of her as his dick throbbed for a few more beats.

He stared down into her eyes and she stared back up at him, both panting, their skin slick with sweat. Her blue eyes widened and then she burst out laughing.

Laughing. What the fuck?

"What's funny?"

Then she whacked him on the shoulder!

"Nothing."

"Why're you laughin'?"

"Because I didn't realize how much I needed this until right this moment. I *sooo* needed this."

As the tightness in his chest loosened, he reluctantly pulled out and fell heavily to her side. "Been a while for you?"

"No."

Her abrupt but honest answer bothered him. He'd hoped she said yes, that she'd been going through a long, *looong* dry spell.

"Then what?"

She turned her head to look at him. "Just the stress of work, that's all. It was nice to just let it all go."

"Nice?"

She reached up and brushed her fingers over his mohawk, then traced one of the tribal tats he had on his scalp.

"Yes, nice."

"Gonna damage my ego, babe."

She smiled as her gaze ran over his face. "You know, you're pretty handsome for a brute of a man."

"No shit."

"Those women are probably beating down your door."

"I tell 'em not to fight over me, there's enough to share."

"So you like more than one in your bed at a time?"

"Had this conversation already."

"Yes, we did."

"Am I just another notch on your bedpost?"

Was she?

She was the first woman he ever brought to his home. Which was why he didn't keep wraps in the house. If he was going to fuck a woman in an actual bed, then it was in his room at church. Never here. He kept a drawer full of wraps at church. For good reason.

"Nope."

"You're just saying that so you get a shot at fucking me again before I leave."

His mind started to spin. "When you plannin' on leavin'?"

She shrugged. "When we're done."

And if we're never done?

"We're not done," he confirmed.

"No," she said softly. "Not yet. But eventually I have to get back to—"

Your life, he silently finished for her.

She sighed and then gave him a soft smile, lifted up onto her elbow and stared down into his face. "There's another elephant in the room..."

"I'll get my gun," he muttered.

"I have to know... Do you use condoms with the rest of the women you're with?"

"Always."

"Oookay. But you didn't with me. I have to admit that worries me, Hawk."

"No worries. You're covered."

"Yes, but..."

He reached up, curled his hand around the back of her head and pulled her down until her forehead touched his. "No worries. Always use it with others. Keep my shit clean. No kids. No clap."

She blinked. "Right."

"Right," he echoed, then kissed her long and hard until she was whimpering into his mouth, pressing herself against his side. Without letting her mouth go, he cupped her tit and rubbed his thumb across the tip.

He hooked his leg around her and rolled until she was on her back again. He trailed his tongue over her throat, then realized he forgot something he needed to do.

Lifting his weight off her, he told her, "Roll over."

Without hesitation, she flipped onto her belly and he straddled her waist, pulled her hair away from the back of her neck and sank his teeth in hard.

She cried out, gripping a handful of sheet in each hand. He sucked her flesh, making sure there would be a mark left behind. Something to remember him by, but something she could hide when necessary.

If she was his woman, he'd make her get a tattoo of his name at the nape of her neck. Mark her as his permanently.

Finally, he released her and her hand automatically came back to touch the spot where he bit her.

"Like that?" he asked.

She looked over her shoulder at him, "Not at first, but then... Yes, it... I don't know. Maybe it was the adrenaline rush. I... Damn. I've never been bitten like that before."

"Bit me when I was fuckin' you."

"I did?"

"Babe... that wasn't the only thing you did." He twisted to show her his back. He couldn't see the scratches but he could feel the burn where she clawed him. He just hoped his tats weren't fucked up too badly.

Her eyes got wide and she sat up, pushing at his shoulder, but he couldn't turn any more than he already was without getting off her.

"I'm so sorry. I... Wow, did I screw up those tattoos? They look like the patches on that..." she wrinkled her nose, "vest of yours."

"Worth it if you fucked 'em up. Crow'll fix 'em."

"Crow?"

"Brother who slings ink."

She nodded as if she understood what he just said. Which amused him a little, since he wasn't sure if she did.

"Blood brother?"

"No."

"Do you want me to clean those up for you?"

"Only if I get to fuck you in the shower."

"I meant with alcohol and antibiotic ointment."

"Then fuck no."

"I'm really sorry about that."

"Babe, like you leavin' your marks on me like I left mine on you. Means the sex was good."

"Does it?"

"Wasn't it?"

"I'd have to give it two thumbs up." She gave him a double thumbs up to prove it.

He smiled with satisfaction. "Gotta give me a few so I can give you a repeat performance."

She was quiet for a moment, then said, "Speaking of brothers, I'd ask you how you and your brother got your unique names, but I met your father. Is Ace his real name?"

He shook his head. "Andrew. Though surprised Doc didn't name 'im Ace from the get-go."

"Doc's his father?"

"Yeah."

"Was he a biker, too?"

Fuck yeah, his granddad was a biker. One of the originals. "Built this club from the ground up, babe. Him an' Bear were the founders. Buddies in 'Nam. Got out, settled here. Set up shop. Both survived the war an' then Bear got killed on American soil."

"Oh, sorry to hear that. How did that happen?"

"Warriors an' Angels have had a beef for a long time, babe."

"Warriors?"

"Shadow Warriors," he clarified.

"The bikers you got into a fight with at the pub?"

He grunted. "Same ones."

"How long has this been going on?"

A long fucking time. "Since before I was born."

"Damn," she whispered. "Is it ever going to end?"

He lifted a heavy shoulder. "Dunno, babe. Maybe when the last of the Warriors are gone. Or the last of DAMC."

"Gone?"

"Dead an' buried."

"Oh. Is it that bad?"

"Ain't good. Try to rise above it but those motherfuckers keep pullin' us back in. No escapin' it."

"Is your grandfather still alive?"

"Sorta."

She arched one of her brows his direction. "What does that mean?"

"Can't say doin' life in the joint is actually livin'." Wasn't that the fucking truth.

Her eyes got wide. "He's serving life?"

"Yeah."

"For what?"

"For evenin' up the score."

She frowned. "Eye for an eye?"

"Could say that."

"So, for every action there's a reaction."

"Could say that, too."

She sighed. "It'll never end then."

"Probably not. As long as they're around an' they keep takin' cheap shots, we ain't gonna just let that shit go."

"Well, you could."

He cocked an eyebrow. "Babe."

"Rise above it."

"Can't rise above when Z did ten years for shit when they set 'im up. Can't rise above when they almost snagged his ol' lady. Not sure what would've happened if they'd been successful."

"They tried to kidnap someone?"

"Yeah. Broad daylight. Middle of town. Z standin' right there with his woman."

"Oh good lord," she mumbled.

"Destroyed one of the nicest bikes I've ever seen. Yanked Jag's custom sled down the street with a chain 'til it was nothin' but scrap metal. Still hasn't recovered."

"He hasn't recovered just from a motorcycle being trashed?"

"Babe, Jag sunk two years of work an' forty large ones into that sled. Ain't no 'just' about it."

She nodded quietly. Hawk wondered if forty grand was a drop in the bucket for her.

"'Nough talkin'. Time for me to leave a mark on your ass like I did your neck."

Though she smiled, her answer was, "No."

"Wasn't askin', babe."

"Hawk," she breathed

"Say 'Hawk, fuck me.'"

She swallowed hard enough that he could see it. Then she said in a low, husky voice, "Hawk... fuck me."

With a growl, he tackled her. When she squealed loudly and laughed, it shot right to his dick.

He was ready to get down and dirty once again.

Chapter Five

KIKI'S EYES popped open in a panic. For a second, she had no idea where she was. She only knew she wasn't in her own bed and was pinned against something solid and warm.

She also had no idea what time it was but she could tell it was early morning due to the dim light creeping in from the uncovered dormer windows.

She lifted her head and glanced down at the man she had fallen asleep on.

Oh good lord. She had wanted to leave last night after their third round of satisfying, and completely mind-blowing, orgasmic sex. But somehow that never happened.

Apparently, she fell asleep in his arms and he never woke her up to kick her out. Which she found interesting. She couldn't imagine him being a cuddler. Or wanting to have a woman sleep in his bed beside him all night.

He didn't seem like a man who'd want anything tying him down. Though, owning a house and a business would do just that.

His eyes remained closed and his breathing sounded steady. At least he hadn't snored, even though he was sprawled on his back with her draped over him. Hopefully, she hadn't, either.

She tried to extract herself carefully, not wanting to wake him. But just when she was making some progress, he grunted, his arm tightened around her waist and he jerked her back tightly against his side.

His eyes hadn't opened yet, but she was pretty sure he was awake. She didn't have to lift the sheet to see he was awake below the waist, too. It had risen on its own.

As much as she wouldn't mind taking a fourth crack at him, she really needed to get home, clean up and get ready for work. She had a lot of prep to do for an upcoming criminal trial.

Though, she had to admit that curling around him felt nice and secure. The man was as solid as a rock.

But even so, he didn't fit into her life. Well, it was fun while it lasted...

"I have to go," she whispered into his hard chest.

His fingers trailed up her spine, then back down, brushing over the crease in her ass. She quivered beneath his touch.

He grabbed her hand and shoved it under the sheet, curling her fingers around his hard length. "Gonna help me with that before you go?"

She sighed with regret. "Sorry, I can't. Unfortunately, you're on your own. I have to go get ready for a long, boring day of researching case law and putting together a compelling argument of why my client should be exonerated."

"You'd have more fun with this," he said as he guided her fist up and down his erection.

"I'm sure I would, but that doesn't pay my bills."

"Right," he grumbled.

"I had fun last night, though."

"Right," he grumbled again.

"I appreciate the stress relief."

He lifted his head as she again attempted to pull away. This time he let her go.

"Right," he said once more, this time with a frown.

"I'm sure we'll cross paths again the next time you decide to knock someone out cold and leave them bloodied and beaten in a heap."

"Gotta oversee my community service."

She slipped from the bed and searched the room, gathering her clothes but ignoring her shredded stockings. He could keep them for a souvenir.

She stepped into her panties and pulled them up, avoiding his gaze. "Oh, that's right. Yes... uh. Me or one of my paralegals." She found her bra and quickly corralled her breasts. Ignoring his intense gaze, she leaned over and shook them until they settled more comfortably into the cups.

"You."

She stepped into her skirt, which now was in need of a good dry-cleaning. "Well, I..."

"Babe."

Her head popped up after zippering her skirt closed. "Yeah?"

"Tryin' to scrape me off?"

Scrape him off?

She snagged her wrinkled blouse off the floor and slipped it over her shoulders, fastening the tiny buttons as rapidly as she could. "Uh... no. I just..."

"Light of day, see your mistake?"

"No! *Nooo*... I enjoyed myself. We... both enjoyed ourselves. It was great." And it was, it was just done and over with.

He pushed into a seated position, his eyes narrowed on her. "Right."

"I would love to hang around while you serve me Eggs Benedict Florentine in bed, but I really have to go."

He finally chuckled. "Might get a Pop-tart."

"As long as it's the kind with the frosting... Honestly, Hawk, I have to get going. It was fun."

His amusement quickly fled. "Got you."

Well, it was good that he finally "got her." But now she felt a bit guilty taking off so abruptly. Usually it was the man trying to hightail it out the door after meaningless sex.

Times have changed.

"When's our next appointment?"

She froze in mid-motion while pulling on her shoe. Next appointment?

Like hookup?

Oh shit. She needed to make him aware that this wouldn't happen again. "I'll get someone from the office to contact you in regard to your community service."

"Babe."

She straightened up after finally slipping on her second shoe and she glanced over at the bed. He was sitting up in bed, totally naked, the sheet long gone.

Oh. Good. Lord! Even with his body full of tattoos he was hot as sin. Pure testosterone. She didn't think he had an ounce of fat on his muscular frame and he was well-hung. Not too big, not too small. But just right.

He'd be the complete package if he wasn't a biker, didn't have a record, and had a better command of the English language.

And didn't nail anything that moved with a vagina.

He did seem fairly intelligent and ran a modestly successful business. But still...

She shook herself mentally. *Kiki, you are not going there. Say thank you for the nice time, for the great orgasms, and get the hell out of there before he slaps a couple Pop-tarts into the toaster.*

"I really have to go. Thank you for the wonderful evening."

"What the fuck," he muttered, shaking his head.

With a last smile shot in his direction, she rushed down the stairs, hanging onto the handrail so she didn't break her neck by falling down them.

When she hit the small foyer, she snagged her suit jacket from the floor and her key fob from the decorative shelf by the door and yanked it open.

Rushing out the front door she almost ran smack into Jazz.

"Shit! Sorry!" Jazz cried out, grabbing her arm to keep from slamming into Kiki and dropping the cardboard coffee cup holder with three large to-go cups of coffee. Jazz gave her a look of surprise. "I wondered why your badass car was still out in the driveway. Hawk must be slipping."

Kiki blinked. "Why's that?"

"First, he never, and I mean *never*, brings any females back to the house. And even when he hooks up with sweet butts, or whoever, at church, they never spend the night together."

"Never?" She suspected the first part because what virile, single man didn't have condoms by the caseload in his bedroom?

"Fuck no."

"Wait. What are sweet butts?" Before Jazz could answer, Kiki raised a palm. "Hold on, do I really want to know?"

Jazz grinned. "If you're gonna be Hawk's ol' lady, then you'll find out soon enough."

Ol' lady?

She was smart enough to guess what that may mean in biker terms. She hoped she was wrong, but was afraid she wasn't. "There's no chance of that."

"Uh-huh."

She looked at the young woman in front of her. It was early. Where was she coming from? Had she gotten up at the crack of dawn just to run for coffee? "You okay here?"

Jazz tilted her head. "What do you mean?"

"Do you mind living here? Being this house maid or house mouse or whatever it is?" She waved a hand toward the coffee. "Running errands?"

Jazz threw her head back and laughed. "Yeah. I don't mind it. I like living here and helping out. I get to live in this awesome house for free. Hawk helps pay for my college and books, he's way more lenient than my parents or grandparents, and he's hardly home so I get the house to myself mostly. Plus, he's got an awesome big screen TV with every channel available. Can't forget the Wi-Fi. I have it better here than at home or even in a dorm."

"He doesn't try to touch you or anything?"

Jazz mouth dropped open. "Eww. No! Why would you even ask that?"

Ah, crap. "I just wanted to make sure you didn't need... help or anything."

"I'm free to come and go as I please. Hawk's like having a cool uncle."

Relief flooded through Kiki. "Okay, that's good. Sorry. I never heard of this house mouse thing before so I got a little concerned."

"Kiki, right?"

Kiki nodded.

"Let me just make something clear. I'm DAMC. We take care of our own. Most people think bikers are low-class scum, but I've got it better than a lot of people. I can't complain."

Kiki felt like a complete idiot. "I'm sorry. I didn't mean to make assumptions."

Jazz pulled one of the coffees out of the holder and held it out to her. "I get you're out of your element with Hawk, but don't make assumptions about him, either."

Kiki stared at the cup for a moment then lifted her head and met Jazz's eyes. "No assumptions to be made. We had fun. Now I have to go."

"Just like that."

"Yes, I have to get back..." Her voice trailed off before she finished that sentence with "to my own life."

Then she realized Jazz was still holding the coffee between them. Kiki accepted it. "Thanks, I could use some caffeine about now."

"No problem. Figured you could use a pick-me-up this morning. Even with my earbuds in, it was hard to miss the headboard banging against the wall. My only hope is that when I find a man I want to keep, he has that kind of endurance."

Kiki's mouth dropped open and heat crept up her throat into her cheeks. So much for her not listening.

"I have to go." Kiki turned and headed down the walkway at a quick clip, hoping the morning air would cool her face down.

"Right. Hope to see you again soon," Jazz called out from the doorway. "I can make you two dinner next time and I'll hang something behind the headboard to cushion the wall."

Oh good lord.

Kiki hit the locks on her key fob, slid into her car and after bringing the Vette to a roaring start, she got the hell out of there.

HAWK WANDERED AROUND HER BIG, fancy office in her big, fancy firm in a big, fancy brick office building in downtown Pittsburgh.

He did not belong here.

He did not fit.

Kiki was pure class.

He was...

Crass. And sometimes an ass. Ask anyone, they'd probably say more than sometimes.

Her fingernails clicked impatiently, or possibly even nervously, on her too-neat desk. "Hawk," she started.

"Yeah, babe?"

He didn't miss her eyes flick to her open office door. She didn't want anyone to hear him call her that. Which cemented his suspicion.

"Regret bringin' it down a notch?"

"A notch?" she asked, confusion crossing her face.

"Okay, a shitload of notches."

"I don't understand..."

"The other night." He turned to face her, hands on his hips. "Bein' with me."

Her breath hissed out of her and then she bit her bottom lip, which made his dick twitch in his jeans.

She might be out of his league but she did it for him and he'd do anything to get a second shot at getting her back in his bed. Even if it meant having to patch the drywall behind his headboard again.

She frowned at his sudden grin. "Why are you here, Hawk?"

He shrugged. "Have an appointment."

"Yes, my assistant announced that when she escorted you into my office, so I'm well aware of that. Though, you didn't need to make one, I could've talked to you over the phone."

"Wanted to see you."

"Now that you've seen me, is there business you need to discuss?"

"Yep."

His feet began to move him around her office again since he was too restless to take a seat.

She flipped a hand toward one of the expensive-looking chairs that sat in front of her expensive-looking desk. "Would you like to sit down?"

"Nope."

"Hawk," she said in a tone that reminded of him being scolded. Which brought his thoughts back to her wearing her glasses and looking like a naughty librarian. His eyes landed on her discarded glasses to the left of her computer keyboard.

"Need to put your glasses on?"

She blinked slowly at him then said just as slowly, "No?"

Too bad.

"Hawk," she repeated and his dick kicked in his jeans, which now brought his thoughts to how badly he wanted to drive it deeply inside her.

She was scrambling his brain. "Need to make another appointment."

Her eyebrows rose. "For what?"

"Babe. You know for what. Need one for tonight."

She was silent for a moment. Hawk watched an expression cross her face he couldn't recognize.

"You have no other available prospects?"

He ignored that. "Want you in my bed tonight."

"Uh... Okay, I'll let you know. Is that the only reason you're here? I have a lot of work to do."

"Nope."

She dropped her head and sighed. He grinned. When she finally lifted it she asked, "What else, then?"

"Wanna plan the community service I need to do." This was his excuse to come see her. Not call. Not text. Not even fucking email. Walk into her office and see her in flesh and blood. Wearing one of those *sexy-as-fuck* skirts. Somehow, he needed to convince her to stand up and strut across the room, swinging her hips. Though, if she did that he might have to slam the door shut and fuck her against the wall.

"I read the judge's order. You have three months to complete one hundred hours of community service. You have time."

His brain did a one-eighty and slammed into reality. "Gonna knock that shit out." He didn't like this community service bullshit hanging over him. Get it done, and get rid of that noose hanging around his neck.

"How?"

"Gonna do a Dogs an' Hogs fundraiser." He had already run it past the executive committee during their meeting yesterday and they voted on it. The brothers thought it was a good idea. Not only would the money go to a charity that the club liked to support, it was good community relations, too.

"A what?"

"Dogs an' Hogs."

"What are you fundraising for?"

"Charity that supports vets with PTSD. Rescues dogs from the shelter an' trains 'em up for these guys."

"And it's a valid 501(c)(3) charity?"

A what? "Yeah." At least he hoped so.

She planted both palms on her desk and gave him a great big kilowatt smile. "Well, that's a great idea! What's the plan?"

"Pig roast with some extra shit."

She laughed and his eyes were glued to her mouth when she did it. He wanted to take that mouth right now. Who cares who saw it.

"So, a typical biker party."

"Open to the public. Not havin' it on club property. Gonna rent the fairgrounds."

"In Shadow Valley?"

"Yeah."

She nodded. "Okay, that sounds like a good plan."

He was relieved to see her on board. "Gonna help me."

"Who?"

"You."

Disappointment gripped him when her smile turned into a solemn frown. "I need to help you?"

"Yeah, judge said I'm your responsibility."

Her frown deepened. "Well, no... that's not exactly—"

"Heard it with my own two ears, babe."

"Right. He was just being a hardhead. He clarified the order later that I just need to make sure that you—"

"Babe."

"Yes?"

"You gotta sign off on my doin' time, right?"

"Yes, I—"

"Then you gotta make sure I'm doin' my time."

"But I—"

"Babe."

Kiki sighed. "Look, if you need help, I'm willing to help. It's a good cause and I'm pleased you're picking that particular one."

He moved around the desk and stood over her, looking down into her face as she gazed up at him. Her red lips parted and he could almost hear her panting. Damn, he wanted to unzip his jeans and have her suck his dick right here in her office. Leave a lipstick ring right at the root. His eyes bounced to her open door again then back to her.

He lowered his voice. "Good to hear, babe. Tonight, come over, we'll start discussin' details."

"We have to do it tonight?"

No, I gotta do you tonight. "Yeah, lots to plan. Gotta get started if we wanna get somethin' done in the next few weeks."

KIKI STARED up at the man who now stood behind her desk. She wished he would either sit down or leave. She couldn't get her thoughts straight with his bulk standing over her like that.

She swallowed. Hard.

She fought not to drop her eyes because if she did, she'd be looking *right there*. And she knew what was behind that zipper. She knew it well after the other night. But her neck was starting to cramp.

"Hawk," she began. Then her head twisted to follow his gaze when her coworker and fellow attorney Mike Hepler walked into her office, a look of macho concern on his face.

Shit.

"Are you okay, Kiki?"

Shit.

Mike to the rescue. As close as Hawk was, she could sense when his whole body went solid.

Double shit.

When Mike drew himself up to his full height—which was about six feet, a good four inches shorter than Hawk—Kiki's heart started to pound.

This might not be good. This might not turn out well. Especially for Mike.

She pushed from her seat to her feet and had to put a hand on Hawk's stomach so she wouldn't lose her balance on her heels, since he hadn't moved an inch from where he stood.

Which meant she was pinned between her chair, her desk and him.

Triple shit.

Mike's gaze dropped to where her hand was and she automatically jerked it away, curling her fingers.

She cleared her throat. "I'm fine, Mike."

"Doesn't look like it." Mike took a step closer to the desk.

"I'm fine." She gave him a weak smile. "Really, everything is fine."

Mike's eyebrows shot up but he didn't back down.

She glanced up at Hawk. "Can you just..." She pushed against his stomach again, hoping he'd step back and give her some breathing room.

"No," Hawk grunted, his eyes not leaving Mike, his jaw tight.

"You want me to stay?"

"Really, Mike, he had an appointment. You can leave."

Hawk snorted loudly as if he was egging Mike on. "Is your bitch ass gonna stop me if I do somethin' to hurt her?"

The other man's chest puffed up and Hawk shook his head, barking out a laugh. "See you're wearin' your hair down, babe. Wanna tell ol' Mikey here why?"

Her hand automatically went to the back of her neck and her cheeks became hot. "I have a rash."

"Right," Hawk grunted.

Mike asked sharply, "Is he a client?"

"Yes."

"Is he part of that biker gang Tom assigned to you? I told him—"

"Club."

"What?" Mike asked.

"Club," Kiki repeated. "It's a club not a gang."

Hawk placed a hand on her shoulder and squeezed. "Babe," he said softly, his jaw no longer tight, his gaze no longer hard as steel.

Well, chalk one point up for her, apparently.

She studied the man in front of her. He was wearing black jeans, his black leather vest, a thick leather cufflet on his right wrist, and a bulky silver belt buckle with the letters DAMC at his waist. His fingers sported a half dozen clunky, silver rings, a black bandana hung loosely around his neck, and a long, leather wallet tucked into his back pocket was hooked to a belt loop at the front of his jeans by a long chain.

And he smelled like fuel, exhaust, and some other indescribable thing she didn't want to analyze.

But still, everything about the biker before her turned her on. Maybe she needed to go to a psychologist and get her head examined.

She glanced over at Mike, who was the complete opposite. He wore a tailored suit that had to put him back at least a grand, with a tie and a neatly pressed dress shirt with actual cufflinks, not buttons. His shoes were polished, his Rolex gleamed on his wrist, and Kiki felt comfortable betting a week's salary that he didn't have one tattoo on his Elite Gym membership body. And there was no way the man was straddling an engine with two wheels between his legs. He parked a brand-new silver Porsche Cayenne S next to her Vette in the parking garage.

He'd been trying to get up her skirt for months now, ever since his wife left him. For what, she didn't know, nor did she care. Nice enough guy, a little pretentious, but again, the type she's been dating for a while now and had become bored with.

In bed. In conversation. In life.

But, she had to remind herself, she didn't need to go from one end of the spectrum to the other. She needed to be on the lookout for a nice guy, who was financially responsible, was intelligent and...

"Babe," Hawk murmured in her ear and she jerked.

How long were they all standing there saying nothing?

Shit.

"One of us gotta leave. Gonna go if you agree to—"

She cut him off before he said something outrageous that would spin Mike into a tizzy of macho bravado. "Our appointment later?"

He snorted and his eyes slid to Mike. "Yeah, if that's what you wanna call it."

She sighed. "Fine. Later."

His eyes crinkled at the corners and he pressed his mouth to her ear. "My place. Be there or I'll come find you."

Kiki's thighs quivered and her nipples peaked at the thought of him hunting her down and doing whatever he wanted to do to her as his "punishment" for not showing up.

And for a crazy second she thought that might be fun...

She closed her eyes for a moment and bit her bottom lip. No. No. No.

"Okay. Eight," she said with an acquiescent sigh.

He shook his head. "Six."

"Seven thirty."

"Seven."

Kiki grimaced. "Fine."

With a smile, he finally stepped away, inspected her outfit and then said, "Wear that, lose the panties."

Great.

Her gaze jumped to Mike who stood there with his mouth hanging open. He snapped it shut when Hawk approached him on his way out the door. As Hawk closed in on him, Mike took a step back and his face got pale.

Just like Hawk said, Mike wouldn't be able to fight Hawk off if he'd been trying to hurt Kiki.

But it was the thought that counted, right?

Hawk stomped a foot toward Mike, who jumped back another step, then he laughed and walked out of her office door.

"Six-thirty," he shot over his shoulder.

She shook her head, collapsed into her chair and pressed her hands to her face, groaning.

"Are you seriously meeting up with him tonight?"

She peeked at him through her fingers. "Really, Mike?"

"Yes *really*, Kiki. I've asked you repeatedly out to dinner. To a really nice restaurant, in fact. Not a hot dog cart like he'll take you to. And you haven't agreed once. Not once. But then this... this *guy* comes in here, bosses you around and suddenly, the strong, outspoken, independent Kiki that I know acts passive, like she lost her backbone, and agrees to meet with this..."

"Guy?" she suggested before he called Hawk something that would piss her off.

Mike frowned. "Sure, whatever."

After looking over his shoulder, probably to make sure Hawk really left, Mike moved around to the side of her desk. Not as close as Hawk had been, but too close for just a co-worker.

"Do you have any idea what you're doing?"

She dropped her hands and frowned up at Mike. "Is this even any of your business?"

He raked his fingers through his short, dark hair. Short, but not mohawk short. "I'm worried about you."

"Don't be."

"Jesus, Kiki, if you're just looking for a quick fling..."

She looked at him in surprise. "Are you volunteering?"

"I'm not looking for only a fling, but if..."

She raised her palm to him. "No, Mike, don't even go there."

"The man's been arrested for being violent. He's not an upstanding citizen, Kiki."

"He's only violent when pushed." As that came out of her mouth, she hoped what she said was true. But even so, she was done with this line of conversation. She didn't need the wakeup call Mike was attempting to give her. Even if she did, she certainly didn't need it from him. "And he's a successful business owner." Why did she feel the need to defend Hawk? Or was she only doing it to make herself feel better about her bad choices? "Are we done here?"

"If he hurts you..."

Kiki wasn't sure if he meant physically or emotionally, but either way... "I've recovered before. Not my first rodeo."

Shaking his head, Mike turned on his heel and headed out of her office. "Hope it's worth it."

Hot, built body, even if marred by dozens of tattoos? Lots of mind-blowing orgasms?

Yes, it might be worth it. Just for one more night.

Chapter Six

AT 7:45, Kiki stood on a Harley door mat in her three-inch heels, stabbing the doorbell with her finger. She'd figured Jazz would answer the door, so she was surprised when she heard heavy footsteps approaching instead.

The door swung wide and she lost her breath.

No vest. No boots. No shirt. *Good lord.* Simply a pair of worn jeans. She licked her lips and swallowed to prevent the drool from dribbling down her chin.

"Babe."

She expected him to bitch about her being late, but he said nothing. But then, she couldn't imagine he normally was a prompt individual himself.

His bulk remained blocking the doorway as he took her in from top to toe. Then he searched the wood porch near her feet. "Where's your bag?"

"I don't need a bag since I'm not staying the night."

"Yeah you are, babe. Next time bring a bag."

Next time bring a bag?

Seriously? Did he think this was going to be a regular thing?

"You sleep naked next to me, but you gotta go downstairs, put on one of my tees. Got me?"

He was laying down the rules already. She wondered if all bikers were this overbearing. With her boss, Tom, handing over the club to her, she guessed she'd find out soon enough since they kept the firm on retainer. And their retainer was not a small one, either.

She sighed. "Are you going to let me in?"

His lips twitched. "Depends. Got panties on?"

"You're not going to find out unless you let me in."

He chuckled, shaking his head as he stared at his feet for a moment, then he took a step back. Once she crossed the threshold, he shut and locked it.

"Babe," he said softly from where he stood behind her.

"Yeah?" She winced. Damn it! Why did she keep answering him when he called her that?

"Lemme see." His voice, a low grumble, sent a shiver down her spine.

She turned to face him. "Nothing to see."

"That's my girl."

Kiki blinked. *That's my girl?* "I haven't been a girl for a very long time, Hawk."

"Longer we stand here yappin' the older we're gettin'. So let's get crackin'."

Kiki pinned her lips together, holding back her laughter.

She glanced over her shoulder into the empty living room. "Where's Jazz?"

"Friend's. Kicked her ass out tonight."

"You didn't have to do that."

"Wanted some privacy. Not holdin' back tonight."

She raised her eyebrows. "Were you holding back the other night?" Because if so... *damn.*

Hawk pushed off from where he leaned against the door and snagged her waist to haul her to him. The air hissed out of her lungs as his big body came in full contact with her. Jesus, there wasn't anything soft about this man. Not that she was complaining.

He plunged his fingers into her hair, fisted them, then tilted her head back to stare down into her face. "Gotta ask you somethin', babe.

Somethin' that's been botherin' me." He lowered his head until his lips hovered above hers.

"What's that?" she whispered, desperately wanting him to close the gap and take her mouth.

"You do 'im?"

Kiki blinked, confused. "Who?"

"The guy in your office."

The guy... "Mike?" she squeaked.

"Yeah."

"Are you going to ask that about every man I know and you meet?"

"Yeah. Expect it, babe. Wanna know my competition."

"There isn't any competition."

"Good to hear."

Of course, he ignored her meaning on purpose. "Because there's nothing to win," she clarified.

"Plenty to win." And with that, he crushed his mouth against hers, jammed his tongue in between her lips and kissed her so long and thoroughly that a groan bubbled up from the back of her throat.

When he finally released her, he was breathing just as heavily as she was. Though, she might have him beat, but not by much.

"Babe," he whispered, like he was surprised at his own reaction.

"Yeah?" she breathed, feeling a bit stunned that this *far-from-polished* man could kiss so well. But then his kisses weren't neat and polished, either. They were demanding and raw and they lit her up like a string of Christmas lights.

"Pull your skirt up."

Right here? She swallowed as her pussy clenched hard at his words. "I... I don't think I can. It's too tight."

"It's hot as fuck." He reached around her and yanked at the zipper. She slapped his hands away so he wouldn't break the delicate tab in his haste. She unzipped it and before she could slip the skirt down, he was shoving it up around her hips instead.

She gasped as his hand found her wet center, stroking between the folds before sliding two fingers deep inside her.

Oh lord, did he have wonderfully long fingers.

He curled his tall body over her and shoved his face into her neck. "No panties, babe. *Fuck.*"

She whimpered as he worked her, thumbing her clit, fucking her with his fingers, while he grabbed a handful of her ass with his other hand and squeezed.

She just might come that quickly...

"Get my dick out."

Her mind had become nothing but mush so it took a second for his words to penetrate. As soon as they did, she undid the top button, unzipped his jeans, and quickly shoved them down enough so she could take his cock into her hand and cup his balls.

Her thumb grazed the crown and she swirled the precum over the hot velvety satin of his skin. He was just as ready as she was.

Suddenly, his fingers disappeared and he grabbed her ass in both hands. She yelped when he jerked her up his body. She wrapped her legs around his waist as he lowered her enough to line the tip of his cock up with her center.

Then someone groaned, she wasn't sure who, when he let her fall a little more until he impaled her deep.

He blew out a breath and held her still as she snaked her arms around his neck to hold on.

"Fuck yeah," he grunted. "Get no deeper than that."

When she opened her mouth to agree, nothing but a ragged breath escaped.

She had never been with anyone before that was strong enough to hold her weight like that. She wasn't the most petite woman, though she felt like one next to Hawk's bulk, but still... He could hold her weight without even a slight tremor and she didn't fear him dropping her.

When he started to lift and lower her, she wrapped her arms tighter around him and shoved her face into his bare chest, inhaling his masculine scent. "Hawk," she groaned against his skin.

"Yeah, babe?" he groaned back.

"Hawk," she said again, her mind spinning.

"Yeah," he breathed.

"Hawk... I'm going to come."

"Yeah, feel you squeezin' me tight. Fuckin' come all over me."

His words became the tipping point and she did. She rippled around him, her toes curling, and she cried out his name again. Still quivering in his arms, he shifted and moved until her back was against the nearest wall.

Then he pumped into her hard. Over and over. Her body taking the brunt of his thrusts since the wall didn't give even a little bit. Every one of his deep thrusts was accompanied with a low grunt and she closed her eyes to let his sound and movement push her over the edge once more.

"Coming," she warned him.

"Feel ya, babe. *Fuck*!"

"Come in me, honey."

"Gonna. *Jesus*. So fuckin' hot, wet an' tight. Makin' that pussy mine."

His words rolled through her, making her shudder.

With another grunt, he jammed his hips powerfully against her, driving deep and staying there. He panted heavily, holding her tight. After a few seconds, his words rumbled in her ear, "Called me honey."

Kiki blinked and thought back. She was not responsible for what came out of her mouth when Hawk was driving her mad. "No, you were hearing things."

"Nope. Heard it. Can't deny it."

"Oh, I can deny it."

His body shook against hers as he chuckled. Without releasing her, he stepped away from the wall. "Was just a quickie. Now time to get down to business."

"Need a few minutes?" she teased.

He guided her up and down on his still-hard shaft. "Feel like it?"

"No, but—"

A cell phone rang loudly nearby and he tensed against her.

"Fuck," Hawk muttered. He shifted his grip on her ass and said, "Cell phone. Back pocket."

Still hanging onto him with one arm, she reached around and felt around the back of his undone jeans until she located his smart phone. She slipped it from the pocket.

"Show me."

She flipped the face of the phone toward him and he looked at the caller ID.

"Fuck me," he muttered. "Hit the speaker."

She turned the phone toward her and tapped the speaker phone button, then held it between them.

"What," he barked.

Kiki tapped Hawk's shoulder and his eyes lifted to hers. "You can put me down," she mouthed.

He shook his head and went back to scowling at the phone. "This better be good."

A gruff male voice filled the tiny foyer. "Gotta guy in here. Rode up on a sled. Not wearin' colors but he's just sittin' in the corner observin'. Gettin' a weird feelin'... like maybe he's a Warrior an' casin' the joint."

"Fuck. Get Diesel."

"Can't get a hold of 'im."

"Where's Z?"

"On his way. Told me to call you, too."

"Yeah," Hawk grunted and closed his eyes for a moment. "Fuck. Okay. See who else you can round up. Don't approach. Observe. Got me?"

There was a hesitation.

"Fuckin' got me?" Hawk barked.

Finally, "Got you."

"On my way." He frowned. "Hang up."

She didn't know if he was talking to her or the guy on the phone, but Kiki jabbed the End button and disconnected the call.

With an irritated sigh, Hawk growled, "Know I run a bar, babe. Usually there at this time of night. Figured I could go one night without me babysittin' it."

"Who was that?"

"Abe."

"Abe?"

"Yeah. Don't know his fuckin' real name an' don't care to know. Right now, he's just a prospect. He's even lower than p—" His eyes slid to hers, then quickly away. "We gotta go."

"Oh, no. You finish that sentence."

"The fuck I will." He dropped her gently to the ground, breaking their connection, and then smacked her ass. "Let's go, woman."

"I can just go home. We can do this another time." She pulled at her skirt in attempt to adjust it back in place.

"No. Comin' with me."

She zipped the skirt closed. "I don't need to do that."

"Not done here, babe. Soon as this business is dealt with, we have our own business to finish."

She'd just had two awesome orgasms but the promise of more tonight made her hesitate.

Was she seriously thinking about going with him to his bar? *Oh good lord*. She was. And she was sort of curious on what it was like.

"I think I'm overdressed."

"Not sure I want you goin' in there with no panties. Got 'em in the car?"

"Yes."

He eyeballed her outfit. "Should be on the back of my bike, but that skirt won't do. How 'bout grabbin' some of Jazz's clothes?"

"She's a bit slimmer than me, Hawk." And much younger, meaning she couldn't imagine Jazz had anything Kiki would want to be caught dead in public with. Even at a biker bar.

"Yeah."

She arched a brow at him. "Yeah?" she repeated.

"Like it. Don't want a skinny bitch. Need somethin' to hold on to when I'm ridin'."

"Wouldn't I sit on the back of your bike and I'd be holding on to you?"

"Meant in bed, babe."

A smile crept across her face. "We should go."

"Gotta take your ride."

She sighed and snagged the key fob off the foyer shelf where she had placed it earlier. She automatically held them out. "Guess you're driving then."

"Damn straight." He plucked them from her fingers and shoved them into his pocket. "Gonna get dressed." Without waiting for her to respond, he jogged up the steps. Kiki couldn't help but watch his ass as he did so.

She hoped the business at his bar didn't take long at all.

WHEN HE CAME BACK DOWN, she was already outside waiting in the passenger seat. That pleased him to no fucking end.

He shook his head to himself as he approached the low-sitting, expensive sports car. Beautiful woman, smart, successful.

He never expected to be sliding into the driver's seat of a practically brand-new Vette with a woman like Kiki next to him.

Fuck no.

Shit wasn't going to last long. She was way too independent to want to deal with his shit. But he was going to milk it out as long as he could.

He liked having class sliding up and down his dick.

When he settled into the seat next to her and pressed the start button, the 6.2-liter engine powered by six hundred-fifty horses roared to life.

Damn. That right there was enough to give him a hard-on.

"Your vest is inside out."

"Yep." He felt her gaze on him as he put the car in reverse. He twisted his head to back the car out of the driveway.

He had to be careful with his big-ass feet and bulky boots on the accelerator. With the power this baby had, it was super responsive to even the slightest touch. "Don't wear your colors in a cage."

"Colors?"

"Cut," he clarified as he backed into the street and shoved the shifter into drive.

She shook her head.

He yanked at his leather vest. "Cut. Colors."

"*Ah*. Why's that?"

"DAMC ain't a car club, babe."

"Got it."

He grinned at her and squeezed her bare knee. "Good. Glad you're gettin' it."

He mashed down on the gas pedal and the back tires chirped then they shot forward. Hawk chuckled at Kiki's gasp.

"Gonna drive this bitch like it's stolen," he declared and did just that.

Chapter Seven

HAWK KEPT a hand at the small of Kiki's back as he guided her through the front entrance of The Iron Horse. The normal, familiar bar smells and sounds hit him as soon as they walked through the door. Smoke, beer and fried bar food wafted through the air. The clack of pool balls sounded in stereo since busy billiard tables filled both sides of the bar.

He spotted the two prospects, Abe and Moose, behind the bar that stretched along the back of the room. He was relieved to see one of their new prospects, Moose, tending bar tonight since he was just like his nickname, as big as a moose. And Abe wasn't a hot head so he was good at breaking up fights or talking people down before a brawl broke out.

So, if Diesel wasn't there to have his back, at least two of the better prospects were.

He kept his eyes set on his destination and deliberately didn't look to where the suspicious biker sat. In the car, he had told Kiki to do the same. He was proud that she managed to keep her gaze forward. Though, he was sure her eyes were sliding back and forth as she checked out his business.

When they hit the bar, he steered her to an empty bar stool. "Babe, sit. Get her anythin' she wants," he directed Abe.

The young prospect nodded and slid down the bar to stand in front of her, giving her the eyeball.

Waving a hand, she dismissed the offer. "I'm good, thanks," she told the prospect.

Hawk leaned down and muttered, "Get a drink, babe. On the house."

Then it hit him that she probably didn't drink beer or whiskey, or anything he normally stocked behind the bar. Her alcohol selections probably consisted of expensive wine, champagne and fancy martinis.

"Just a whiskey neat, then." Kiki said.

Well, damn, that was his girl. Abe grinned wide and slapped an empty shot glass in front of her, another one in front of Hawk and poured them each a double shot of Jack.

As he was serving them, he leaned toward Hawk and said low, "Back right corner. Jeans, black tee, been nursin' the same beer for a good while now."

Hawk jerked his chin up slightly, then casually turned around, leaning back against the bar between Kiki and the empty bar stool next to her. Pressing against her side, he made it look like he was about to have a conversation with her while his gaze sliced through the semi-busy room.

It wasn't packed tonight, but it wasn't dead, either. But there was no mistaking the guy in the back corner sitting by himself.

From what Hawk could see through the haze of smoke in the open floor space, the man was at least in his late twenties if not early thirties, had two full sleeves of tats, and his neck was covered, too. His hair was short and tight, like military or law enforcement tight, not shaggy in the least. If it wasn't for the neck ink, Hawk may have leaned toward believing the guy was a plant for some law enforcement agency and not another club.

Either way, Hawk didn't recognize him and like Abe had said on the phone, he didn't wear a cut. The bar didn't have a "no colors" policy and they welcomed other clubs as long as they didn't stir up shit. So, if he belonged to a club other than the Warriors he should be wearing his patches.

Maybe he was just a lone wolf.

Before he could straighten up and approach the guy, Zak pushed through the swinging doors from the kitchen area that divided the private clubhouse and the public bar.

Z's gaze pinned on Kiki as he advanced, and it wasn't difficult to see he was trying to hide his surprise. He came around the bar to clasp hands and bump shoulders with Hawk.

"Chicken Hawk," Z greeted with a grin.

"Z."

Zak's gaze dropped to Kiki, who Hawk noticed had her deep blue peepers glued to the club's former president. He tamped down the jealousy that stabbed at him like a knife.

"He's got an ol' lady, stop eyeballin' him."

Kiki's eyes widened for a second then her brows dropped low and she said, "Are you going to ask me if I did him, too?"

Zak let out a long, low whistle then laughed. "Damn."

"Know you didn't do him, don't gotta ask."

Kiki held out her hand to Zak. "Kiki Clark. Since he's not introducing me, I'll introduce myself. I'm your club's new attorney."

Zak's eyebrows shot to his forehead. "What happened to Pudwhacker?"

"Tom passed you guys on to me."

Zak took Kiki's offered hand and instead of shaking it, he lifted it to his grinning mouth. Hawk couldn't stop the little growl that slipped from his lips.

Zak's eyes shot to him and he laughed again. Releasing Kiki's hand, he whacked Hawk's shoulder. "Got it, Chicken Hawk."

Kiki's gaze shot to him, too. "Got what?"

"Ain't lookin'. Got my ball an' chain," Zak said, his eyes flashing with amusement and ignoring Kiki's question. "Definitely don't need another one."

Grabbing the double shot that sat in front of him, Hawk downed it, then wiped the back of his hand across his mouth. Once the warmth of the whiskey rushed into his gut, he pushed that jealousy aside to deal with what was currently going on.

Without even looking, Zak asked, "Guy in the far right corner?"

"Yeah," Hawk grunted. Z must have pegged the guy as soon as he came through the double swinging doors.

"Wanna approach? Have words?"

"Who else is around?" Hawk asked.

Zak lifted a shoulder. "Can't find D. Crow was in church earlier but left to go chase a piece of pussy. Grizz was planted on his ass in his normal spot when I came through. Need 'im?"

Hawk cocked a brow.

"Didn't think so," Zak said. "Just gonna have a coupla words. Don't need anyone else."

"Right," Hawk grunted.

Zak looked down the bar at Moose. "Got that big fucker down there if we need 'im." He jerked his chin toward the corner. "But that guy ain't takin' both of us if it comes down to it."

"Right," Hawk grunted again. Z was right. Hawk alone was bigger than the stranger. He was bigger than most guys, except for his brother, Diesel, and Moose might not be taller, but he definitely had some substantial girth.

Hawk's gaze slid to Abe. "Watch her." He tilted his head toward Kiki. "Anything happens send in Moose first. Got me?"

"Gotcha," Abe said with a chin lift.

He looked down at Kiki. "Babe, don't move from this seat unless shit goes down. Abe'll send you through those doors there." He jerked his chin toward the kitchen's double doors. "Keep goin' 'til you find an old fuck sittin' at the club's bar. He'll take it from there. Got me?"

Kiki's eyes widened. "Are you serious?"

"Yeah, babe."

She grabbed his forearm. "Did you forget you're on probation?"

His gaze dropped to her warm, delicate fingers wrapped around his thick, tattooed arm. The contrast between the two of them hit him hard. "Nope."

"Do you think I'm going to be able to get your ass out of jail as easily as last time?"

He peeled her fingers from his skin and gave them a reassuring squeeze. "Yep. That's why we pay you the big bucks."

Kiki did a soft little snort and shook her head.

Zak elbowed him into action and they headed toward the back corner. Hawk watched as the stranger sat upright in his chair and straightened his shoulders, now on notice and, though his face was a blank mask, his eyes were active, aware. He had no doubt that the two brothers were headed his way with a purpose.

When they got to his table, the guy greeted them with a chin lift which neither he or Z returned. Then the lone biker used a booted foot to kick out one of the empty chairs from under the table. "Have a seat."

With a quick glance at Z, Hawk pulled the offered chair out further and sank his weight into it. Zak grabbed another chair from a nearby table, spun it backwards and settled on it, arms crossed over the chair back.

"Hawk. That's Zak."

The guy did another chin lift toward the both of them. "Slade."

"That your sled out front?" Hawk asked him. It was a sweet Harley that was well taken care of. Hawk couldn't help but respect a man who took pride in his ride.

Slade leaned back in his chair and crossed his arms over his chest. "Yeah."

"Watcha doin' here?"

"Just enjoyin' a beer."

"Beer's probably flat an' warm 'bout now."

"How'd you know? You just got here a little while ago."

"True. We got eyes."

Slade nodded, his eyes flicking to the bar and then back to Hawk. "It's a biker bar. Ain't bikers welcome? That's what the sign says out front."

"You read it right. You ain't wearin' colors, though."

Slade lifted an eyebrow. "That a requirement for a beer?"

"Nope. You attached?"

Slade ran a finger down his beer mug and shook his head slightly. "No, man."

Hawk studied the man before him. "Know who we are?"

"Yeah. Heard of your club."

Hawk continued his questioning since the man didn't seem to be taking offense to it. "You from 'round here?"

"North of the 'burgh."

Hawk noticed a thin metal chain around Slade's neck, but whatever was hanging at the end of it was tucked into his worn Iron City Beer T-shirt. That type of chain was easily recognizable so it sparked his curiosity. "Dog tags?"

Slade's hand automatically went to this chest where there was an unmistakable outline under the thin cotton. Yeah, that's what they were.

He wasn't a hundred percent sure of this Slade, but Hawk was pretty confident he wasn't a Warrior.

"Army?"

Slade pulled up one sleeve and on his right bicep was a USMC logo tattooed into his flesh.

Marine. *Oorah.*

Zak made a noise then shifted in his chair. "Should join us. Lookin' for some good recruits."

Slade's eyes landed on Z. "Did some time with another club. Not lookin' to do that time again."

Z tilted his head, his interest clearly written across his face. "Were you patched in?"

"Yeah."

"What happened?"

"Club went in the wrong direction. Wasn't lookin' to do time in a concrete cage. 'Specially for stupid shit."

Z blew out a breath. "Hear ya on that. DAMC's goin' the other way. Lookin' for solid people."

Slade shrugged. "Think about it. Not sure I wanna be tied down."

"Hear ya on that, too. Club can be like a naggin' bitch sometimes. A noose 'round your neck."

"Amen to that, brother."

Zak rapped his knuckles on the table. "Think about it."

"Won't prospect."

Hawk grunted. "Gotta prospect."

Slade's dark eyes swung to him. "Definitely not interested then. Too old for that shit."

Now that he was close, Hawk reevaluated Slade's age. He now guessed thirty or so. "You find you're lookin' to settle, stop in. I'm not here, whoever's behind the bar will find me."

"You president?"

"No, VP."

Slade's gaze hit the bar again. "That your woman?"

Hawk twisted his neck and followed his gaze. Kiki was still where he left her but she had swung around to observe them. His lips twisted into a frown. The woman had a great pair of legs and they were hard to miss since she had them crossed as she leaned back against the bar on her elbows. One foot encased in those fucking heels was swinging, drawing most of the bar clientele's attention in her direction.

Not that he blamed them, he just didn't like it.

Fuck that. He hated it.

"Workin' on it," Hawk muttered. He ignored the startled look Z sent his way.

"Aimin' high," Slade murmured.

Hawk sucked at his teeth as Kiki raised her shot glass to him, winked, then downed what looked like another double.

Shit.

He needed to get her home and out of those clothes now that things proved okay there at the bar.

He pushed up and out of his chair, motioned to Moose, then yelled across the room, "Get this Marine a fuckin' beer."

A few "Oorahs" rose up through the bar and Hawk grinned. He offered his hand to Slade, who slapped a palm against his and then shook it firmly. "See combat?"

"Yeah."

"Drink free here anytime, even if you don't join us."

Slade nodded. "Appreciate it, brother."

Hawk looked at Zak who remained seated. "Comin'?"

"Nope. Slade don't mind, wanna hear some war stories."

Hawk grunted and strode back to the bar. He snagged Kiki's elbow and helped her from the stool. "Let's go."

Her eyes dropped to her shot glass that Abe was apparently keeping topped off. "I have a—"

Hawk grabbed the glass and downed the double shot of Jack, hissed through the burn, then said, "No, you don't. Let's go."

He guided her back to the entrance of the bar, giving Slade and Z a last chin lift before they walked out the door.

"Last time I tell you to wear a skirt," he grumbled.

KIKI'S WARM, wet tongue glided up his throat as Hawk buried his dick even deeper into her slick heat.

He couldn't get enough of that tight cunt of hers. Dropping his head, he latched onto her nipple and drew it hard into his mouth. Her long nails dug deep into the flesh of his ass as he powered up and into her over and over again.

Her eyes were squeezed shut and the sounds that came out of her hit him directly in the balls, which were already painfully tight.

He was ready to blow his load. But he wasn't ready for this to end.

He plowed his fingers through her hair and pulled it tight. "Look at me, babe."

Her eyes popped open, but they remained unfocused. She gasped when he thrust hard again into her tight heat.

"Like this?"

"Yes," she hissed.

"A lot?"

"Yes."

"Best you ever had?"

"Yes, honey."

Yeah, it was. He grimaced as he powered up once more, driving hard. "Can't get enough of you."

"I know," she whispered.

"Gonna come?"

"Soon."

"How soon?"

She hesitated, then she tensed and cried out, "Now."

He gritted his teeth as she clenched down tight around his dick. The throbs seemed never ending and he was trying not to lose it. Not yet.

Not yet.

He had to make it last.

He wasn't sure how many more times he'd be able to talk her into coming to his house, climbing into bed with him, offering herself to him... *Hawk.* To her, he may very well be some low-class biker that was only scratching a temporary itch. But, fuck it, he'd take every second she gave him.

So tonight, he had to make it last. He might not have tomorrow.

Her body loosened around him as she came down from her climax.

"Gonna make you come again."

She smiled up at him, "That would be nice."

"Fuck nice."

She laughed. "Give me a badass biker orgasm then. Ride me rough and hard and give me all you fucking have."

Fucking goddamn.

He took that dirty mouth of hers. Every time she cursed it surprised him. It didn't seem that classy mouth of hers should expel anything obscene. But when she did...

Fuck.

He kissed her long and hard, exploring every inch of her mouth until she was groaning and rocking her hips against him once more.

Goddamn. She was making it hard for him to last.

He pulled away. "Babe."

Her eyes fluttered open. "Yes?"

"On top."

Without breaking their connection, he rolled and when she settled on top, her dark brown hair fell loosely around her face and over her shoulders. Not neat, fuck no. Wild and wavy. Her deep blue eyes flashed. Her tits tempted him as they hung heavily, her nipples tightly puckered.

He reached up and brushed his thumbs over the hard tips. She arched her back and drove herself down, taking him impossibly deep.

Fuck, they fit just right. How could two people from two different worlds fit together so perfectly?

"Love bein' buried inside you, babe."

"Perfect," she groaned as she ground her hips down on him again.

That it was.

"So goddamned wet you're drippin' down my balls."

"You make me that way."

His chest got tight as he stared at the woman straddling him. He sucked in oxygen, trying to keep his thoughts from turning sour.

He had to just take here and now. He couldn't do anything about shit that would happen afterward.

"Hawk, honey," she murmured, cupping his cheeks, holding his gaze.

Fuck him when she called him "honey." It hit him way harder than it should.

"Yeah," he grunted.

"Something wrong?" She rode him slow, lifting all the way up until just the tip was at her entrance, then she slid all the way back down, taking his whole length.

"Everythin's right when you're on my dick."

"Mmm, yes it is." Her eyes fluttered closed and she circled her hips.

He should be doing something other than just lying there, staring in amazement at her, and thinking how fucking lucky he was right now.

He put his fingers where they connected, feeling how slippery she was, how slick she was making his skin as she rose and fell on him.

Pressing his thumb to her clit, she gasped and tilted her hips, now gliding back and forth on him.

Oh fuck.

He didn't think he'd ever been with a woman that got this wet or maybe he just didn't take the time to find out. Get off, get out, get gone.

With his other hand, he ran a finger through her juices and then reached around and slipped his finger into the cleft of her ass.

She stilled, planted her palms on his chest and leaned forward, blowing out a breath. Her eyes locked on his.

Hawk took that as encouragement and circled her puckered hole. However, she was clenched tight.

"Relax, babe."

"I... I..."

"Relax," he whispered while he pressed.

She tried again, "I don't..."

"Gonna feel good. Promise. Just gotta relax."

"Promises, Prom—"

Her words were cut off by her gasp when he pushed his finger slowly inside her tight canal. And it was fucking tight.

"Oh... I..."

Yeah, she liked it. Fuck him, so did he. Now he wanted something other than his finger inside her back there.

"I never..."

"Can tell, babe. Fuck. So tight."

"Jeez, that feels... Fuck! Keep doing that..."

A chuckle rumbled through him. There was no way he was going to stop. Especially when her pace quickened and she began to ride him like a wild woman, throwing her head back and the noises she was making...

For fuck's sake, he might come before she did.

He grunted when she slammed down on both his finger and his dick, grinding hard against his thumb that was still pressed to her clit.

Then her whole body spasmed around and against him.

Thank fuck.

"Tell me," he growled.

"I'm coming," she cried out.

"Yeah, fuckin' me, too." He bucked his hips up and shot his load deep inside her. Her pussy was pulsating around him; his dick was throbbing. And, holy fuck, he was going to die right then and there a happy man.

Chapter Eight

KIKI SAT under a pavilion in the courtyard at church, aka the DAMC clubhouse. A bonfire was blazing, beer was flowing freely and she was surrounded by a bunch of bad boy alpha bikers, almost all of them wearing similar black leather vests. Some were fully decorated with the patches that Hawk had tattooed onto his back, some with just a few. It was easy to spot the prospects from the fully-patched members.

Never in her life had she pictured herself in this type of environment. She certainly didn't quite fit in even though she had donned a pair of her oldest designer jeans, an old T-shirt she found at the back of her drawer from her college days that now fit a *bit* snugly, and a pair of flip-flops that she only wore around the house and to the beach.

At this point, it wasn't a party per se, but more of a meeting to plan the upcoming fundraiser. Hawk told her that all of the brothers were required to attend this meeting and participate on the day of the event.

She looked around. There sure was a lot of them and there were a lot of women here as well. A few wore these "cuts," too. Though, their patches said "Property of" at the top, then had what she assumed was a club member's name at the bottom. Hawk had called it a "rocker."

She shook her head. She couldn't understand why any sane woman would want to be the property of anyone.

"Babe," she heard next to her. The low, gravelly voice sent a shiver down her spine. And it wasn't a bad shiver, either.

She turned her head to glance at Hawk, who was studying her. "Leather vests ain't your style?"

She must have been openly wearing her thoughts on her face. "Can't say it is. Though, not only the style but the meaning behind it."

Hawk didn't say anything, instead just lifted a bottle of beer to his lips and took a long pull. Kiki watched his throat undulate and felt her pussy do the same thing.

It was just insane, but this man, this biker, turned her on like no other had ever done before. Even her ex-husband, who was a pretty handsome guy.

A single look from Hawk could make her quiver. His deep, rough voice made her wet and wanting. And his body...

Her heart pounded in her chest and warmth ran through her belly to land in her core.

For now, the awesome sex they had was worth dealing with his misogynist ways, but she didn't know how long she'd be able to put up with it.

The one good thing about him though, besides his skills in bed, was there was nothing superficial or slimy about the man. What you saw was what you got.

And what she got the past couple of weeks was a whole lot of wet panties and erotic dreams.

A shout came from the one end of the pavilion. "Everyone's ass here?"

Hooting and hollering rose up from the picnic tables that filled the covered, concrete area.

Kiki noticed most of the men sat on top of the tables, their knees spread, with a woman—*their* woman?—sitting on the bench in between their legs. Just the way Hawk sat with her. Though, there seemed to be a lot of men without a woman, too. One table was overrun with what Kiki could only imagine were strippers. She knew about the gentlemen's club the DAMC ran. She frowned in the direction of the overly made-up and under-dressed women, which wasn't missed by the man sitting above her on the table and his low chuckle rumbled over her.

"Hawk, get up here an' do your thing," the man shouted again.

He pushed to his booted feet and surprised her when he planted a kiss on the top of her head before walking away. "Be back, babe. Stay here."

Where else was she going? He had brought her here on the back of his bike. It was the first time she'd ever been on a motorcycle. Though, she had to admit the ride was exhilarating, and holding on tightly to Hawk was just as exciting. She could see herself enjoying a long ride out into the country while being plastered against the large man on a beautiful day. So, unless she called an Uber, she wasn't going anywhere.

Within less than a minute, Hawk's voice boomed across the pavilion. "This is what we got so far... Sophie an' Bella's doin' a bake sale. Dawg's girls are doin' a kissin' booth an' settin' up a tent for private lap dances."

Cat calls and whistles echoed through the courtyard and the women at the strippers' table all stood up, grabbed their breasts and shook them, then waved and blew kisses.

Oh good lord.

Private lap dances? At a fundraiser for vets? Kiki's eyes bugged out and she searched the crowd to see if anyone else thought that was odd. Nope, just her.

She sighed.

"Gonna have kegs set up for beer."

Oh shit. Alcohol and a bevy of bikers. She pressed the heel of her palm into her eye socket and sighed again.

"Gonna have Jag head a Poker Run." Whatever that was.

"Nash's band's gonna play. Crow's gonna set up a spot to do some tats. Anything else?"

"Gonna have a pig roast an' Mama Bear's gonna get some other food together to sell. An' Ace is gonna donate some shit from the pawn shop for a silent auction," the tall, slightly older man next to Hawk said loudly.

"Yeah, that, too. Got the grounds rented. Gotta get notice out, especially to other clubs in the area. Make it big. Bring in some heavy scratch. Gotta work hard an' make me look good in front of my woman, the club's new lawyer. Show her what a difference we can make in this community."

His woman?

"What?" she whispered.

All eyes landed on her and Kiki felt the blood drain from her face. She turned her gaze back to Hawk, but he ignored her.

"Keeks' gonna set up a table an' take donations for answerin' legal questions."

She was?

Her mouth dropped open.

"Anyone got any other ideas, bring 'em to me ASAP."

"You heard the man. Now, enough of that shit." The man next to Hawk jumped up on a nearby picnic table and yelled, "Let's get down an' dirty!"

The stomping of boots, whistling, hooting and shouts of "'til dead" went up, making Kiki wince at the loudness of it.

That was the extent of their planning? They all gathered for that two-minute speech?

Suddenly everyone was scattering over the courtyard, hitting the kegs that had been set up near the fence and from somewhere, she had no idea where, a band started warming up on what seemed like a makeshift stage on the other side of the bonfire.

Good lord, she was suddenly in the midst of a real biker party. Her heart raced.

"Pierce."

Kiki twisted her neck and her eyes rose up the tall tattooed man that had been standing by Hawk. "What?"

"I'm Pierce, club prez. Heard 'bout you but hadn't needed your services. Hopin' not to any time soon."

She noticed the President patch on the front of his cut. She plastered on a smile. He *was* the head of her biggest clientele after all. "Nice to meet you, Pierce."

Kiki tried to get up, but he was standing so close she had a hard time climbing out from between the picnic table and its attached bench. Suddenly his hand was on her arm, hauling her onto her feet.

Without letting her go, his gaze roamed her from head to toe. Kiki shivered, but this time it wasn't a good one. Pierce's look was predatory.

"My VP landed himself a hot piece of ass."

Kiki's body jerked and she gasped as Pierce's hand was knocked off her elbow and Hawk's firm grip replaced it. "Thanks, *brother*, for lookin' out for her. Got it from here," was his low rumble.

There was no mistaking the older man's jaw getting tight and Kiki's eyes jumped from Pierce's tense body to Hawk's. They were having a stare down.

This was not good.

Kiki covered her mouth and coughed out a word that sounded like "probation" causing Hawk's eyes to drop to her, breaking the standoff.

She smiled at Hawk. "Pierce was just telling me—"

"Yeah," he cut her off. "Let's go inside an' get you a drink. Doubt you wanna beer."

Kiki looked at a miffed Pierce who still stood staring at the two of them, hands on his hips.

"Yes, that might be a good idea," she murmured.

Hawk snaked an arm around her shoulders, yanked her against his side and took off striding through the courtyard. In flip flops, Kiki struggled to keep up. She pulled back. "Hang on, you're walking too fast."

"Keep up, babe. Or I'm gonna plant my fist in that fucker's face."

"Why would you punch him?"

"Touched you."

"Yes, but only—"

Hawk abruptly stopped and grabbed her chin, tilting her face up to his. "He. Touched. You."

Okay, then! Someone was feeling a bit strongly about it. "Just my elbow," she whispered.

"Ain't gonna touch a single hair on your fuckin' head. Got me? Not a single... fuckin'... one."

"Is he dangerous?" Kiki tried to look back from where they came, but Hawk was having none of that and tightened his grip on her chin.

"I will be if he touches you again." His eyes dropped to her chest. "Buy some bigger tees. Shirt's too tight across your tits."

"I hardly wear T-shirts."

"Right. You can wear mine."

"I would swim in yours."

"Good."

Kiki sighed as he began to propel her to the side entrance to the clubhouse. He yanked the door open and with a hand on her ass pushed her inside.

She stopped just inside the door and surveyed the large common area which was not nearly as nice as The Iron Horse side. And the public side was no five-star place, either.

A long bar, similar to the one at The Iron Horse, sat to her left along the wall. Pool tables were scattered to the right. An opening to a stairway was on the far wall going to who knows where. Dart boards hung on horribly decorated walls. She actually couldn't tell if some of the motorcycle parts displayed were supposed to be decorations or if they were just a convenient but tacky way to store spare parts.

Couches that looked like they should be burned lined the exterior walls. She scrunched her nose up. She would not be cuddling up with Hawk on those couches any time soon. Or ever. In fact, she planned on giving them a wide berth.

Her gaze landed on what seemed to be restrooms at one end of the bar. One door was marked "dicks" and the other "chicks." She rolled her eyes.

"Hawk."

"Yeah, babe," Hawk answered.

She lifted a hand toward the bathrooms. "I need to use the facilities."

She noticed his lips roll in and his face get tight like he was struggling to keep his composure.

"Sure, babe. Use the *facilities*. Meet me at the bar. I'll get you a whiskey."

"Neat."

"Yeah, neat." He snorted and shook his head, lumbering off toward a group of people who gathered at the other end of the bar. She didn't miss the fact that there was a very pretty woman with long, dark hair behind the bar serving drinks.

Kiki tried not to let the jealousy bug bite her. Nothing to be jealous about, she reminded herself as she rushed toward the women's room.

She shoved the door open and—

"Oh, excuse— *Oooh! Damn...*"

An extremely large man with a very pale ass had what she guessed was a woman pinned against the wall. He looked like Hawk's brother but she couldn't be sure since she couldn't see his face. He wore a cut with all the patches like Hawk's and his jeans hung down around thick thighs. Kiki couldn't see the woman since the man was so much bigger, but she certainly could hear her. And there was no doubt she was enjoying every powerful pump of that very pale, but muscular ass.

Wow, he had one spectacular rear end.

Kiki tilted her head to study it some more. When the man looked over his shoulder at her, she realized it *was* Hawk's brother, Diesel.

Holy crap!

He gave her a chin lift then turned his attention back to the woman who had her legs tightly wrapped around his hips.

For some reason, Kiki couldn't pull herself away. Or even unglue her eyes from the muscles that flexed powerfully in his ass.

God, she was no better than the woman who was encouraging him to fuck her faster and harder. She should be ashamed. She should just back out, close the door and give them their privacy.

"Diesel in there?"

The question that came over her shoulder startled her into action as heat rose into her cheeks for being caught. "Yes."

She started to retreat just as she should have done from the get-go, but the other woman pushed against her, peering over her shoulder.

"Let me see!" The woman then sighed out a "*yessss.*"

Kiki tried to back up but the woman blocked her escape. "We should give them their privacy."

"D doesn't care, do you, D?"

A loud grunt came from the man in answer.

"See? His ass is like the eighth Wonder of the World. Every woman should see it at least one time in her life. To miss that sight would be a travesty."

Kiki actually had to agree with this woman, whoever she was.

"I'm Sophie, by the way."

"Kiki."

"Hawk's new lady, right? The new club lawyer?"

"Well, the second part is correct, at least." She couldn't believe they were standing there having this conversation as Hawk's brother was screwing some woman, who they couldn't even identify, against a bathroom wall.

But there they were. And nobody seemed to even care.

A barked "Woman!" came from somewhere behind them.

"Oops. Busted." Sophie laughed then blushed. "Can't blame a girl..." With one last look at Diesel's derriere, she murmured, "No, I'd say not."

"Is Hawk's like that?"

Okay, she needed one more peek for good measure. "Haven't seen it from that particular viewpoint yet."

"Well, let me know."

"He doesn't do the bathroom thing?"

"Not that I'm aware of."

Well, that was good to know.

"Babe!" a man bellowed again.

"Shit," Sophie muttered. "I'm being paged."

"You certainly are. Is that your man?"

"Yep, that's Zak."

Kiki grabbed the doorknob to pull the door closed, but it was ripped out of her hand and the door was slammed shut.

She turned in surprise to face Sophie's man, Zak, who she'd met the other night at The Iron Horse.

She had to admit Sophie was one lucky woman. The man had a hip swagger that would make any woman wet. Kiki had watched it closely when he and Hawk had approached the stranger in the bar.

He was a little on the rough side, but in a rugged good-looking, panty-soaking way. And he had eyes that could either pierce your soul or make you drop your clothes instantly.

Kiki shook herself mentally. The air in this clubhouse was too thick with testosterone.

"After watchin' that, you in the mood, babe?"

Kiki raised surprised eyes to Zak and was relieved to find that he was asking his woman and not her. Because she might have just mindlessly answered, "Yes."

"You know it, baby," Sophie teased, smiling up at her man and pressing a hand to his belly.

Zak's hand curled around Sophie's and he tugged her into his arms, pressing a kiss to her temple. "Home or upstairs?"

"I think I can wait until we get home. Though, we've done it on the bike before."

Zak smiled. "True, babe. Might be an option."

Kiki's eyes widened. She shouldn't be in the midst of this intimate conversation. But then, she shouldn't have been standing there watching a man having sex against a wall, either.

Hell, her life had certainly taken an odd turn.

Zak looked at Kiki and said with a wide, genuine smile, "Gotta go knock up my woman."

"Oh, you're trying to get pregnant? How exciting!"

Sophie scrunched up her face. "No, I'm on birth control."

Kiki blinked slowly in her confusion.

"Doesn't stop him from trying, though," Sophie clarified then laughed.

Zak grabbed her hand and tugged her away from the tiny alcove where the bathrooms were located and Kiki slowly followed.

She watched the two walk hand in hand across the large room and, before they exited out the back door, Zak flicked two fingers over his shoulder as a kind of wave goodbye.

Huh. The man had some sort of badass coolness about him. She could see why Sophie was clearly infatuated with him.

"Babe," was barked from the other end of the bar. Kiki's gaze swung that direction. Hawk sat on a stool with a beer mug in front of him, surrounded by some other bikers. He crooked his finger at her.

And, holy hell, didn't she automatically start moving in his direction. The sense must have been knocked out of her on Hawk's headboard. She never thought a day would come where a man would crook his finger at her and she'd respond. At least not without a knee to the 'nads.

When she reached him, he spun on his stool with his thighs spread wide and he pulled her in between them, hands firmly planted on her hips.

Even surrounded by people, her nipples beaded to hard points and her pussy clenched hard. Being sandwiched between his thick thighs made her think dirty thoughts.

And this was exactly why she had walked across the bar when he crooked his finger.

His eyes dropped to her chest. "New T-shirts," he muttered.

She looked down and her hard nipples were pushing against the snug cotton.

"Since my cousin is too busy staring at your tits to introduce us... I'm Bella."

She turned toward the dark-haired, smiling woman behind the bar. "Kiki."

Bella's brows rose sharply but she quickly recovered. "Pannebaker passed us on, huh?"

"Yes."

"Lucky for Hawk since you got him off," said a man standing nearby, then whacked Hawk on the arm and chuckled.

Since Hawk ignored the double entendre, so did she.

Bella lifted her chin in the direction of the wannabe comedian and the beautiful redheaded woman who was plastered like icing on a cake to his side. "That's my sister, Ivy, and her ol' man, Jag."

Kiki wondered if all of the bikers in this club were as hot as the men she'd already met. Maybe it was a prerequisite along with having a body full of tattoos. "You don't look old to me."

Jag gave her a wide smile, then looked at Hawk. "Better pass on Soph's Biker to English dictionary. She's gonna need it."

Ivy leaned toward her, "You'll get used to it. You'll have to if you're going to represent us."

"I prefer you all don't get arrested or in any legal jams, but then, I do have bills to pay."

"Like that fuckin' sweet Vette I hear you got. Need to take that out for a spin."

Kiki's head turned to the new voice as the man slid onto the stool to the left of Hawk. He had long dirty blond hair pulled back into a man-bun. Kiki tried not to make a face. Her eyes dropped to the patch over the right side of his chest.

"Your name is Crash?"

"Yep."

"Then no."

Hawk's body shook against her and when she looked back at him, he had his head turned away, hiding his laughter.

Bella slid a glass of what looked like whiskey in front of her. "Neat." Then she smiled, her eyes sparkling with amusement.

"Thanks." Kiki grabbed the drink and downed it in one swallow.

"Damn. Didn't make a face or even cough," Crash said, seemingly impressed.

"I'm good at mixing drinks, anytime you want something other than whiskey neat, just ask."

Kiki placed the glass on the bar carefully and nodded at Bella as the warmth of the whiskey slid into her belly. Her eyes slid to Hawk as the hand at her back slipped down over her ass and squeezed.

That reminded her...

She leaned into Hawk's broad chest and put her lips to his ear. "We need to head back to your house."

His fingers flexed over her ass again and his warm breath swept over her cheek. "Not that I'm complainin' but... why?"

"I need you to fuck me against a wall in front of a full-length mirror. Do you have one of those?"

"Think Jazz got a long mirror. Should I ask why again?"

"No." She yanked on his arm. "Can we go now?"

Hawk's eyes narrowed on her, his gaze lifted to over her shoulder, then a knowing look came over his face. "Take it that the bathroom was occupied."

"Yes," she whispered.

He nodded, his eyes crinkling at the corners. "His ass is legend 'round here. But we're brothers, babe. Built the same."

"I'll be the judge of that."

He jerked his chin up, smiling. "Got you. Let's go."

She took a last glance at Bella. The other woman was staring down at something behind the bar and wiping at whatever it was really hard with a towel. Kiki didn't miss the huge smile Bella wore.

Kiki stepped out from in between his legs and he followed after quickly downing the rest of his beer. As they made their way through the common area to the back door, she looked up at him and said, "By the way, the next time you crook your finger at me, you better only be wearing your tattoos." She let him get a stride ahead then she slapped his ass hard.

He threw his head back and boomed with laughter.

HAWK CLIMBED the steps to his bedroom. His ass was dragging after a long, busy, typical Saturday night at the bar. It was bad enough when he had to break up two drunken fights and barely missed getting clocked in the head, but then he had to throw out a group of underage college kids with fake IDs. And, of course, they acted offended and entitled when they demanded he should let them drink. Right.

He wanted his lawyer beneath him squirming, not beside him at a defense table in a courtroom.

At least he had something to look forward to. He couldn't miss

Kiki's fancy red Vette parked in his driveway when he parked his sled in the garage. Jazz must have let her into the house again.

As he reached the second floor, his gaze fell on the bed. This was not the first time that he'd come home in the early hours of the morning to find her curled up asleep under his sheets.

It shocked the shit out of him. He never expected her to be the one to keep showing up in an effort to continue whatever was going on between them.

Which, he wasn't quite sure what it was besides her just showing up to take part in the awesome sex they had.

Problem was, he was getting used to her being in his bed. But he knew it wasn't going to last. They were just too different, their lives completely opposite.

It didn't go unnoticed that she hadn't asked him over to her condo in Pittsburgh. It was probably in some fancy high-rise building with a door man and filled with rich, nosey neighbors. She wouldn't want to be embarrassed by taking someone like him up to her place.

She wouldn't want to be caught lowering herself to his level.

What-fucking-ever.

As long as she kept showing up at his front door, he wasn't going to turn down the opportunity to stick his dick in her.

And if he was busy doing that, then that pretty much guaranteed that no one else was.

Fuck.

He sat on the edge of the bed and began to unbuckle his boots. He set them to the side quietly, yanked off his socks, wiggled his toes, then peered over his shoulder.

She was sound asleep, her long dark hair draped over one of his pillows. Her face was turned toward him, her eyes shut, her breathing steady, her lips parted just slightly.

Fuck me.

She was mind-blowingly beautiful and no matter how tired he felt she always gave him an instant hard-on. He glanced over at the full-length, free-standing mirror he hadn't bothered to give back to Jazz yet. They had come home the other night and he did what she had demanded by fucking her against the wall with the mirror behind them so she could watch his ass as he pumped hard and fast into her.

She had come three times back to back. He grinned. And she confirmed his ass was as nice as his brother's, so there was that.

He pushed to his feet, the exhaustion really sinking into his bones now as he tugged off his cut and threw it over the nearby chair, yanked his shirt over his head and unbuckled his belt. He headed into the bathroom, started the shower and dropped his jeans to the floor.

Before stepping into the glass shower stall, he stopped in front of the sink and looked at himself in the mirror. He brushed his palm over his short mohawk and then studied the black tribal tats on the sides of his scalp.

He would never fit in with her type. He frowned at his reflection. Why would he even want to?

A little bit of pussy shouldn't be making him question himself or his life. He had a good one full of family, brotherhood and loyalty. He'd never wanted anything else. Never dreamed about anything else, either.

His pop was a biker; his granddad was a biker. It was in his blood. It was only natural he was a biker. He grew up in the club. He was vice president, for fuck's sake.

And if Zak didn't take the presidency back from Pierce soon, Hawk might go for it himself. They should be proud of how far this club had come. Now with this fundraiser, they would be once again giving back to the community, giving back to the veterans who deserved it.

This was why their club was so engrained in Shadow Valley. No one, other than the Shadow Warriors, had ever tried to push them out. Not even the cops. Yeah, they sometimes had some run-ins with 5-0. Sometimes they deserved it, sometimes they didn't. But for the most part, the cops left them alone. DAMC ran legit businesses and they were successful ones, too. The townspeople never hesitated to use their services. Even the strip club.

Just a couple months shy of thirty-five, his life pretty much felt complete. The only thing missing was a good woman. And maybe some kids, eventually. Though, he had plenty of time for that. He was in no rush to be tied down with rug rats.

He wasn't sure if the woman asleep in his bed was even the motherly type. She seemed to be focused on her career, not on getting a ring on her finger and a baby in her belly. She didn't need a man to support her, either.

Since the mirror had fogged up, he could no longer see himself. He needed to stop thinking such heavy thoughts, get cleaned up and climb into bed with his woman.

He grinned. He liked thinking of her in that manner, even if it was only temporary.

He pushed away from the sink and let the hot water soothe his thoughts and his tired muscles.

Chapter Nine

HE WAS HAVING the best dream ever. A hot, wet mouth wrapped tightly around his dick, sucking him as hard as a Hoover vacuum. His hips rose off the bed and he dug his fingers into the mattress.

Damn. He couldn't come, he'd mess up his sheets.

Fingers wrapped firmly around the root and pumped him as a tongue lapped at the tip. Then soft lips encased the head, capturing the precum that kept escaping the end.

Fuck.

He didn't want to wake up because he didn't want it to end.

Nails scraped over his balls and he grunted. He couldn't believe how realistic this dream was.

Then, somehow the dream took a turn and a slim finger was up his ass, stroking his prostate. He bellowed—and it wasn't in protest—as his eyes popped open and he came hard, his dick throbbing intensely and his cum spurting endlessly down her throat.

At last, his body relaxed, melting into the mattress, and he looked down at the woman who had swallowed every drop of him. The woman who *had a finger up his ass*.

What. The. Fuck!

Kiki smiled up at him around his cock. He didn't return it.

"Spent ten days in jail recently an' no one got near my ass. Then wake up to you violatin' me."

She rubbed the shiny, wet crown of his dick along her grinning lips. For fuck's sake, he had to admit that was hot and if he hadn't just blown his load, he'd be ready to blow it again.

"Aw, you didn't enjoy that?" she teased.

"Feel like crawlin' into a ball in the corner an' cryin' like a fuckin' baby."

She had the nerve to laugh. Laugh! Fuck that.

"I guess you never had that done to you before."

"That would be a big fat fuckin' no," he grumbled. He gave her the stink eye. "Mind removin' it from my ass now?"

She giggled again. "Sure." She wiggled her finger and he jerked away from her, dislodging the offending digit. She slipped from the bed, then padded barefoot and naked into the bathroom. He heard the sink run, the toilet flush and then she was back, climbing into bed with him, snuggling against his side.

He wrapped an arm tightly around her and sighed with contentment. "Where'd you learn that?"

"The Internet."

"Right," he grunted. As many times as he'd shoved his fingers and his dick up a woman's ass, he'd never had it done to him, the dick part he never would.

But he had to admit, she had a touch that made him lose his shit.

"Don't ever tell anyone you did that."

She giggled softly again, patted his stomach, and snuggled closer. "Okay."

"Never goin' to ask you to do that again."

She lifted her head and he avoided her gaze. "I see how you worded that."

"Right," he grumbled.

"So... you liked it."

He grunted, and twisted his fingers within the long length of her hair. When he finally sneaked a peek at her, she was grinning from ear to ear.

"Got it," she whispered.

"Good," he answered. "How'd you get in here?"

"Jazz."

Of course. He looked over at the clock on the nightstand. "You're up early."

"Hawk, it's ten."

He wound a strand of her hair around his finger then tugged it. "Yeah, early. Bar's open 'til two. Work 'til three. Don't fall asleep 'til four."

Her fingers brushed over his chest and she circled a fingertip around one of his nipples. When she scraped the tip of it with her nail, he shuddered. *Goddamn.*

"I know."

Against his better judgement he stated, "Weren't here last night." There was nothing obligating her to sleep in his bed while waiting for him to come home, but he was always pleased when she was. And he hated to admit he was disappointed when she wasn't.

"I had some late clients."

He cocked a brow. "How late?"

She slid farther up his side, placed her thigh over his, and nuzzled her nose into his neck. Damn, he liked that.

"I had dinner with one and drinks afterward with another."

His body tensed and he stilled his fingers that were tracing the curves of her waist and hip. "That normal?"

"I try to avoid it when I can. Sometimes I can't."

"Don't like you goin' out at night with a man. Dinner *or* drinks."

"Who said they were men?"

Right. He tried to catch her gaze but she was avoiding it. "Were they?"

She sighed. "Yes."

His nostrils flared and his blood surged through him. He blew out a forceful breath and shut his eyes until his temper cooled down a few degrees.

Pressing her lips against his throat, she laid a path of kisses along his skin. "I can't be here every night, Hawk. I don't live here and we're not even what I'd consider dating."

He opened his eyes and stared at her. It fucking killed him how beautiful she was. She shouldn't be in his bed. She should be in some rich fucker's bed, bearing his well-off children, and being spoiled with overpriced jewelry, expensive cars and fancy vacations.

He could give her none of that.

The only thing he could give her hung between his legs.

God-fucking-damnit.

"I have my own life, my own career, and my own place. I can't always be away from it."

The air rushed out of him and the disappointment rushed right in. "Right."

"It is what it is."

His jaw tightened. He fucking hated that saying. "An' what is it?"

"I don't know," she answered so softly that he almost didn't hear her.

That was a bullshit answer. "Right," he repeated.

"Hawk..."

"Quiet, Kiki."

He felt her lift her head, but he stared at the ceiling. His chest was tight; his blood pounded through every vein and artery in his body. A sharp pain shot through his brain.

"Hawk," she started again.

"Seriously, shut it." She needed to stop talking, otherwise he might go ape shit and say something he might or might not regret. Either way, it wouldn't be good.

"Right," she echoed him, now just as tense as him. "Maybe I should go."

"Right."

"I guess I'll see you at the fundraiser," she said softly.

His breath rushed out of him. The *Dogs & Hogs* fundraiser was a month away. *Fuck.*

"Yep."

He continued to stare at the ceiling as he listened to her gather her clothes, get dressed, and head downstairs. Though, he had to strain to hear the soft click of the front door closing.

He squeezed his eyes shut and forced himself not to jump out of bed to chase her down as her Vette roared to life and he heard her back out of his driveway. Her tires chirped for a split second when she gave the six hundred-fifty horsepower engine gas and accelerated at a high rate of speed down the street.

Hawk flipped over onto his belly and punched the pillow, then shoved his face into it and screamed.

HAWK'S GAZE swept the fairgrounds and landed on the area where he knew Kiki's pop-up tent and table would be set up. He was surprised to see a line of people snaking out from under the tent. His eyes shifted to the kissing booth not twenty feet from her location, then flicked back to the "legal aid" table, then back again to Dawg's girls in the booth.

What the fuck?

Her line was longer than the kissing booth's, but like the kissing booth it was made up completely of men.

He never should have gone on the Poker Run this morning. But he needed to clear his head and he thought taking his bike out to enjoy the early morning air would help. It didn't.

Why? Because he knew he'd finally see Kiki again after a whole fucking month of not. Which was bullshit.

But for the best.

Sure. *Fucking goddamn.*

His bed had been empty for almost thirty days. Even his bed at fucking church. He didn't touch anyone else for almost thirty whole days. That was worse than doing the ten days in County.

Right now, he couldn't stomach any of the pussy that had been offered up. Maybe after today things would go back to normal. He would see her, remind himself that she was way out of his league, that her not showing up in his bed was for the best, and get back to quick and meaningless fucks.

Once he dealt with seeing Kiki today, she'd sign off on all the hours he put into this fundraiser and he'd be free from the court's judgment. For the most part.

And she'd be free of him, too.

He'd just need to keep his nose clean awhile longer and get off probation.

He strode across the trampled fairground grass, pleased that they had a great turnout, but annoyed that he had to push through so many people to get to her.

When he got to the crowd at her tent, he shoved his way through.

"There's a line," came a grumble behind him.

Hawk ignored the gripes, groans and bitching as he worked his way through the line to move around to the back of the table. She had a clear plastic barrel, with a sign taped to it that read "donations," sitting at one corner of the table and it was stuffed full of dough.

As he stepped beside her, deep blue eyes slowly rose up his body until they hit his face.

"Hey," she said softly. Then turned her attention back to the guy sitting in the chair on the other side of the table.

Hey? That was all she had to say?

He let his gaze roam over her like a starved man. It felt like he hadn't seen her in more than a month. More like a year.

Fuckin' A.

Now that he was up close and personal, he could see exactly why she had such a crowd. It wasn't because it took longer to give free legal advice than a kiss. It was because she wore tight jeans with frayed holes strategically placed, and a super snug black DAMC camisole which did nothing but emphasize her fucking tits. She had to be wearing some sort of push-up bra, or even no bra at all, since her cleavage was mounding out of the top begging to be stared at. Or even touched.

Her tits had to be almost as big as some of Dawg's girls, but hers were one hundred percent natural. Soft, squeezable, and certainly fucking suck-worthy.

His fingers clenched into fists. He was going to lose his mind.

"Where'd you get that?" he growled.

Her eyes jumped from the guy she was talking to back to him. "What?"

"What you're wearin'."

Her fingers automatically went to one of the thin straps that curved over her bare shoulder. His eyes and probably every other man's in eyeball view went the same direction. Too bad it wasn't winter when she'd have to wear a turtleneck and a thick coat.

"One of the girls gave it to me. We're all wearing the same thing."

"Didn't they have your size?"

"This is my size."

No way. It was *way* too small for her. "The fuck it is."

Her eyes narrowed and her eyebrows dropped low. "Hawk... I'm in the middle of—"

"Know what the fuck you're in the middle of. Need to go change."

"I didn't bring anything else."

"Fuck me," he muttered. He looked over at the line of all men. "Closin' this down."

"No, you're not."

"Yeah, I am."

She slammed her palm down on the table, making the man sitting across from her jump. She pushed to her feet and drew herself to full height, even though it was a good eight inches shorter than his six-foot-four.

She sucked in a deep breath, which, of course made her tits look even bigger, and let it rip. "I'm in the middle of raising money for this event. *You* were the one who volunteered my time to do this." She jabbed him in the chest with her finger. Her eyes narrowed and became heated. "*You* were the one who didn't even have the courtesy to ask me first. *You* were the one who got arrested and it was because of *your* actions that you needed to do community service. I'm here because of *you!*"

He winced.

Shit.

His eyes once again went down the line of men, who now all stood smiling and looking like they were about to cheer her on.

"So..." she continued loudly. "I'm going to finish what I started and you're not going to say *shit* about it. *Got me?*"

Fuck him.

The whole time she was yelling at him, her tits jiggled wildly and he now had a half of a hard-on.

He ought to just throw her over his shoulder, toss her on the back of his sled and haul her ass home to fuck the shit out of her.

That's what he should do.

That's not what he did.

"Whatever," he grumbled. "We'll talk later."

"Fine," she snapped, then settled back into her chair and apologized to the man she had been helping.

Clearly, he had been dismissed.

With a last look at her, he realized he needed to have a little discussion about those jeans she was wearing, too.

He pushed back through the crowd and saw Zak standing on the other side of the line. He was not fighting back his laughter. Not one bit. When Hawk approached, Z held his hand out, palm up.

Hawk frowned at it. "What?"

"Hand over your fuckin' man card."

"Fuck me," he muttered and headed toward the beer tent, hoping he had enough cash on him to get shit-faced.

Chapter Ten

KIKI SAT BACK in her plastic folding chair, stretched her arms overhead, and released a long, weary sigh. Not only was she beat, her ass hurt from sitting all day, and her muscles were stiff.

The *Dogs & Hogs* fundraising event had been extremely successful. At least from what she could see since she had been tied to her tent almost the entire day. The donations she collected for answering simple legal questions, that for the most part could have been answered by Google, filled up ten of those clear plastic pretzel barrels. Ten.

For any questions or cases that were more complex she handed the person a business card, telling them that she'd give them their first hour of consultation for free.

Tom would have a coronary, but she didn't care. She'd do it on her own time if she needed to.

All day long, the air was filled with catchy rock music from a club member's band, Dirty Deeds, the roaring of loud motorcycles, and the smells of a roasting pig and fried food.

Her stomach was growling since she only ate a pulled-pork sandwich and some fries that Bella and Jewel had brought her earlier in the day when they came to check on her. Which was nice. The DAMC women had all been very warm to her, accepting her into their fold easily. And, of course, Ivy had been kind enough to supply the day's "uniform" of the black DAMC camisole that Hawk had a conniption over.

She looked down. Yes, it fit a little "too well." But she figured if that was what helped fill ten whole barrels with cash, then so what. The money was going to a worthy cause by supplying trained service dogs to veterans.

Surveying the fairgrounds, she noticed quite a few bikers still hanging around. Some wearing DAMC cuts, some wearing "colors" proclaiming them to belong to the Dark Knights. Then there were a few clean-cut men wearing vests that said the Blue Avengers.

Wasn't hard to figure out they were law enforcement. She dealt with cops way too often in her job, so she could spot them a mile away. A few times during the day she had spotted Bella and one of the Blue Avengers standing close and talking very animatedly.

She wondered what was up with that. Guess she could ask Bella herself since the woman was headed her direction.

"Done here?" the dark-haired beauty asked.

"Yes." Kiki sighed. "I'm tired. I'm hungry. I need a long nap."

Bella laughed. "We're all going back to church to get grub. Prospects are going to stay behind to break down all of the tents and tables."

It seemed that prospects were little more than slaves. They did whatever they were told, no matter how menial the task, to prove themselves worthy of "patching" into the club. Kiki compared it to hazing into a college fraternity.

Amazing what she could learn in one day of being surrounded by bikers and their women. She knew more now about the biker life and motorcycle clubs than she ever wanted to. At least it gave her some insight for future defense purposes. Not that she wanted to have to defend any of the "brothers" any time soon.

"Diamond come collect your money yet?"

"No, and look," she lifted the long fabric tablecloth away from the ground and lowered her voice. "There's a lot of it."

Bella leaned over, peering under the table. "Damn, you raked it in.

Guess the combination of a beautiful woman who can get your ass out of a jam is a good one!"

Diamond strolled over, wearing a huge smile. "I think Hawk would agree with that." She pulled one of the clear plastic barrels from under the table, held it up and turned it three hundred-sixty degrees, whistling. "Need to do this for all of our fundraisers."

Oh good lord, now she was going to be stuck doing more of these?

"How much do you think you collected?" Bella asked.

"I don't know." She'd been so busy, she never had a chance to count.

"Shit, this thing is full of twenties, not ones and fives like the Dawg's strippers over there," Diamond tilted her head toward the now abandoned kissing booth. "I think someone threw a bunch of pennies in theirs."

Bella and Diamond snorted while elbowing each other.

"I take it that you ladies don't like the club running a strip club?"

Diamond shrugged. "Wouldn't be so bad if Dawg didn't drag them into church all the time and to all our gatherings. It's bad enough that there are sweet butts constantly hanging around, spreading their legs every time a brother glances their way. That's why you hardly catch me at church for the parties."

Just then a loud rumbling came out of nowhere. All three of the women's heads spun toward the sound to see a few men on motorcycles headed their direction, riding hard and fast through the center of the event area and over the grass. Their faces were covered with dark goggles and black bandanas, their heads with skullcaps.

"Fuck!" Bella shouted, her face suddenly pale. "Warriors!" Her head spun toward Diamond. "Put the money down, Di."

Diamond hugged the barrel closer to her stomach. "No, they're not getting Kiki's hard-earned money."

"Fuck that, Di. Put the money down!"

"No—"

Diamond's words were cut off when she gave an angry scream as a biker snatched the barrel out of her arms and then kicked her squarely in the gut with his boot. Diamond dropped to the ground with a cry, grabbing onto her middle.

Four unknown bikers circled the tent on their bikes, knocking a couple of the poles down. A bike came so close to Kiki that she fell backwards and landed on her ass, the air rushing out of her.

Bella faced off with another one of the bikers and when he got close enough to her, he put out his arm like he was going to snatch her up.

Kiki watched in horror as Bella screamed, "Not today, fucker!" Her face was now flushed, her eyes glittering. She pulled back her arm and punched him in the side of the head. The bike wobbled but didn't go down.

"Fuckin' bitch!" the Warrior yelled, then swung at her, punching her in the face. Blood spurted, her head whipped back and she fell to her knees.

Before Kiki could scramble to her feet, Diamond screamed at her, "Don't let them get the money!"

Kiki quickly crawled on her hands and knees under the table, throwing her body over as many of the barrels as she could, which wasn't many.

Then there were hands everywhere, grabbing her, yanking painfully on her hair, pulling her off, snatching the money. She grabbed the closest barrel and curled her body around it.

They were not getting all the money. No way.

"Fuckin' bitch! Let it go!"

She shook her hair out of her face and glared up at the masked biker. "No!"

"Fuck it then, I'll take you with."

Oh shit.

The man grabbed her bicep and started dragging her from under the table. Even with that, Kiki refused to release the money.

Holy shit, if he got her on his bike and rode away with her, she was screwed.

Before she could kick at him, the biker went down. Kiki's eyes followed the biker's fall as he hit the ground hard.

She glanced back up and saw the guy who had been at The Iron Horse that night Hawk took her there.

She never learned his name.

He jumped on the downed biker and started to pound the hell out of him.

Watching his fists fly, Kiki's mouth dropped open, not knowing what to do. She turned her head to see where the rest of the Warriors were and was shocked to see Bella chasing one on foot across the fairgrounds. Then one of the Blue Avengers rode up beside her on his bike and snagged her by the waist, halting her progress. Bella shook her head violently and shoved both palms into the man's chest, almost knocking him off his motorcycle. She was screaming at the top of her lungs, her arms moving wildly, but Kiki couldn't make out what she was yelling. He grabbed her wrist and pulled her close, trapping her arms. Kiki realized it was the same guy Bella had been speaking closely with earlier.

Then the remaining pack of Warriors sped through the grass riding low over their bikes, hopped over a curb and escaped down a nearby side street.

Another group of bikes roared past the tent going the same direction as the Warriors. Kiki only got a glimpse of who they were. It was a mix of Dark Knights, Dirty Angels and Blue Avengers. They were hot on the Warriors' tail.

She spun around, looking at Diamond, who now sat up with Jewel bent over her, brushing Diamond's long dark hair out of her face, asking her if she was all right.

"No, I'm not all right. I'm pissed. Those fuckers got away with some of the money."

"Everyone's going after them," Ivy said, standing close by, hands on hips. "They're not going to get far, hopefully. Especially when the cops are part of the chase."

"How many did they get?"

Kiki looked around at the scattered barrels and counted. "Four." Her gaze landed on the biker who didn't wear a cut. He was squatting next to the knocked-out Warrior. He wiped the back of his hand over his bloody mouth, but only managed to just smear it worse.

Diamond crawled over and sat down beside him. She grabbed his face and turned it toward her. "You okay?"

He nodded, his chest rising and falling rapidly. Whether he was out of breath or just angry, Kiki couldn't tell. His eyes still looked a bit wild.

"What's your name?" Di asked him.

He finally managed to focus on her. "Slade."

"Who do you belong to?"

He didn't answer for a moment, just studied her. "No one."

Then Hawk, Jag, and Zak surrounded them with a mixture of worry and fury on their faces.

Hawk's eyes looked almost as wild as Slade's as he inspected the half-disabled tent, the remaining scattered money barrels and the women. "What the fuck?" he growled.

Jag wrapped an arm around Ivy, pulling her to his side. "You okay, baby?"

"Yes, I only ran over here after I saw what was going down. They didn't touch me."

He nodded, his eyes landing on Slade. "Thanks, brother."

"Only got here in time to get this fucker off her," he tilted his head toward Kiki.

Hawk's gaze landed on her, his jaw tight, then he reached down and hauled her up by her armpits. He inspected her, probably to see if she was hurt. He yanked one of the spaghetti straps of the camisole up higher onto her shoulder. "You okay?"

Kiki brushed off the seat of her ass, ignoring his assessing look. "Yes, fine."

Hawk tipped his chin toward the downed biker. "He touch you?"

"He—"

"Grabbed her arm and was ready to kidnap her," Diamond volunteered.

Oh brother. She was going to try to play it down to Hawk, knowing that information might put him into a tailspin and she wasn't wrong.

His nostrils flared and he began to move toward the unconscious male. Kiki grabbed his arm and shook her head. "Hawk, no. You're on probation, let the cops deal with him."

Zak whacked him on the back. "Good idea. Need all boots on the ground. Won't do us any good if you're tossed back inside."

They need all boots on the ground? For what? Some sort of war? A spark of fear ran through her.

Hawk's gaze jumped from her to the Warrior. "Good thing Slade got to him before I did. Fucker wouldn't be breathin' right now."

Jesus.

Zak stepped closer to Slade. "Said this once before, brother, you should join us."

Slade wiped the back of his hand over his bleeding mouth again. "Not gonna be a prospect."

Zak held out a hand. Slade grabbed it and Zak helped pull him off the ground. When Slade got to his feet, with their hands still clasped, Zak bumped shoulders with him. "After today, don't need to be. Jumped in to protect our women. Got our appreciation."

Hawk went over, nodding. He clasped hands with Slade and bumped shoulders with him, too. "Thanks, brother. Owe you one."

Slade just nodded and raked a hand over his short, dark hair, staring at Diamond. "You okay? Got kicked in the gut."

Diamond's hand went to her belly. "Hurts like hell. It'll probably bruise, but yeah, I'm okay. Thanks."

Slade nodded again. He dropped his gaze to the fallen Warrior, then nudged him not-so-gently with his boot. "Whataya gonna do with this piece of shit?"

Hawk went over and gave the unconscious biker a firm nudge with his boot, too. Kiki was pretty sure Hawk wanted to kick him a lot harder. "Nothin'. Too many 5-0 around. Like Keeks said, gonna let them deal with this one. We'll deal with the rest."

"Didn't 5-0 ride off after 'em with some other brothers?" Slade asked.

"Yeah. Ain't gonna do anything right now," Hawk murmured, his eyes sliding to Kiki.

She frowned. "You're not going to do anything later, either. Otherwise, you're going to land back in County," she reminded him.

"Right," he muttered, returning her frown with an even bigger scowl.

"Right," she huffed.

A prospect, apparently named Rooster by the look of his name patch, ran up out of breath. "5-0 on their way."

He had a mohawk, too, but his was a lot longer and messier than Hawk's well-maintained hairstyle. It actually flopped to the side somewhat just like a cock's comb. No wonder he was called Rooster.

"Gonna get these women outta here," Zak said. He turned to Jag. "Make sure your sister gets home. Probably needs to rest."

"I have no way to get there," Diamond interjected. "And I don't want to go home anyway. I want to go back to church."

"Where's your car?" Jag asked.

"Most of us women carpooled over from church."

Jag's eyebrows shot up his forehead. "Why the fuck did you do that?"

Kiki couldn't miss the dark cloud that crossed Jag's sister's face. "*First off* to not clog up the parking and, *second*, we met at church this morning. While *you all* were on your fun Poker Run, we were all working."

Jag swatted a dismissing hand in his sister's direction. Kiki didn't miss the look Ivy gave him.

"So, who's got their cage here?" Jag asked.

"Bella drove us," Kiki volunteered.

"Get Bella to take you wherever then," Jag said impatiently to his sister.

"Bella took off after one of the Warriors—"

"What the fuck?" Hawk shouted, causing all eyes to turn his direction.

Di frowned at him. "If you'd let me finish! Bella took off on foot after one of those assholes that stole the money. Axel chased her down, snagged her mid-stride, and they disappeared. Who knows where they went off to," she finished.

"Fuckin' Axel," Hawk muttered.

Kiki was dying to ask who Axel was, but didn't think it was the appropriate time. She just figured he was one of the cops but had no idea how he was connected to the club.

Though, Hawk sort of cleared that up when he pointed at Zak. "Your fuckin' brother needs to keep his hands off Bella."

Zak raised both of his palms. "Preachin' to the choir, brother. Don't want that dick anywhere near DAMC property."

Hawk grunted and nodded. He turned towards Kiki. "You parked at church?"

"Yes, I—"

"Ridin' with me."

She ignored his bossiness. She could find another way back to church to get her Vette.

"Jag, you take Di," Zak said.

Jag shook his head. "Can't. Ivy got here on the back of my sled."

"Fuck," Zak cursed. He looked toward Hawk, who shook his head and tipped his eyes toward Kiki. "Fuck," he muttered again.

"I'll take her."

All eyes turned to Slade in surprise.

"Can take her on the back of my bike."

"Brother, that's my sister," Jag said with narrowed eyes and a warning clear in his voice.

"Yeah, got that. I'll be careful."

Jag nodded reluctantly and glanced at Zak. "He okay to come back to church?"

"Yeah, not a problem. If the committee agrees, want him to patch in anyway. Got a feelin' everyone's gonna gather there once the chase is over. Be a good opp to introduce him."

"Wait! What the fuck? He gets to patch in without being a prospect?" Rooster squawked.

Hawk's gaze landed on the younger man. "Yeah, got a problem with that, hand over your cut."

Rooster clearly had a problem with it but kept his mouth shut.

Though, by the way his face contorted, it looked like he struggled with it.

"Stay here an' watch this asshole 'til the pigs get here. An' if you got a problem with that, too, tell me now."

Roosters lips thinned at Hawk's words.

Hawk cocked an eyebrow at him and gave him a few seconds to change his mind, then he directed his gaze to Kiki. "You're on the back of my sled."

She sighed. "I can wait for Bella."

"You're on the back of my sled," he repeated, more firmly this time.

She opened her mouth to argue, then snapped it shut. "Fine," she relented.

"Yep, sure is. Let's go." He put a broad hand to the small of her back and gave her a gentle shove.

Kiki took a couple steps, then stopped to look over her shoulder. "The money."

"Z will take care of it."

"Why are you so fucking bossy?" she whispered loudly, not masking her annoyance.

"Tell you when we get to my ride."

"Tell me now."

"No."

"Hawk."

"Let's go." He grabbed her arm and she cried out when he grabbed the same spot that the Warrior had. "What the fuck?"

Crap. She needed to get Hawk away from the unconscious biker before he saw the bruise which was starting to bloom on her arm. He may lose his shit when he spotted that. She started walking fast over the grass to where a few bikes were parked, figuring one of those was his. "You want us to go, so let's go."

He jogged after her, catching up in an instant. "Babe, what's wrong?"

"Which one is yours again?"

His mouth flattened as he moved to his bike and straddled it. "Get on."

She planted a hand on his shoulder and mounted behind him, glad the seat had a back to it that she could lean on.

He kicked the starter, the bike roared to life and within seconds they were off. Then not a minute later, he pulled behind a building at the far end of the fairgrounds, shut the bike off, kicked the stand down and dismounted. He turned, hands on hips and stared at her.

When his eyes dropped to her arm, she got a little worried. A thunderous look crossed his face. "That fucker do that to you?"

She looked down and noticed the bruise on her bicep beginning to take the shape of a hand. "I'll be fine."

"Yeah, you will. 'Cause Slade stepped in." He brushed an agitated hand over his short mohawk. "Shoulda been there by your side all day. I fucked up."

"I don't need you by my side watching over me like a sentry. Not only do I not need it, I don't want it."

His head jerked back and his expression got even darker. "Woman, seriously. Not in the mood for you to push my buttons."

"Oh, you're not, are you?"

"No."

She planted a hand on her hip. "What are you going to do about it?"

Again, his head jerked back and his eyes narrowed. Kiki yelped as he grabbed her elbow and hauled her from the back of the bike. He pulled her over to the building, pressing her against the concrete block wall.

"Show you what I'm gonna do," he grumbled. Then dropped his head and took her mouth.

Her lips parted in a gasp and he took advantage of it by sliding his tongue deep into her mouth, laying claim to her once again.

Her stomach fluttered and a warmth rushed through her landing in her center.

God, she'd missed this. Missed him.

She'd gone a whole month without him. Without any contact. She didn't want to admit it, at least not until now, how much she truly missed him.

It was absolutely crazy that she needed a man like this. Like Hawk. Someone who *so* did not fit into her life.

Before him, she had felt empty for a long time with only her career driving her. And the stunning realization that this man could fill her soul hit her hard.

She thought she could live without him, that he was just a temporary fix to fill a particular need. But, no. He was more than that. His bossiness annoyed her, no doubt. But that was him. That was Hawk.

He'd probably never change.

Even so, a little part of her liked it. Hell, *loved* it. It thrilled her when he took control, got demanding. Became possessive of her, acted like she was his, felt the need to protect her like she was something delicate and breakable.

Even though she was far from that.

Wrapping her arms around his neck, she pushed to her tiptoes to deepen the kiss, groaning into his mouth.

She could have sworn he groaned, too.

His hips pinned her to the wall, and that left no doubt how hard he was.

She didn't care that they were out in the open for anyone to come upon, where anyone could see what they were doing. At this moment, she only cared about him, what his mouth was doing, how good he felt pressed against her.

She yanked his T-shirt out of his jeans and slid her hands up his belly, over his warm, firm skin and solid muscles. He thrust against her and she whimpered.

He pulled back until his mouth was just a hair's breadth away. He was breathing hard as he pressed his forehead to hers, cupping her cheek. His chest rose and fell rapidly under her palms.

He'd missed her, too.

"Hawk," she breathed.

He rocked his head side to side. "Babe, gotta get outta here before I fuck you against this wall. Unlike my brother, I care if my lily-white ass is on display."

"Are we going back to your place?"

He released her and stepped back. "No. Gotta go to church to wait for word. Got a room there."

"Won't everyone be there, though?"

"Yeah."

"I guess we'll have to make it quick then."

He grinned. "Yeah."

Chapter Eleven

HAWK RAN his tongue between the folds of her slick pussy, tasting her tangy sweetness.

He missed this shit. Missed his wild hellcat.

With one arm braced over her hips, he kept her from squirming too much. Slipping two fingers inside her hot, wet cunt, her hips jerked once again. He pressed his lips to her clit and sucked hard.

"Oh God. Oh God. Oh God," she whimpered, which made him even harder than he already was, and precum began to bead faster at the tip.

He needed to be inside her. And he needed that soon. Otherwise, he was going to blow his load all over his bed at church. And that would be a waste.

He wanted to savor her taste, make her come at least once before driving his dick home.

Home.

This woman felt like home to him. And that was fucking crazy.

Curving his fingers, he located that little spot inside her and she threw her head back, crying out. Her muscles clenched around him as he continued his assault.

Pulling back enough to see the glistening pink of her pussy, he smiled at how soaked she could get. Her fingers dug into his scalp and she pressed his face harder into her cunt.

He chuckled.

"Not funny... keep going..."

"Gonna make you come, babe."

"Not if you keep talking!"

He chuckled again and teased her clit with the tip of his tongue as he fucked her faster with his fingers.

"That's it, honey."

Hawk closed his eyes when she had breathed the word "honey." Just for a moment, he wanted to imagine that they did this every night, that she woke up next to him every morning and they'd do it all over again.

Her legs, draped over his shoulders, stiffened. "I'm going to..."

Yeah, she was.

He pressed his mouth harder against her clit, stroking his tongue repeatedly over that stiff little nub that made her hips jump wildly under his arm. Then he felt it. Tasted it. The gush of wetness that he'd only ever experienced with her.

For fuck's sake, he couldn't take any more. He rose up, covered her with his body, and drove his cock deep until he hit bottom.

She turned into his little wildcat, scratching, biting and mewing her encouragement as he powered in and out of her as hard and fast as he could.

Somewhere along the way, he lost his fucking mind. Everything disappeared except for her.

His eyes locked on hers and held. He could no longer feel her nails ripping at his skin, he could only feel how hot, wet and tight she was as her insides gripped his dick like a fist. He could only hear the hot, sexy sounds that escaped her parted lips. He could only see her face change with each thrust.

And, fuck him, he was a goner. A complete fucking goner.

She had stolen his soul, captured his heart. He didn't think he'd ever be able to recover from that.

He couldn't imagine anyone else for him other than the woman who was wrapped around him, taking every inch of him, making his chest swell and fill with something he never, ever fucking felt before.

Jesus, he was *done.*

"Gotta come, babe," he growled, not slowing down. Each thrust pounded her body. Every little gasp she made, he answered with a grunt of his own.

"Gotta come, babe," he warned again. She needed to come soon, or he was going to leave her behind and he didn't want to do that. "Tell me when... Tell... me..."

"Now!" Her head bowed back, her mouth opened wide and a wail escaped her that pulled his balls so tight, he had no choice but to let go.

With one last grunt, he sank deep, holding her tight as his cum shot from his dick in powerful spurts.

He shoved his face into her damp neck. He needed a moment to get his shit together. Not his physical shit, this unexpected emotional shit.

Jesus. Might as well neuter him and take his motorcycle license. Turning into a goddamn emotional pussy.

He pressed his lips to her throat and tasted the salty tang of her skin. He inhaled deeply, picking up her scent as well as the strong scent of sex in his small room.

His room was one without its own bathroom since he didn't live here full-time or even spend a lot of time up here. Keeping it was only a means to an end. A place to get laid or to crash when he was too lit to drive home after a party. Unfortunately, he would have to head down the hall to the communal bathroom to get something to clean her up with. Because there was no way she was hitting the hallway just wearing his tee or anything similar.

In a minute though, he told himself, since he still wasn't ready to break their connection.

"Hawk," she sighed.

"Yeah," he mumbled against her skin.

"You're not very light."

"Yeah, babe." He didn't move.

Five seconds ticked by. "Hawk."

"Yeah, babe."

"You're crushing me."

With a groan, he fell to her side, leaned over to snag a dirty T-shirt off the floor and wiped off his dick. He tossed it back where he found it.

Kiki had watched the whole thing with bugged-out eyes. "Really?"

"Wanna use a T-shirt to clean up or do you want me to go get you a wet towel?"

"A wet towel, please. Your house is as neat as a pin. What the hell happened to this room?"

He glanced around and saw it through her eyes. It was filthy. No other word for it. The only reason his house was clean was due to having a house mouse. This room wasn't nearly good enough for his woman. And he had stupidly gotten her naked and fucked her in this pig sty. That wouldn't happen again. "Shouldn't have brought you up here."

"I still don't understand how your two places could be so different in... cleanliness."

"Jazz."

Her mouth dropped open. "Oh my God. Without Jazz your house would look like this?" She waved her arm around the room.

That's when he spotted it. In the past hour or so her bruise had turned a few different shades of purple. It was worse than he thought.

"Fuck," he grumbled, grabbing her arm to look at it closer. "Don't you ever protect something like that again."

"Like what?"

"Fuckin' money."

"I wasn't going to let them steal it all."

He held her arm in front of her face so she couldn't miss the results of her being stubborn. "Fuckin' woman. Let 'em have the fuckin' money. Ain't worth it."

"Hawk."

"No. No lip. Not gonna do that again."

She broke free of his grip and pushed herself up into a seated position as she clutched the sheet tightly to her chest. He hated the fact that she felt the need to cover herself up from him.

He more than hated it.

"No, you're right. That's not going to happen again because I won't put myself in that type of situation *again*."

He sat up abruptly and shot a scowl in her direction. "Whataya mean?"

She tossed a hand out. "I was only obligated to make sure you did your community service. You did it. It's done."

It's done.

Right. "Then why you in my bed right now?"

She blinked at him, then pressed the heel of her palm onto her forehead. "*Gah!* Why are you so hardheaded?"

"Born that way, babe. Ain't gonna change." He grabbed her shoulders and pushed her onto her back, rolling his body back over her, planting his face inches from hers. "It ain't done, babe."

"What?" she asked softly.

"*It. Ain't. Done.*"

Her eyebrows furrowed. "Your community service is done."

His muscles relaxed slightly.

"Wait... you thought... There's nothing to be 'done,'" she clarified. "It is what it is."

"Oh, for fuck's sake. Here we go with that fuckin' 'is what it is' shit again."

"Well, what is it, then? Huh? Tell me."

He rolled away from her to sit on the edge of the bed, his back to her. He scrubbed both hands over his face. With his face turned away from her, he closed his eyes, and tried his damnedest to keep the tone of his voice flat when he asked, "What do you want it to be?"

If she said, "what it is," a blood vessel would burst in his brain. When she was silent for way too long, he glanced over his shoulder at her.

She sat there, eyes closed, chewing on her bottom lip. Jesus, that didn't bode well for him.

He sucked a deep breath through his nostrils, pushed to his feet, swiped his jeans from the floor and shoved his legs in. He zipped them closed but didn't bother to fasten the top button.

"Gonna get you a towel," he mumbled. He strode from the room, shutting the door behind him with extra care, because he really wanted to slam the shit out of it.

He brushed a hand over his hair, let out a silent but searing curse, then headed down the hallway to the bathroom, hoping he could find something clean in there for her to use.

He never should have brought her back here. His room at church just reminded her who he really was. What his life was really like. And that they were worlds apart.

Fuck.

THE CLUBHOUSE WAS busy and loud as both bikers and women milled about, drank, and played pool, all of them hanging around to find out what happened with the chase involving the Warriors. And, more importantly, whether any of the stolen money was recovered.

However, no one knew where Bella was. Still.

Kiki, knowing she was probably with that cop, Axel, wasn't worried. The woman seemed more than capable of taking care of herself. But the thought of Bella disappearing with Zak's cop brother seemed to disturb most of the men for some reason.

As long as she was safe and not being held against her will, then they needed to get over it.

As they waited for word, Kiki couldn't help but eyeball the man who sat to her right on one of the bar stools one more time.

He had shiny black hair that flowed over his back like a waterfall. His hair was so long that she was extremely jealous of how long it actually was. And his face was... Oh lord, she had no other word for it but... stunning.

Perfect caramel skin, almond shaped eyes, cheekbones which also made her jealous. He'd be considered pretty if he was a woman. But he certainly wasn't. There was no mistaking he was anything but *all male*.

His dark, almost black, eyes landed on her as she stared at him and smiled. He didn't return it.

Whatever. He was pure eye candy and she would still stare at him. He could move elsewhere if he didn't like it.

She shifted his way a little more. She read the patch on his vest. "Is your name Crow?"

He put down the whiskey he'd been slowly sipping for the past fifteen minutes and twisted his head toward her again, his pitch-dark eyes burning into her soul. "Maybe."

God, his voice was like warm, sticky honey, too.

"Please don't take this the wrong way, but..." Kiki sucked in a breath. "You don't seem to quite fit in here."

His expression remained the same, which was pretty much a blank but beautiful canvas when he said, "I'm a biker."

"I get that." She twisted slightly on her stool and swung her arm out, indicating the rest of the crowd in the room. "But I'm just surprised that—"

His gaze pinned to her arm and she startled when he grabbed it. "Who did that?"

The man went from emotionless to fierce in a second flat. She opened her mouth but nothing came out.

"Hawk didn't do that." It wasn't a question, but more of a challenge for her to refute that.

"No! No. He didn't. One of those Warriors did."

"Six feet under," he muttered.

"What?"

His gaze hit hers, his eyes sparkling like black diamonds. "Six feet under. That's where those bastards need to be."

"Uh... By the way, I'm the new club attorney. Although there's something called attorney-client privilege, I'd rather not hear things like that." She leaned towards him, and lowered her voice. "Just in case."

He raised his glass to his lips and instead of sipping, he took a gulp of the amber liquid. "Know who you are."

"Well then... I'd appreciate it if you'd not tell me stuff like that. Again... just in case."

"Hawk's woman."

"What?

"He gonna take it to the table an' claim you?"

"Claim me? As what?"

"His ol' lady."

His ol' lady? Unfortunately, she now knew what an ol' lady was. No question about it. You couldn't hang around the DAMC women for even a minute and not figure that out real fast. And it wasn't hard to miss quite a few of the "Property of" cuts that women wore from the Dark Knights, Dirty Angels and other various clubs that had shown up at the *Dogs & Hogs* event.

She had no plans to ever wear anything like that, nor would she willingly become the property of a man. What year was it, anyway? Women had worked hard to become independent and still to this date must fight for equality. She didn't understand this biker way of thinking at all.

Besides, relationships should be an equal partnership, not one partner lording over the other.

Kiki realized she never answered. "No. I have no reason to become someone's *ol' lady*, Hawk's or otherwise."

Crow just smiled in response.

He smiled. And it was *cream-your-jeans* worthy.

Damn, whispered through her head. She shook it to clear it.

"Women," he finally grumbled in the way that sounded like the word "silly" should be in front of it.

Then his eyes dropped to her jeans and he made a guttural noise. She had worn the designer pair that had fashionable frayed rips cut into them. From the factory, of course. She didn't wear jeans enough to wear a pair out and have them look that cool. She had bought them to try to fit in a little more today. Of course, the boots she also wore were nothing like a biker boot, but were stylish at least.

She jerked in surprise when he ran a finger over the skin above her knee that peeked out of the rip. "You buy 'em like that?"

Her heart leapt into her throat and suddenly began pounding, like it was trying to escape her neck. "Y-yes." She tried to swallow it back down into her chest.

He trailed his finger up her leg and poked it into the small frayed hole at the top of her thigh. "How much they set you back?"

She realized she was holding her breath and released it in a whoosh. "Why?"

"Coulda done that for nothin' with my blade." He patted the very large knife that hung off his belt in a sheath, but was kept mostly hidden by his cut.

"A hundred and twenty."

He shook his head. "A buck twenty. For fuck's sake," he muttered.

Suddenly, he jerked his wandering finger away from her like he had touched fire. A second later, his black eyes tipped up just as two large hands landed on her shoulders.

"Said she ain't gonna be your ol' lady, brother, so she's available," Crow said to whoever stood behind her. And she knew exactly who stood behind her without looking.

Even though she couldn't see his face, Hawk's fingers tightened, pressing into her bare flesh.

His words were low, grumbly and held a clear warning. "She's full of my cum right now, brother. Got me?"

Kiki's mouth dropped open and heat rushed up her throat into her cheeks. She was just going to die right then and there. Yes, it had been no secret that they had come from upstairs together. Most of the crowd had already arrived and all eyes had been on them. But still...

What he said was just plain rude. He might as well have lifted his leg and peed on her.

Crow dropped his gaze to her face. A smile slowly crept across his as he stared at her but talked to Hawk. "Just fuckin' with you, brother. You know I'm not lookin' to deal with any mess." Then he turned to the bar, downed the rest of his whiskey and pushed to his feet. He wacked Hawk on the shoulder as he passed, laughing sharply and saying, "Also not lookin' for you to kick my ass."

Kiki twisted on her stool to watch him walk away... or more like it, watch the swing of his narrow hips. When she looked up at Hawk, his eyes were boring into her.

"That was rude."

He cocked an eyebrow at her. "What?"

"What you said."

"Truth."

She closed her eyes and sighed. "Rude, Hawk. Embarrassing."

"Were you embarrassed when we came downstairs together after I just got done fuckin' you?"

She didn't answer.

"'Cause if you don't think everyone knew, you're fuckin' dead wrong."

"You don't have to announce that I'm full of your..." She lowered her voice. "DNA."

His lips twitched. "Yeah you are."

She rolled her eyes. "That's the last time I go upstairs with you."

"Got that right."

She gave him a surprised look.

He continued, "Not here, not again. My house. Your place. My bike. Not your car, though. Too tight."

Her eyes sliced through the crowd. Crow was no longer in sight.

"Done fuckin' 'im with your eyes?"

She ignored that. "What's his story?"

"Not mine to tell. Will tell you that if you want ink he's the man. One of the best ink slingers in the state."

"I'll keep that in mind when I'm ready to tattoo 'Mom' on my right breast."

"I'd prefer you get 'Hawk' on the back of your neck. But lemme make somethin' clear, the only thing you'll get from him is ink, got me?"

Lemme make somethin' clear.

"Do women really like this old school misogynistic crap? Because *lemme make somethin' clear*, I'm not really feeling it, just so you know."

"Whataya mean?"

She waved a hand in his direction. "This bossiness crap. Like you're *the man* and I'm just a *lil lady* who is helpless. And *lemme make somethin' else clear...* Just because you have a dick hanging between your legs, doesn't mean you get to act like one."

He opened his mouth and she gave him *the palm*. "I'm not done. And just because I have a vagina doesn't mean I need a man. Because I certainly don't."

She heard a loud snicker behind her and she spun in her seat to look at the older man with a long scruffy gray beard, a protruding beer gut, and lots of wrinkles, wearing a cut that had seen better days.

He slammed his beer mug on the bar and looked over at Hawk, pointing a gnarled finger at him. "Got your hands full with that one." He shook his head and muttered something that Kiki couldn't understand, then grumbled, "Hope the pussy's worth it."

Just great! They had an audience.

Hawk moved between them to where Crow previously sat. "Yeah, old man, the pussy's worth it."

Oh good lord.

She was grateful when the back door to the clubhouse opened with a *bang*, and that conversation was diverted.

A group of bikers funneled through the door. All of them wearing DAMC cuts. Kiki sighed in relief when she noticed they carried the four missing barrels of money. She recognized Hawk's brother Diesel, the club president, Pierce, and the brother named Crash. The rest she had no idea who they were.

Pierce wore a big smile as he lifted one of the barrels over his head and shouted, "Got the fuckin' money. Ditched it not far from the fairgrounds. With us an' the pigs hot on their tail, didn't have time to get it outta the barrels."

Shouts rose up, along with whistling and hooting.

Hawk's arm snaked across her collarbone and he pressed his front to her back. He spoke close to her ear. "Shit's good. We can get outta here now. Gotta check on the bar before we leave, though."

He thought she was going back to his place. Before she could respond, Diesel was there, towering over her, but had eyes on his brother.

"She good?"

"Yeah. Fucker grabbed her arm." Without releasing her, Hawk lifted her arm to show Diesel the bruise. His eyes narrowed on it and his lips flattened into an angry slash.

"Shoulda kept after them then. Need to crack some fuckin' heads."

"Uh," Kiki started but Hawk cut her off.

"You go to station?"

"Hadta follow the pigs back to station to wait for 'em to make a fuckin' report an' release the scratch."

"Axel there?"

Diesel's eyes tipped up to Hawk, who was still pressed against her back. "No. Why?"

"Think he got Bella."

Diesel's face turned dark and scary as he pulled a cell phone from the back pocket of his jeans. His big fingers jabbed at his phone and he'd apparently put it on speaker phone since the ringing sounds filled the air.

After three rings, her voicemail picked up and his jaw got tight. After the beep, he yelled into the phone, "Bella! You call me ASAP. Got me?"

He jabbed at the screen again, staring at it for a moment. He glanced up to survey the crowd until he found who he was looking for. "Jag!"

"Yo!" came the answering shout.

"Your ol' lady hear from Bella?"

Two seconds later he answered, "Nope."

Jag's so-called *ol' lady*, Ivy, was standing right next to him. The fact that the massive man didn't ask Ivy that question directly once again hit home for Kiki that things were somewhat backwards in this male-dominated world.

"Anyone hear from Bella?" Diesel barked loudly and the busy room became quiet.

Diamond pushed past a few people as she approached Diesel, Slade close on her heels. Besides a fat lip and a bruise across his jaw, Slade didn't look any worse for wear.

"Last we saw, she was with Axel. She's fine."

"Gonna go find her," Diesel growled.

Diamond sighed as Zak joined them. "D! Really. If she's with Axel, she's fine."

"Fuck that pig. Gonna go find her."

Diamond turned pleading eyes to Zak. "Z…"

Zak shrugged. "D wants to flatten my asshole brother, then more power to 'im."

Kiki felt like she should be shoving her fingers in her ears and singing, "La la la la!" She did not need to hear about anyone being flattened, put six feet under, or being threatened with a head cracking.

With a grunt, Diesel shoved his way out of the group and headed out of the clubhouse.

She glanced over her shoulder at Hawk. "He's going to end up back in jail. Especially if he assaults a cop."

Hawk's eyes dropped from his brother's retreating back to Kiki as he contemplated her words. "Right." He sighed. "Stay here."

Then he followed his brother out of the door.

"I'm going to go," Kiki said to no one in particular.

Zak turned to her. "Hawk said to stay here."

Kiki raised her eyebrows at him. "I heard him."

She pushed herself from the stool, checked to make sure she had her key fob then hurried past them all before someone stopped her.

She had enough drama for one day.

Chapter Twelve

SHE KNEW Hawk wouldn't be happy that she left the clubhouse last night after his *command* to stay there. In fact, without a doubt, she knew he'd be pissed. But she needed to leave. She needed to think.

The problem was, as much as she tried to convince herself that they were no more than a hook-up, she was afraid it had become so much more.

She couldn't deny the attraction between them, even though it still surprised her. She also couldn't deny the desire to spend more time with him.

The scary part was that she caught herself thinking about a future with the man. To do that, she'd have to tie up any loose ends.

The biggest one being her ex-husband who really wasn't her ex. At least, not yet. And not for a lack of trying. She'd been pleading with him to sign the divorce papers for the last two years. In fact, ever since she filed them with the court.

They had no children, each of them had well-paying jobs which meant neither needed spousal support, they had equally divided the furniture when she left, so he had no reason to not sign and close out that chapter in their lives.

He simply didn't want to let her go.

He'd said that too many times to count in the past couple years.

Still, she had no idea why he wanted to hang on to something that had been irrevocably broken the day she came home to find him fucking their neighbors' nineteen-year-old daughter in *their* bed. In *their* house.

Had he apologized? Sure.

She *might* be able to forgive, but even if she dug deep she couldn't ever forget what she saw. Especially in the position she caught them in.

Which, she had to admit, wasn't very flattering for Landon, her hopefully soon-to-be-ex.

Tonight would be her last push at getting him to sign the papers. She had bitten the bullet and invited him for dinner. She figured it was better to meet him in a public place than at her condo, his place, or the office. This way she could walk away if she needed to.

She cleared her throat and straightened her skirt as she saw Landon approach the table.

Dressed to impress, his suit was top of the line, his blond hair trimmed and gelled perfectly, his gait confident.

He looked better than ever and it reminded her why she had been attracted to him in the first place. He had swept her off her feet and it wasn't long after they had started dating that he proposed. At the time, they were both up and coming attorneys who planned to conquer the world. Or at least the city of Pittsburgh. And they planned to do it together.

"Hello, sweetheart," he greeted, a large smile on his face.

She pinned her lips together and frowned when he slid his hand under her hair and curled his fingers around her neck, leaning down and brushing a kiss along the top of her head.

"Landon."

"Yes?" he murmured near her ear.

"Sit, please."

He gave her a look, his green eyes narrowed with his impatience. She bit back a sigh of relief when he finally complied.

"Can I order you a drink?" he asked, his gaze crawling over her face, hair and then her breasts, where he lingered.

He'd always been a breast man. Karin, the neighbor, had some young, perky ones. Or at least she did two years ago.

"Yes, please." She was going to need one.

He waved at a nearby waiter, who rushed over. "Glenlivet Eighteen on the rocks for me. Vodka martini for the lady."

"No." Both sets of male eyes landed on her. "Whiskey, neat. Thank you."

As the waiter rushed off, Kiki met Landon's surprised eyes. "Really?"

"Yes, I've acquired a taste for it."

"Since when?"

"Since..." She took a breath. "Landon, things are different now. I..." Oh good lord, how did she explain any of this to him? He certainly wouldn't understand and might recommend her doing a stint in the loony bin. "Although, I invited you to have dinner at one of our favorite spots, I... I'm here asking for the last time for you to sign the papers. Please don't drag this out any longer."

He frowned and leaned forward over the table, grabbing her hand. "Kiki. Jesus. I've asked for your forgiveness. I've asked for you to take me back. I made a mistake. A grave one. I realize that. I... Well, I had a weak moment."

A weak moment.

"Right," she murmured.

"But what we had was something good."

"Not good enough apparently."

Landon closed his eyes for a moment then blew out a breath. "I was hoping with time, you'd see the error of your ways."

"The error of *my* ways?" The last two words came out a little higher pitched than she expected.

The waiter returned in a rush, placing a glass filled with dark amber liquid in front of her and sliding another one with ice in front of Landon. She gave the waiter a half-smile of thanks. After Landon's words, that was all she could muster.

"What's bringing this about now?"

Now. Like she hadn't been bugging him forever.

"Well, how about this... It's been two years. I'm tired of asking. And..." She drifted off as she took a deep inhale to bolster herself.

"And?"

"I'm seeing someone."

He sat back in his chair, reaching for his expensive scotch and downing almost half of it. She couldn't miss the gold Cartier watch on his wrist as he did so. When he placed his glass back down on the table, she noticed his nails were still neatly manicured. She bet there wasn't a speck of dirt under even one of them. "Who? Do I know him? Is he part of the bar?"

At his question, she paused her glass halfway to her lips. "Not the bar you're thinking of..." She took a sip and the warmth she was quickly getting familiar with slid down her throat. She waited for the burn to subside before continuing, "He's not a lawyer."

"Oh."

"You definitely don't know him."

Landon pursed his lips as he studied her, mindlessly fiddling with one of his cufflinks as he did so. "Do I get to meet him?"

Kiki's head jerked and she blinked at him across the table. "What? Why the hell would I have you meet someone I'm seeing?"

"Because I worry about you."

"You weren't worried about me when you were," she leaned closer and lowered her voice, "on your knees behind Karin giving it to her good. Not to mention you were telling her how she was the best you *ever had*. I also can't forget how you were telling her how tight her—" Kiki stopped abruptly. Not only because her blood pressure was starting to rise, but she looked around to remind herself where they were.

He frowned and cleared his throat. "Sweetheart, I've apologized a million times."

Kiki ignored his term of endearment. "I know."

"If I could take it back, I would."

"I know, Landon, but you can't."

"And once again, I'll say that I'm sorry that I hurt you."

Though he sounded sincere, she believed he was more sorry about getting caught.

A clearing of a throat that was not Landon's came from next to them. "Sorry to interrupt, would you like to hear our specials?"

Kiki rolled her eyes when Landon said, "Of course."

The waiter proceeded to rattle off the overpriced specials of the night. Though, she had to admit, the food was top quality here, even if a little pricy.

The waiter looked her direction. "Ma'am?"

As Kiki opened her mouth, Landon cut in. "The lady will have the filet, medium rare, with a spinach salad, house dressing on the side, and the grilled asparagus. I'll have the squab with the roasted vegetables and a Caesar salad."

"Very good, sir."

Kiki held up a hand. "Uh, no." She narrowed her eyes at Landon. "You need to stop ordering for me." She tilted her head toward the waiter who, as professional as he was, managed to keep a blank expression. "I'll take the lobster risotto, and a house salad, please and thank you."

"Very good, ma'am." The waiter gave a sharp nod and scooted quickly away.

"Seriously, Landon."

"Sorry, sweetheart. Old habits and such."

"It's been two years."

"So, tell me about... *him*."

She hesitated. Maybe she could make a deal. "Only if you agree to sign the papers. I'd like to call you my ex-husband and have it be true."

"Can I hear about him first and then decide?"

"No."

Landon's lips twitched. "Can I change my mind after I hear about him?"

"No."

With a shake of his head, he reached across the table, snagging her hand and squeezing. "Keek, I still care about you. More than I can express. I only want what's best for you."

Great. If she told him about Hawk, he definitely wouldn't think

---

that man was best for her. Hell, she couldn't even say that. But, no matter what, it wasn't his decision.

"He's a successful businessman."

Landon's eyebrows rose. Out of surprise or jealousy she didn't know or care.

"Yes? And what type of business?"

If she was thinking about any kind of future with Hawk, she couldn't be embarrassed to talk about him. He was who he was. He never claimed he'd change and she would never ask that of him. For the millionth time she told herself she needed to accept him as he was or move on. Or at least after a few more rounds of awesome sex.

Landon squeezed her hand harder and it brought her back to the restaurant's table.

"He owns a bar."

"Like a piano lounge? A cigar bar?"

Oh good lord. "No. Like a *bar* bar. With pool tables and... stuff."

"In Pittsburgh?"

"No, Shadow Valley."

Something she didn't recognize slid across Landon's face. It was there, then it was quickly hidden. "I've been to that town a few times."

She looked at him in surprise. "You have?"

"A client had a real estate transaction there. Cute town, but I heard there's a biker gang that owns quite a few properties there. I advised my client against the purchase. He argued that he didn't think owning an apartment building next to a gang-owned business would affect the value. I beg to differ." He shrugged. "What's the name of the bar?"

Oh shit. "I'm sure you wouldn't recognize it," she quickly answered.

He tilted his head. "Try me."

Her heart did a thump and a skip. "It's a roadhouse."

"A roadhouse..." He frowned.

Jesus, just rip the Band-Aid off, Kiki. "Yes, it's The Iron Horse Roadhouse."

Suddenly, Landon released her hand, dug into the interior pocket of his suit jacket, and pulled out his phone. He activated the screen, hit a few buttons, typed something in as Kiki watched frozen from her seat. His gaze scrolled over whatever he pulled up. And then his eyes hit her.

Hard.

He turned the phone toward her. She stared at the website for The Iron Horse where it was clear—so clear it was crystal—that it was a biker bar and that motorcycle clubs were welcome.

"Are you talking about *this* roadhouse?"

"Mmm."

"What was that?" His eyes tipped back down to his phone, he swiped, tapped, swiped, then froze. He lifted the phone closer to his face and scowled.

Kiki's stomach flipped as she waited for him to show her his screen. She didn't have to wait long.

"Kiki," he breathed. "Is this him?"

Kiki opened her mouth then snapped it shut as she stared at a photo of Hawk, *clearly* wearing his club's colors, *clearly* sitting on his Harley, *clearly* in front of The Iron Horse. And, of course, he had his bulky arms crossed over his wide chest, muscles bulging and his tattoos *clearly* on display. She'd be remiss in not noticing the really cool set of dark shades that covered his deep brown eyes.

Oh shit.

Well, at least he looked hot in the photo. Her heart did a little flip again, but for a totally different reason. She'd have to ask Hawk for a copy. Her eyes flicked up to Landon's as she lifted her glass to her lips and took a long, *long* sip. "Maybe."

"Are you delusional? He's in a freaking biker gang, Kiki."

"Club."

He waved a hand. "Semantics. He's dangerous."

She stared at the liquid in her glass as she swirled it around. "A complete kitten."

Landon slapped his palm on the table, making the silverware jump. "Have you lost your mind?"

His question made her snap, "Great orgasms tend to do that to me.

It had been a while since I had a good one. I tend to lose my mind when I do."

Kiki glanced up at the waiter holding two salads, a spot of red in both cheeks. *Whoops.*

The server slid the plates in front of them, then scurried off like his pants were on fire. She stared at her almost empty glass and realized she really, really needed to order another round. Or two.

"Do you think you could wave that poor man back over here and get me another drink?"

He made a noise of disbelief. "Do you think this is humorous?"

It sure didn't feel like she was laughing. She wasn't even finding any of this slightly amusing. "Not at all. I also don't appreciate you insulting a man you know nothing about."

They both ignored their salads and Landon scooted his chair closer to the table to lean toward Kiki. "How the hell did you meet him?"

"He's a... client."

At her words, Landon slapped a hand over his eyes and shook his head.

Honestly, he was acting way too dramatic. She scowled at him.

"Not a surprise he's been arrested. And I'm sure more than once."

No point in fudging the truth about something that was public record. "Sure has."

"He wears a black leather vest with dirty patches all over it."

Landon wasn't telling her anything she didn't know. "Not when he's naked."

His eyes narrowed at her answer. "He's solid tattoos."

"Not completely." She wiggled her eyebrows at him trying to lighten the mood, though failing miserably. She scanned the busy restaurant for their waiter. She'd flag him down herself if need be. But right now, water wasn't going to cut it.

"Jesus, Kiki."

There he was, hiding in a corner. Kiki waved her hand at their server in an attempt to get his attention.

"No, not Jesus. But Hawk does make me call out Jesus' father's name sometimes. Well, a lot, actually."

"*Hawk.* What's his real name?"

"Hawk."

"Who names their kid Hawk?"

Who names their daughter Kiki? "A biker named Ace."

"Does he have a brother named Falcon?"

"No... Diesel."

"Get the hell out of here," Landon muttered.

She'd had enough of this line of questioning. They needed to get back to the reason for her dinner invitation. "Landon, please. I'm done talking about this. I brought the papers for you to sign. Will you do that for me, please?"

"Kiki..."

"Landon, no. You're out of my life, or will be when you finally sign the papers. What I do is no concern of yours. Who I'm with isn't either. I'm not stupid."

"I don't like it, sweetheart."

"I'm sure you don't."

"I only want you to be happy."

"Then sign the papers."

Landon leaned back in his chair and sighed. "After we eat. If this is our last meal together, I want to enjoy it."

Kiki grabbed her fork and stabbed her salad. "Then let's eat." Though she doubted she was going to enjoy one bite.

AFTER SHE IGNORED his demand to stay put last night, Hawk fought the temptation to chase after her. Even though he had no fucking clue where she lived. In the time they'd spent together, she had never once revealed that information or invited him to her place.

Which was telling.

So, last night despite his instinct to find her, throw her over his lap and spank her for not listening, he let it go. If she wanted him, she knew where he lived, where he worked, where he played.

But today he finally broke down and asked Ivy to do her Internet magic. To dig up her address. And if she couldn't or wouldn't, then he'd get one of Diesel's connections to dig up the information he needed.

Surprisingly, Ivy complied. He had expected her to give him a bunch of shit since the women tended to stick together and have each other's backs. Which was good for them. Not so great for the men.

His first mistake was going to Kiki's condo in Pittsburgh. He couldn't get into the lower level parking garage since it was keycard access only. From outside alone, he knew she was paying a pretty penny to live there.

As he rounded the block twice looking for a place to park his sled, he caught a glimpse of red leaving the garage.

His second mistake was weaving through traffic while trying to catch up with her Vette since she drove like a madwoman. He planned on having a long talk with her about that. He was cut off once by a cab and almost T-boned by a city bus. He fucking hated everything about the city.

Now he hated it even more. He ground his back molars so hard, the muscles in his jaw felt like they popped.

At first, he thought she may be meeting a client. Especially since the restaurant was upscale. Kiki was definitely dressed for work with her typical tight skirt that fell just above her knees, her *sexy-as-fuck* stockings, and those *higher-than-hell* stilettos. And that fucking blouse... What man could concentrate with her tits hanging out like that?

Maybe one who wasn't straight. But when he saw the man who approached her, there was no doubt he wasn't gay. Nope. It took everything in Hawk's power not to bust into the restaurant right then and there when the man in the suit wrapped his hand around her neck and kissed her.

Yeah, there wasn't any tongue and it was on the top of her head, but fuck if any man should be touching her. At all.

And when the suit settled into the chair across from her, it wasn't hard to miss him eye-fucking her.

Seeing how this guy was dressed reminded him, once again, she was way out of his league. He couldn't even begin to compete with a man like the one who joined her at her table.

Hawk needed to leave. It did him no good to pace back and forth in front of the restaurant's wide picture window like a crazed stalker.

The two valets stationed at the stand by the front door kept eyeballing him like he might rip their throats out. And, fuck him, he just might. Especially when the suit reached out and grabbed Kiki's hand.

That fucker had intimate knowledge of her. And if he didn't, he was trying to.

A low growl escaped his lips.

Ain't gonna happen. No fuckin' way.

Within three strides he was at the double doors to the restaurant, his hand gripping the handle hard.

"Uh..." one of the valets began. Hawk shot him a look and the valet's jaw snapped shut.

Smart choice.

He yanked the door open and paused at the entrance when the hostess' mouth dropped open.

Jesus. These people acted like they never saw anyone with a couple tattoos.

As he strode past the hostess stand, she called out, "Sir! Do you have a reservation?"

Hawk snorted and kept moving, his boots heading him in the right direction while his brain focused on the table in the far corner of the busy restaurant. The din that hit him when he first opened the door became a low murmur as he moved between the tables. Or maybe he was just that fixated on his destination.

Since eyeballs tracked him, he figured the first one was more likely.

Kiki's fork, with lettuce and a tomato slice speared on the tines, was paused halfway to her mouth when she turned as if in slow motion. Her eyes widened when she saw him.

"Oh, look, it's your boyfriend," the man murmured with a frown, dropping his fork onto his plate with a clatter.

Hawk ignored him, his eyes pinned on Kiki as he stepped up to the table. "Yeah, babe. Got it."

Kiki carefully set her fork down without breaking his gaze. "Got what?"

"The truth."

She swallowed hard enough he could see it. "Hawk, what truth?"

He ripped his gaze from her throat back to her eyes and threw a hand out. "This is you. You don't belong in my life."

"What?" she whispered, her face becoming pale and her eyes wide.

"All this, babe. Can't give it to you. Don't wanna give it to you. Ain't me. But it's you. Deserve better. Deserve this kinda shit. Don't deserve my kinda shit."

"Jesus. Does he even speak English?"

Kiki's gaze flew to the man across the table from her. "Landon!" she snapped.

Landon.

Right. Fancy name for a fancy guy. A guy with some serious scratch. One who could give Kiki what she needs and deserves.

It was clear to Hawk what she needed wasn't a biker like him.

"Are you going to introduce me, sweetheart?"

Sweetheart? What the fuck.

His lip curled.

Some man in a monkey suit approached them and warily sidled up to Hawk. "Sir," he whispered. "You're creating a disturbance. I'm going to have to ask you to leave."

Hawk looked down at the man, whose Adam's apple bobbed wildly. "How am I makin' a disturbance? Just standin' here."

The man's face twitched. "About that... we... uh... we also have a jacket policy, sir."

Sir. Hawk snorted. He tugged on his vest. "Wearing a vest."

"Something with sleeves. And... preferably not in leather."

"Got a problem with cows? Can't imagine that, seein' you serve them on a plate here."

Kiki pushed her chair back and started to rise. "Hawk..."

"No, babe. Stay here. Have your fancy dinner with your fancy guy here. I'm headin' back home. Kept tellin' myself we're too different. Needed to be slapped in the fuckin' face with it. Got the truth now. I'm good."

"Hawk..."

"Can't give you what he can. Need to be with him." Jesus, it killed him to say that but it had to be said.

"See, sweetheart? Even he agrees—" *Landon's* words stopped when Kiki glared at him. *Landon* raised his palms up in surrender.

"Don't pass on somethin' good, babe. You got it, keep it."

"Plan on it," he heard her murmur as he spun on his heel to stop embarrassing the fuck out of himself. He needed to get some pride and move the fuck on.

Hearing her say those last words made his chest cave in, his stomach churn, and his heart freeze as he weaved through the occupied tables on his way back to the front door. All eyes followed him on his exit, too.

"Nothin' but a freak to 'em," he grumbled under his breath as he shoved the door open and stepped out into the night air.

He struggled to breathe as he stalked to his bike, kicked the starter and raced off into the night.

Chapter Thirteen

A WHOLE WEEK later and she had balls big enough to show up at *his* bar on a busy Friday night. For what?

She needed him to scratch another fucking itch?

Did she get bored with the suit, *Landon*, that quickly and get shot of his ass?

Maybe pretty boy couldn't give it to her hard enough, rough enough for her liking and she had to come slumming to get some good coming.

He had known the second she walked in the door and his eyes had been automatically drawn to her. He could've met her halfway but he didn't. He wasn't giving her that. She had to come all the way to him.

However, he wasn't the only one who noticed her immediately. The urge to beat the fuck out of every man who eyeballed her was strong as she swung her hips on her journey across The Iron Horse floor to where he was.

What she was wearing now wasn't much better than the DAMC camisole-thingy she wore at the *Dogs & Hogs* event. As he watched her full tits bounce with each step, he had to put the mug he was drying down before it shattered in his hands.

She wore a white, snug button-down blouse that had such a deep V he was surprised her nipples weren't playing peek-a-boo. Tight jeans hugged every line of her hips and thighs. Brown high-heeled leather boots covered her legs all the way to the knees. A brown leather belt cinched her waist, emphasizing her hourglass curves.

Curves he couldn't get enough of.

Fuck me.

This woman had crawled under his skin and was now deeply infused in his blood.

He thought he could let her go after last week. Just like he foolishly thought he could let her go after she walked away the month before.

Watching her approach the bar proved just how wrong he had been. Once again.

Even though there wasn't one empty bar stool along the bar, when she stepped up, three men jumped to their feet offering theirs.

Figures.

Hawk gritted his teeth as the men fumbled over their introductions to her. The normally drunk and rude motherfuckers suddenly became perfect gentlemen. However, she only had eyes for him.

He ignored that pull and ripped his gaze from hers, grabbed a clean glass and poured her a Gentleman Jack on the rocks. Tonight, nothing was going to be neat.

He slid the glass in front of her. "On the house," he muttered.

She reached for it before he could let it go and her fingers brushed against his. He allowed it for a moment then pulled away.

"Thanks." Her voice, husky and low, shot right down into his dick. Which was exactly what she wanted.

"Get lost?" he asked.

"No. I know exactly where I am."

She sure did. She was on the "wrong side of town" for one reason and one reason only.

And, fuck him, he wasn't going to be able to resist giving her what she wanted.

"Wanna deal with my shit only when it benefits you," he muttered.

"It's going to benefit you, too," she said softly with a small smile.

Yeah it was. Fuck him.

"Talk," he muttered with a frown. He couldn't believe he was encouraging a woman to talk, usually he was trying to get them to shut up.

"It wasn't what you think it was."

"Wasn't thinkin' much of anything."

She gave him a look. She didn't believe him. Hell, he didn't believe him, either. That's because he was lying out of his ass. He'd hardly slept in the last week. He hated coming home to an empty bed as much as he hated waking up in one, too.

He looked at the woman in front of him. It wasn't just coming home to an empty bed. It was coming home to a house without Kiki in it.

Fuck him. She had him by the fucking balls and she probably didn't even know it.

"Landon's my ex-husband."

Hawk cocked an eyebrow, but kept his mouth shut.

"I didn't invite him to dinner to get back together with him, Hawk. I was there to get him to sign the divorce papers."

"He sign 'em?" Because if the asshole didn't, both he and Diesel could help him hold the pen.

Kiki sighed. "Yes. Finally. Two whole years of asking and it took you showing up to convince him."

"Didn't convince him of shit."

"No, but I did. Because of you."

Because of you.

"Makin' a mistake, Keeks. Can't give you any of that shit."

"You don't have to give it to me, I'm capable of getting it on my own if I want it."

Hawk's jaw tightened. He was the one who was supposed to provide for his woman, for his ol' lady. She wasn't supposed to be forced to get it on her own. Jesus. He might as well tuck his balls up into his pussy. "Don't work that way, babe."

"In my world it does. Take it or leave it."

"Right," he grunted. He'd have to think on that one. He knew he wouldn't be thinking too long or too hard on it. He took care of his woman. Period. "Why'd you get shot of his ass?"

Her fingertip traced the rim of the whiskey glass, her eyes avoiding his. "He slipped and fell into a nineteen-year-old named Karin."

"Fuck," he muttered. Who wanted a teenager over a more mature woman who knew what she was doing in bed and did it well? And who had a body that wouldn't quit with all its soft curves and who got wetter than the Allegheny River.

His dick twitched.

A stupid fuck, that's who.

"So, what're you here for?"

"You," she said softly, peeking at him from under her eyelashes.

Fuckin' goddamn. His dick wasn't just twitching. He now sported a full-blown hard-on.

Just what he thought, she just wanted some dick. Well, fuck him, he was going to give it to her.

Digging into his jeans' pocket, he pulled out his house keys and slapped them onto the bar next to her glass. "Got an hour before I can get outta here. Go get yourself warmed up."

Her gaze rose from the keys to lock onto his. The look in her eyes made his gut twist.

"I can wait," she murmured.

He shook his head. "No." He wasn't going to get anything done if she sat there surrounded by men who would fall all over themselves in front of her.

"I can wait, Hawk," she repeated, this time more firmly, but still more quietly than normal.

Her feistiness seemed to be gone tonight, leaving behind a soft, pliable woman who was subdued. Not at all like her normal self. It made him wonder what was up.

Maybe she wasn't proud of herself for having to come down to his level to get laid.

She might not want it any longer from her ex but he couldn't imagine that ol' Mikey from her law firm wouldn't offer up his.

It is what it is.

"Don't want you here. Want you in my bed waitin'."

She took a sip of her drink, avoiding his eyes.

Something was definitely up. He softened his tone. "Babe. Do this for me, yeah?" Otherwise, he'd be dealing with an unruly cock, too.

Her gaze tipped back up to him. And there was something behind her eyes he couldn't quite get a bead on. "Okay."

Relief flowed through him. "An hour. Tops."

"Okay," she repeated. Tipped her glass to her lips, drained the liquid, then pushed to her feet.

Then he and the rest of the men in the bar watched his woman walk back out the same way she came in. Everyone seemed to take a collective breath once the door closed behind her.

Fuck him.

KIKI PULLED into Hawk's driveway, put the car in park and sat staring at the house. The living room was lit up so she assumed Jazz was home. Her eyes flicked to the keys she had thrown onto the passenger seat. She didn't need his keys after all.

"Don't pass on somethin' good, babe. You got it, keep it."

And that's exactly why she went to the bar tonight. Even though her brain kept telling her that this was a mistake, that it wouldn't last, her heart kept laughing at her and saying otherwise.

There had been a hole inside her for the past week after watching him walk out of the restaurant and that emptiness had turned into an ache as soon as she stepped through the door at The Iron Horse, as soon as she'd seen him working behind the bar.

She needed to stop denying that pull between them. She didn't even know whether Hawk himself wanted something more than what they had. Something regular. Possibly even permanent.

Now that she was officially free of Landon since she had filed the signed papers this week, permanent was a possibility.

She shook her head and blew out a breath. She had no idea how all of it would work. They lived in two different worlds.

Yes, she was focused on her career right now, but she eventually wanted kids, a family. She looked at the house again trying to imagine raising children in a house like this in the 'burbs. With a man like Hawk.

The doubt niggled at the back of her brain again. It would never work.

Not only were they worlds apart, he was too domineering, too possessive. Would that eventually make her bitter? And possibly even tear them apart?

She unfastened her seat belt and leaned forward, pressing her forehead against the steering wheel.

She had no idea how to approach him with all these things she'd been contemplating. She'd had a million conversations in her head, trying to work through it. She'd hardly slept a wink.

When she decided to head to The Iron Horse tonight, she wasn't sure what her final decision would be. Whether seeing him in his element would cement the fact that they just didn't belong together, like he kept insisting, and that she needed to move on. Or whether when she saw him, she would want to do whatever was needed to get back into his bed, into his life. The decision had been clear the minute she saw him.

Her heart had exploded and warmth of her love for him seeped out of every pore of her body. Now, she could only hope he felt the same way.

And then they'd have to deal with the rest.

That hour she would have to wait for him was going to seem like an eternity.

Without warning, her driver's side door was yanked open and she expected to see Hawk standing there.

Instead, a hand reached in and a deep gruff voice yelled, "Get outta the car, bitch!"

She was grabbed and yanked out of the car and thrown roughly to the ground. Even in the dark, she recognized the Warrior who tried to steal some of the money at the fundraiser. The one that grabbed her and Slade knocked out.

Ice ran through her veins and she screamed, hoping Jazz would hear her and call 911.

"Shut the fuck up!"

"Just take the car!" she cried out as she attempted to climb to her feet.

A heavy boot kicked her in the chest, knocking her back on her ass with an *oomph*. "Shut the fuck up! What the fuck!" His head turned as he looked toward the road.

Kiki looked the same direction, still trying to catch her breath from the kick, and saw a van along the road blocking the driveway with someone in the driver's seat.

That person yelled out of the window, "Grab the car. Let's go!"

"This is the bitch with the money!" the one standing over her yelled back. "I'm taking her with."

Holy shit!

Kiki wheezed as she tried to suck in air. She rolled onto her hands and knees and attempted to crawl toward the house. A boot kicked her in the head, knocking her down flat. "Comin' with me, bitch." Then his voice was low and near her ear. "Paybacks are a bitch, you cunt."

"Just take the car... leave me."

The man laughed sharply. "Shut the fuck up."

"No... I—" Movement caught her eye and she looked up to see Jazz running out of the house toward them, barefooted, hair flying wildly behind her, her cell phone in her hand. "No... Jazz," she groaned.

Fuck. She never should've shouted her name.

Kiki watched in horror as Jazz was tackled by the Warrior that had been waiting in the van. She tumbled to the ground, the weight of the biker on top of her. She turned into a whirlwind as she screamed and scratched, her hands and feet flying.

Then Kiki saw the Warrior who had her pinned to the ground backhand her twice, and as if in slow motion, watched him pull his elbow back and slug her in the face. Her body went limp and Kiki cried out her name.

Holy shit, now would be a great time for Hawk to show up.

The first Warrior squatted in front of her, grabbed a handful of her hair, yanking her head up. "Takin' you with me, bitch. You gonna fight?"

Kiki spit in his face. "Fuck you!"

With his free hand he wiped the spit off his cheek and he dropped her head. She struggled to get back onto her hands and knees. She needed to get up. She needed to get to Jazz. They needed to get away.

That plan quickly went south as the Warrior stood up, a wicked smile on his face, and drop kicked her in the ribs. Kiki gasped, once again losing all her breath as she fell to her side.

Then he kicked her again on the other side. Shards of pain shot through her. Her ribs had to be broken. Her head was spinning and she couldn't breathe.

She had enough energy to lift her hand and give him the finger. He laughed. "Fuckin' feisty bitch. Like feisty. Can't wait to get a piece of you." He looked over his shoulder at the other Warrior.

"Throw her in the van. This one, too."

Oh shit.

Oh shit.

Oh shit.

She and Jazz were done if those assholes took them. No one would be able to find them. Hawk had explained that the Shadow Warriors were nomads. No permanent clubhouse, no home base. Nowhere for the Dirty Angels, or even the cops, to look.

With a groan, she tried to roll to a seat. She couldn't let them take them.

"Jazz," she tried to call out, but it ended up sounding more like a cough. Her hand immediately went to the pain shooting through her ribs. She gasped.

"Leave... us... get... cash..."

"Fuck the cash. This car will bring us good scratch. An' after we're done with you, you bitches might, too."

Kiki pushed through the pain to roll to her knees.

"Think you're gonna get away? Think again, bitch."

She never saw what hit her.

Chapter Fourteen

HAWK ROARED INTO THE DRIVEWAY, rolled to a stop and dropped his boots to the pavement.

"What the fuck," he muttered.

Kiki's car wasn't in the driveway and he couldn't imagine her parking in Jazz's spot in the garage.

He crab-walked the bike closer to the garage and kicked the stand down. After flinging a leg over his sled, he went over to punch in the code on the keypad to activate the garage door opener.

He blinked as the double door lifted. His truck sat in its normal spot and so did Jazz's old Honda.

He glanced over his shoulder at the house. Downstairs was lit up, so Jazz was definitely home. Maybe she had talked to Kiki. Maybe Kiki needed to run to get something at a twenty-four-hour store.

Maybe. Or she thought better of coming over to his house and hooking up with him again.

He should head over to her condo, bang on her door and wake up all her fucking neighbors.

He wanted an explanation. And he needed his keys back if she hadn't dropped them off with Jazz.

Didn't make sense, though, why she'd show up at the bar acting like she wanted some dick, and then change her mind immediately.

Unless, again, she came to her senses.

Fuck if he didn't leave the bar early tonight to hurry home to settle himself between her sweet thighs.

Fuck.

Maybe she was playing some sort of game with him.

Whatever it was, he didn't like it.

He fucking hated it.

The more he thought about it the hotter he became as he strode down the driveway and then up the front walk.

Why was the front door wide open? He frowned and walked faster. At least until he stepped on something that crunched beneath his boot.

He hopped off whatever it was and looked down. Even in the dark he could see it was a cell phone. He snagged the crushed phone off the concrete.

Jazz's.

What the fuck.

Cold dread ran through him and turned his stomach as his gaze rose from the broken phone in his hand to the open door.

"Fuck," he barked and ran the rest of the way, up the porch and through the doorway.

The large flat-screen TV was showing some late-night talk show with the sound muted.

"Jazz!" he bellowed. He snagged the remote off the couch and hit the power button.

The only thing that greeted him was his heart pounding in his chest.

"Yo, Jazz!"

His eyes landed on the plate of nachos on the coffee table. The melted cheese had congealed. He touched it anyway just to confirm his suspicion. Cold.

As thin as Jazz was, she had a bottomless pit for a stomach, there would be no way she'd leave a plate of nachos untouched.

No way.

"Jazz!" he bellowed again as he rushed down the hall to her room. Empty. Bathroom. Empty. His gaze swept the kitchen. Empty.

"Jazz! You better answer!"

The silence crept over him creating a blanket of fear. He rushed back to the front of the house and took the steps to his bedroom two at a time.

He let out a curse when he got to the top and saw just what he expected: nothing. Neither Kiki nor Jazz were in the house.

He swallowed hard as his blood started to rush in his ears. His rapid heartbeat rose into his throat.

He pulled his phone out of his back pocket as he hurried back down the steps. He hit the switch for the porch light as well as the floodlight that would shine on the driveway. Kiki's cell phone rang three times then the voicemail picked up.

He hung up and hit redial. Again, no answer. This time at the beep he barked into the phone, struggling to keep his shit together. "Call me as soon as you get this. Got me?"

He jogged back down the porch steps as he dialed Diesel's cell.

"Yo," his brother answered, his voice gruff. "What the fuck? Busy, brother."

"Got a problem."

Silence for a moment. "What?"

He stopped at the location where he had stepped on Jazz's phone. Now with the light on, he could see a dark discoloration on the concrete. "Hang on."

He squatted down and tilted the screen of his cell phone toward the dark area. He quickly put the phone back to his ear. "Definitely gotta fuckin' problem."

"What!" his brother barked, now sounding way more awake than he had when he first picked up.

"Think Jazz was snagged."

"What!"

"Jazz. Not at the house. Car's here. Found her phone on the sidewalk. Door wide open. TV on. Food cold on the table. Dark spot on the concrete. Blood."

More silence on the other end of the phone.

"D," Hawk said, trying not to panic.

"Gettin' dressed."

Really trying not to panic. "Yeah. Gotta move on this."

"Yeah, brother, hear you. Gonna make some calls."

He dropped his head back to stare up at the night sky. "Right. Brother," he began but his throat closed up.

"Yeah?"

He forced the words out. "Keeks was supposed to be here. She ain't. Car ain't. Not answerin' her fuckin' phone."

"Fuck," Diesel muttered.

Hawk strode over to the driveway and looked around where Kiki normally parked her Vette.

"Brother," Hawk breathed.

"Fuck," Diesel muttered again.

"Dark spot on the driveway, too. Nothin' else. No other sign. Can't tell for sure."

"Warriors," Diesel grumbled.

"If so, they're all fuckin' dead."

"All of them," D agreed. "Hangin' up. Gonna get my crew on this."

"Can't move fast enough."

"Hear ya, brother. Her cell phone anywhere?"

"Haven't seen it."

"Could be a good thing. Gonna get a guy to ping it. Owes me a favor."

Hawk blew out a breath.

"Hawk," Diesel started, his voice tight.

"Yeah."

"Gonna find her. Jazz, too. Got me?"

Hawk couldn't answer. He was too busy struggling to suck air into his empty lungs.

"Hawk!" Diesel yelled into the phone.

"Yeah, D. Find her. Your guy gets a bead, gimme the address."

There was no mistaking the reason for the long hesitation on Diesel's end.

"Right, brother," D finally said.

The phone went dead.

KIKI GROANED. Unable to stop herself, she rolled forward and hit something solid but soft. With the way the floor vibrated under her, it seemed that they were in a vehicle and it was moving at a high rate of speed. That's all she knew. She blinked her eyes open but the back of the van was dark. Whatever road they were on didn't have any street lights to help illuminate the interior. She slid her hand out to the object she hit. Flesh and hair.

Jazz.

As she twisted toward the girl, she bit back a sharp cry as pain not only shot through her ribs but rocketed through her head, making her vision spotty and her head spin. Her brain felt like scrambled eggs and her head throbbed.

Unfortunately, she didn't think Jazz had regained consciousness.

Holy shit.

They needed to get out of this vehicle or they...

A loud impact sound came from nearby. Metal crunched, glass shattered, an engine raced.

"What d'fuck? You asshole! Why'd you do that for?" The driver screamed, then slammed on the brakes, sending Kiki rolling into Jazz again.

Oh shit.

Her hands weren't tied. Her ankles weren't either. They had just thrown them into the cargo area at the back of the van. She reached out to Jazz and found her hand in the dark. She squeezed it but didn't get a response. Jazz's hand was limp. At least it was warm, which meant she was still alive.

Kiki winced as more pain shot through her brain when the passenger door of the van was ripped open and someone jumped in.

"Fuck!"

"What the fuck! Just trashed that fuckin' car! That was the whole point of this. Now what?"

"Fuck the car."

"Coulda got good money for it."

"Shut the fuck up. We got them. May be worth more than the car."

The driver put the van into gear and the tires chirped as he hit the gas.

Kiki groaned as the movement caused more pain to shoot through her body.

"Hear that?"

"What?"

"One of 'em's awake."

"Fuck."

"Yeah, pull over for a sec."

The van jerked to the side of the road and before Kiki could react, the passenger was climbing between the seats to the back.

Shit. Shit. Shit.

She squeezed her eyes shut and pretended she was still out. But when the Warrior toed her ribs with his boot, she couldn't hold back her cry.

"Fuckin' bitch is awake."

"Need to tie 'em up."

"Don't got no rope. Wasn't plannin' on takin' nothin' but the car."

"No shit. Which you just fucked up."

"Shut the fuck up. I got this."

Kiki released her grip on Jazz's fingers when the world went black again.

———

"Go," Hawk barked into his phone. He paced restlessly, scrubbing his hand over his mohawk repeatedly.

"Found her car."

He tamped down the rush of anxiety. D didn't sound hopeful. Hawk knew by his voice alone that Kiki wasn't with her car. He didn't even have to ask.

"Good news, cell ain't in the car. Hopefully it's on her. Bad news, brother... Car landed hard in a drainage ditch. Gotta be totaled. Bunch of blood on the driver's side. Not sure if it's hers."

"Your guy got a bead?"

"Yeah. Headed that way. How I found the car. Got a few of my Shadows with."

Got a few of his Shadows with him. Jesus.

Diesel had some guys working for him for In the Shadows Security that could be questionable. But Hawk knew they'd take care of business. One way or the other.

But for fuck's sake, he needed to be there, too.

"Location, D."

Diesel grunted into the phone.

"Location, D," Hawk yelled.

"Got it covered."

"Fuck!"

"Yep."

Phone went dead.

Hawk threw his head back and roared. Then he collapsed to his knees and heaved until his guts had nothing left to give.

Chapter Fifteen

MALE VOICES. Scuffling. A distant whimper. A stale, putrid smell that made her scrunch up her nose and her stomach lurch.

Kiki groaned. She mentally did a body check and couldn't find one part that didn't ache or hurt in some way. She could've been hit by a tractor trailer and felt the same. Propped up into a seated position on the floor, she was leaning back against something hard—a wall maybe —but she listed to one side. She tried to shift, to straighten, but when she went to put her hand down for leverage, she couldn't move it.

They must have found rope or something similar since her hands were now bound behind her back. She tried to wiggle her fingers, but couldn't feel them.

Something warm rolled down her cheek. A tear?

She didn't have time to cry and feel sorry for herself and the situation they were in. She needed to think. She needed to figure a way out of it.

She forced her swollen eyes open. It took an effort and the moment her eyelids opened to partial slits, the dim light caused pain to shoot through her temple.

Her legs were folded beneath her so she tried to shift again. Shit, her ankles were tied together, too. Her boots were gone. She glanced down as best as she could through her hazy vision. Her white blouse was in tatters and stained. So were her jeans.

Her tears weren't dripping onto the floor. That was blood. Her blood. She had at least one head wound from the way her head throbbed and her scalp stung.

She painfully swallowed back the bile that threatened to bubble up.

With care, she turned her pounding head and surveyed the room. It appeared the Warriors had taken them to a house, but it was in such rough condition that there was no way anyone lived there. The drywall had holes, the wood framing was exposed, what wallpaper remained was peeling away in large chunks. The floors were filthy and consisted of exposed stained plywood. Not one stick of furniture could be seen. And, of course, being uninhabitable there would be no phone. No way to call for help. No way to let anyone, even Hawk, know where they were.

Kiki wouldn't doubt the abandoned house sat in the middle of nowhere, too. Somewhere where no one would hear her scream.

She couldn't even muster up any hope of being found. Not one single hope.

They were going to die here. And before she did, she was sure whatever these outlaw bikers had planned wouldn't be pleasant.

Unless... they planned on ransoming her and Jazz to the club?

Her heart pounded with the possibility. That would be smart on their part. But then... Kiki couldn't imagine either of them being intelligent.

She closed her eyes again as heavy footsteps approached. No, two sets of boots.

Grunting. Cursing under their breath. Then something hit the bare wood floor hard. Her eyes opened to barely slits again. She sucked in a breath.

Jazz.

She wasn't tied up. Even better, she was coming to. Her head rocked back and forth, small mews escaping her lips.

"Just in time. Wakin' up for the fun." The taller, older one said, kicking at Jazz's bare foot.

Oh shit.

A piercing scream filled the air, making all the hair on Kiki's body stand on end. Jazz was now fully conscious and struggled to sit up. Her arms and legs floundered in different directions as she attempted to get her body to cooperate.

She was truly in fight or flight mode. As one of the Warriors dropped to his knees to grab her ankles, she kicked at him, making contact with his shoulder once and his gut another time. He grunted in pain and cursed at his partner in crime.

Kiki rooted her on silently. *Fight, Jazz. Fight!*

"Hold her still, goddamn it."

The prospect dropped to his knees at her head, but instead of planting them on the floor he drilled his knees into her wrists, effectively pinning her down.

Her eyes wild, Jazz cursed at them. "They're gonna fucking kill you! Kill you all!"

"Shut up, bitch."

"Skin you a-fucking-live. Making the biggest mistake of your fucking life!"

"Shut the fuck up!" the one at her feet shouted, then looked at the prospect, who remained by her head. "Need to gag the bitch."

The prospect pulled a black bandana from around his neck, nodding in agreement.

"Don't!" Jazz screamed as the prospect balled the bandana up and jammed it into her mouth.

Jazz coughed and thrashed, but it did no good. Kiki had to do *something*.

"Stop!" Kiki screamed. "Don't! Don't hurt her!"

Their heads swung her direction. "You shut up, too. You're next."

"No! No! Take me instead. Leave her alone. Take me, you assholes. Or ransom us. They'll pay good money to get us back unharmed."

"Right. Probably dead either way. Might as well enjoy some sweet pussy an' die happy."

A muffled scream came from Jazz, her eyes wide as she continued to struggle against the prospect pinning her wrists to the floor.

"Get her shirt off. Wanna see her tits," the older Warrior barked.

The prospect took two handfuls of Jazz's baby doll T-shirt and tore it clean in half causing Jazz's torso to jerk in response.

Fuck!

"Please, please, please," Kiki begged. "Leave her alone. I'll give you whatever you want."

The older Warrior looked her way. "Willingly?"

"Yes! Just... leave her alone."

He laughed. "Right. Like the fight." Then he pinned Jazz's legs down with his shins and grabbed her shorts, ripping them down her legs.

Oh shit.

Oh shit.

Oh shit.

She had to do something. Anything. She had to do whatever she could to stop what they were doing. What they planned.

"Fuck you, assholes. You want a fight. I'll give you a fight. She's not a challenge. I am. Fuck me instead."

Once again, the Warrior's head spun her direction and he studied her for a moment.

Then he glanced back at Jazz, who was now naked from the waist down. She only wore her bra, which the prospect had yanked up, exposing her breasts. Her eyes were now squeezed shut and Kiki could see her visibly shaking. She was saying something over and over but Kiki couldn't make it out because of the bandana stuffed in her mouth.

Oh, God, someone help us.

"Nah. Fuckin' want this fresh piece first. Then you."

Oh, God, someone help that poor girl.

Kiki opened her mouth, sucked in a breath and, pushing past the pain, screamed at the top of her lungs. She didn't stop screaming until the room went dark once more.

HAWK HUNCHED low on his bike and pushed her to the limit. Diesel wouldn't give him the address, but he forced it from Zak. He'd address that snafu with his brother another time. Right now, he had to get to Kiki. He understood why his brother wouldn't want Hawk showing up, though his reasoning wasn't good enough.

Zak could understand. He would insist on being involved if Sophie had been successfully snatched by that Warrior all those months ago. Hell, he would've been leading the search.

There was no way Hawk was just going to sit around waiting to find out what happened to Kiki. Or Jazz.

No goddamn way.

And if someone was going to have their head busted in, he wanted a piece of that.

Unfortunately, Diesel and his crew had a head start and would get to the address where Kiki's phone pinged way before he would. Zak was also heading that direction. The last known location was somewhere out in the country southwest of Shadow Valley close to the West Virginia line. At least on his bike, he could take the winding, hilly backroads with ease and speed.

He slowed down for only a split second as he passed the crumpled mess of Kiki's Vette in a ditch alongside the road.

His heart thumped wildly and the sight only made him twist the throttle harder.

He was going to exact revenge if it was the last thing he did.

Nobody touched or harmed DAMC property.

Nobody.

KIKI GROANED as she was dragged along the floor by her bound ankles. This time when she tried to open her eyes to assess the situation, it was nearly impossible. Her eyes had swollen so badly that her vision has been reduced to just pinholes. She could no longer breathe through her nose and had to inhale carefully through her mouth. And due to her broken ribs, it was impossible to take a deep breath at all.

She no longer knew where the pain began and ended. As far as she could tell, there wasn't an end. Everything hurt in one way or another. And things were about to get worse.

"Gonna hafta untie her legs."

"I get a piece of her first this time."

"Fuck you do. Prospects don't get shit first."

"Fuck you, Jack."

"No, fuck you, Squirrel. Grab your fuckin' knife."

Kiki heard rustling around as she assumed the prospect, Squirrel, handed this Jackhole a knife. She listened for any sound from Jazz.

Nothing.

Oh God, she had no idea what condition the girl was in. Alive. Dead. Or even dying. Kiki had no idea how long she'd been knocked unconscious this last time, how long they assaulted Jazz.

She needed to vomit but didn't even have the strength for that. Instead, her guts just churned. When her ankles were cut free, she tried to kick out, but even the slightest movement proved difficult.

She did manage to move her mouth enough to say, "You're not... going to get... shit for us in... this condition."

Instead of receiving an answer, the point of the knife jabbed her belly as whoever held it began to slice open her jeans, starting at the waist.

She fought the cloying fear and let anger surge through her instead.

"Dead... You're... all dead," she said on a ragged breath.

She'd kill them herself. If she got out of this alive, she'd hunt them down and kill them with her own hands.

Kiki felt the air swirl over her bare thighs and knew it was close to the end for her.

This was it.

They were going to do something that would haunt her forever. Her life would never be the same from this moment on.

And she was weak. Helpless.

She couldn't fight them even though she wanted to. Oh, God, did she want to.

This time it wasn't only blood trickling down her cheeks. It was tears. A hot, endless stream squeezing from between her puffy eyelids.

"Wanna see her tits, too. Cut that bloody rag off her. She got bigger tits than that other one." That was Jackhole making demands. She'd never forget his face or his voice.

Both would be forever burned into her brain. She'd find him.

She closed her eyes, not wanting to see the prospect leaning over her to slice her blouse and bra open.

"Fuck yeah. Look at—" The prospect's voice drifted off and both of the Warriors stilled.

Jackhole barked out, "You call anyone?"

"Fuck no, man. Don't wanna share this pussy any more than I gotta. Bad enough gettin' second helpin's."

"Straight pipes. Someone's comin'. Gotta split."

Kiki strained to hear what they did. All she could hear was her heartbeat thumping in her ears.

"We can take 'im," the prospect said.

"Stupid fuck. Listen. Ain't just one."

Kiki gasped in relief when the one released her legs. "They're... going to... kill you."

"Shut the fuck up. Let's get the fuck outta here."

"Should take 'em with."

"Fuck that. Don't want 'em followin' us."

Suddenly, she couldn't miss the loud exhaust of the bikes roaring up to the house. To her it sounded like angels singing.

She just hoped it was DAMC and not some other outlaw MC that were rivals of the Shadow Warriors.

Because she was sure that club had plenty of enemies.

She was trying to roll to her side to see where Jazz was when the front door of the house was kicked in. The wooden door shattered into pieces.

"Fuck!" The pissed-off deep voice sounded familiar but with her fuzzy brain she couldn't place it. "Check the house."

Heavy footsteps thundered past them, making the floor shake beneath her. "Jazz," she croaked.

Then she felt a dark presence next to her. "Jesus fuckin' Christ," came the mutter. The second "Jesus fuckin' Christ" sounded a lot louder. And angrier.

"Out... back," she struggled to say. She wanted to let whoever it was know that the Warriors escaped out of the back of the house.

"Don't talk," the gruff voice said.

"Van. Black primer."

"Got it." A second later. "Got that?"

A couple of deep voices shouted out "yeahs" as they rushed back past her and within moments Kiki heard the roar of the bikes again.

"Don't... leave..."

"Not goin' anywhere," the deep voice was closer this time. Then she was rolled gently to one side, her wrists were cut free and something was laid over top of her.

"Who?" she managed to ask.

There was a long hesitation. "Diesel."

"Thank... you."

He didn't respond for a moment. "Be back. Gotta check Jazz."

Jazz.

Oh God.

Then she heard his voice, her savior's deep voice, from a distance. A one-sided conversation. His words coming low, rapid, and tightly strung.

Then she heard him louder and more clearly. "Sorry, baby. Got nothin' to cover you up with 'cept my shirt. Gotta hang on."

Jazz was alive at least. Which wasn't much to go on because Kiki didn't know just how bad she was.

She couldn't see much, she couldn't roll over, she couldn't sit up. She couldn't even clear her throat enough to ask. But she tried anyway.

"Jazz?" she whispered. But Diesel must not have heard her.

Another loud bike rolled up, easier to hear this time through the broken front door. The air around her swirled with Diesel's movement as he rushed to the front of the house.

"Z," he shouted.

Someone else rushed inside. "Heads up, Hawk's comin'."

"Fuck."

There was a pause, then she recognized Zak's raised voice. "Are you fuckin' kiddin' me? Fuckin' motherfuckers!"

"Hawk can't see this shit," Diesel grumbled.

"Fuckers are gonna die. That's for fuckin' sure."

"Shouldn't've given Hawk the location."

"D... Nothin' would stop you, either."

"Right," he grunted.

"5-0 en route?"

"Pained me to do it, but called your pop direct."

"Fuck," Zak muttered.

"Yeah. Ain't callin' 911. An' we need an ambulance to transport. This shit ain't gonna be fixed with a fuckin' beer an' a Band-Aid."

"They're both breathin' though, right?" Zak asked, his voice sounding pained.

"Yeah. Thank fuck."

Kiki hated the fact that she could hear them talking like she wasn't even there. She called out, "Hawk," as loudly as she could.

The conversation halted and before she knew it, Zak was kneeling by her side. "On his way, babe."

"Don't... want him... to see... me like... this."

"Fuck. Me neither. Don't got a choice, babe."

Diesel's voice came from above Zak. "He's gonna fuckin' blow."

"Ain't the half of it," Zak agreed.

"Fuck, I hear 'im," Diesel mumbled.

"Gotta go out an' tell him to brace."

"You ain't gonna be able to hold 'im back, Z. Call Ace, get 'im to meet us at the hospital. I'll go out an' warn my brother."

"Got it."

"Don't want him... to see me... like this."

A hand skimmed lightly over her forehead. "Babe, just gonna hafta deal. Gonna be like a bull in a china closet. Ain't your fault."

"Call Grizz, too," Diesel shouted from the doorway before disappearing.

Kiki struggled to take a long, but shallow breath. She was afraid things were about to get worse instead of better.

THE BACK TIRE on his bike kicked out as Hawk went from what seemed like a hundred miles an hour to a dead stop. He got it under control and shut her down, kicking the stand down and scrambling off his bike.

His brother was trotting down the steps of a falling down porch. The house didn't have a front door. Most of the windows were broken or missing. What paint was left on the wood siding was slowly peeling away with time and the weather.

It was a fuckin' dump. And so off the beaten path that if those dumb fuckers had known better, they would have tossed Kiki's cell somewhere, left it in his driveway or at least at what was left of the Vette.

Thank fuck they hadn't.

"Talk to me," Hawk barked as he met his brother halfway.

"Gotta brace, brother."

Hawk felt his chest cave as all of the oxygen fled his lungs. He went to push past D but his brother stepped in his way, holding up his hands.

"Brother," Hawk warned.

"Gotta brace, Hawk," D said again, more firmly this time.

"She breathin'?"

"Yeah."

"She gonna live?"

"'Spect so."

Hawk tried to round his brother but Diesel grabbed his shoulders and held fast. Hawk narrowed his eyes and tightened his jaw. "Don't make me go through you."

"Hawk. Ain't good. Just tellin' you now. Ain't good. Jazz is worse. This is the kinda shit neither of 'em may get over. Just sayin'."

His heart stopped, squeezed tight and then began to thud in his chest. He closed his eyes, sucked in a deep breath. He opened his eyes and held his brother's concerned gaze. "Gotta go in, D. Gotta. Now, lemme go."

Diesel removed his hands from Hawk and held his palms out in a show that he would no longer try to stop him from going in. "Gonna be hard to tell, but she's conscious. She'll hear anythin' you're sayin'."

Hawk gave him a sharp nod, pushed past him and felt his brother right on his heels as he ran up the steps and through the door, which was splintered into pieces. He stepped over shards of wood and his eyes immediately landed on a figure sprawled on the floor.

Totally unrecognizable. But even from where his feet had frozen in place at the horrific sight he knew who it was.

Grizz's granddaughter.

Holy motherfuck.

Jazz.

Hawk swallowed hard, trying to wrap his head around what he was seeing. Her face was not only beyond recognition, both of her arms were twisted in an unnatural way. Her legs were spread wide, a pool of blood between them. She was mostly covered by a T-shirt, probably Diesel's, since he had come out of the house not wearing anything above his waist.

A movement caught his eye and he looked up to see Z on a cell phone at the opening to another room. The club's former president lifted a hand and pointed somewhere deeper into the same room Jazz was in.

And like Diesel warned him, he fucking braced.

On legs he couldn't feel, he shuffled forward, his breath coming quickly as he stepped through the doorway of the room. He forced his eyes to land on the other woman sprawled over the filthy floor.

The other woman.

His woman.

Fuckin' Kiki.

D said Jazz was worse. Yeah, she was. But not by much.

Kiki's long dark hair was caked with dried blood, her face was swollen and purple, her eyelids puffed out so badly you couldn't even see her eyes. Blood still trickled slowly from a wound above her forehead.

The remnants of her clothes were peeled away from her, like they were sliced open where she lay.

The only thing covering her battered and bruised body was D's cut. But it wasn't enough. He could still see the deep purples, reds, and blues on both sides of her rib cage. Her breath wheezed from between her lips.

He was frozen. Completely frozen solid inside and out as he stared at what remained of the vibrant woman who had shared his bed and who had wormed her way into his heart.

His eyes closed, he sucked in a breath and then dropped to his knees. With both hands holding onto his scalp, he threw back his head and howled.

"Jesus," D muttered from behind him, planting a hand on his shoulder.

He shoved it off. He wasn't the one who needed help.

It wasn't him at all.

It was his woman before him, laying there in a broken heap, that needed all the help they could give her.

As Hawk reached out, Diesel muttered, "Don't touch her, brother. Ambulance's on the way. Hear the sirens comin'."

Hawk jerked his cut off his shoulders and ripped his shirt over his head, gently placing the tee over Kiki's battered body and D's cut.

He leaned close to her ear. "Help's comin', babe. Gonna take care of you, promise. They're comin'. I hear 'em." He swallowed hard. "You hear me, babe? Gonna take care of you. Hear me? Gonna take care of you. Promise. Gonna..."

D's hand landed on his shoulder again. "Gonna go out to meet the ambulance."

"Yeah."

D turned but stopped when Hawk called out, "D..." Hawk glanced over his shoulder at his brother. "Gotta get 'em."

"Got my crew on their tail."

Hawk nodded. "Keep 'em breathin'."

After a slight hesitation, his brother softly said, "Hear ya, brother." Then with a chin lift he headed out to meet the emergency responders.

Chapter Sixteen

MUTED VOICES. Incessant beeping. The smell of disinfectant and some other indescribable scents assaulted her nostrils.

Something tight was wrapped around her middle. She took a careful breath, testing for pain. She was pretty numb, her head still fuzzy.

She was probably on some powerful meds since the pain had faded to almost nothing. She blinked her eyes open, which surprisingly could now be opened wider than back at the abandoned house.

She blinked at the bright fluorescent lights above her. Then turned her head carefully to the right and stared at her hand. A needle was stuck into one of her veins and was connected to a tube. They were pumping her full of fluids. And, more importantly, good drugs.

She rolled her head to the left and her gaze landed on Hawk. He was hunched over in a chair, his back curved, his elbows on his knees, his head braced in his hands as he stared between his parted thighs.

She opened her mouth. Nothing but a squeak escaped. When she attempted to clear her throat, his head jerked up, his hands dropped and he jumped from his seat, coming to her side.

He looked like shit.

She was sure she looked much worse. Especially since something was wrapped around her head. She could guess it was gauze and bandaging and not a pretty scarf.

Her throat felt scratchy when she said, "Didn't want you to see me like this."

He couldn't hide his wince at her words. "Babe," he breathed. "Don't matter."

"Does to me."

He shook his head. "No, babe. Only matters you're gonna be okay."

She inhaled a breath and whispered, "Am I?"

Something flashed behind his eyes. Pain? Regret? Anger? Whatever it was, she couldn't worry about that now. She wanted to know about Jazz.

She whispered her name.

Hawk's eyes darkened and he shook his head. "Down the hall." He twisted enough to grab the chair and drag it closer to the bed. He sat on the edge of the seat, grabbing her hand that didn't have the IV and raising it to his lips. His mouth skimmed across her skin but she could hardly feel it. She must be on some really, really good stuff.

"Morphine?"

His eyes raised to hers. "Yeah."

"She okay?"

Kiki watched his Adam's apple lift then fall as he swallowed hard. That was telling.

"Gonna be. Might take a while."

"Hawk..." She closed her eyes to fight against the picture that played in her mind of Jazz laying on the dirty floor with the Warriors over her...

"Don't fuckin' say it," he growled. "'Cause if I hear it, I'm gonna freak the fuck out an' I need to be by your side right now. Not chasin' those motherfuckers down. They'll get their due."

"Let the cops handle it."

His lips flattened and his jaw got tight. Fear crept through her at his determined look. He was going to dole out the club's form of justice and he might end up back in jail. Not County, either. State prison this time. Which meant he might never get out.

And, *Jesus*, as she looked at the man sitting by her side, she realized she could not lose him. She couldn't.

"I wasn't raped," she whispered.

His nostrils flared and his fingers constricted around hers. His body was like a tightly wound spring. "Know it."

"Jazz—"

"Babe. *Know it*," he said forcefully. Meaning, don't say it out loud.

"I want to see her."

His eyes raised to the bag of fluid that hung above the bed, then flicked to the monitors that were attached to her. "Ain't goin' nowhere."

"I have to see her…" She swallowed hard, her mouth dry like cotton. "I tried, Hawk. I tried to stop them."

His eyes squeezed shut. "Babe," he said on a rough breath. His eyes popped open as he aggressively scrubbed a hand over his mohawk. "Both got your share of shit, babe."

"Is she awake?"

"Dunno. Been in here. Haven't left you."

The beeping from the monitor became quicker as her heart beat faster at his words.

He rubbed his hand over his jaw, which now displayed a dark five-o'clock shadow. "My fault. Shouldn't have dragged you into my life."

"You didn't drag me. I came willingly." And she did. Yes, he was pushy and domineering, but Kiki would never do something she didn't want to. She had been intrigued by Hawk the minute she walked into that room at County and saw his body just about busting from the seams of those orange coveralls, tattoos on his scalp, and seeping attitude. She immediately saw a challenge and the second he opened his mouth, she had no doubt he was one, too.

He continued as if she hadn't said a word. "Shouldn't have sent you back to the house by yourself."

He was going to second guess every move he made that night. "You couldn't have known."

"Got Warriors fuckin' with us, should've known. Fucked up, babe."

Blaming himself for something he had no control over wasn't going to do either of them any good. "It isn't your fault."

He tried to extract his hand from hers. She held on as tightly as she could, but he was a million times stronger than her, especially right now.

"The fuck it isn't," he exploded. "Bastards got a beef with DAMC. Been goin' on a long time. Should've expected more shit to go down after Dogs an' Hogs. Let my guard down. All of us did."

"But I'm not DAMC."

He blew out a loud, forceful breath. "Yeah, babe, you are. Minute you climbed into my bed you were marked DAMC. Them findin' you in my driveway proved it to 'em."

"They just wanted my car."

"Our women, our money, a sled, a car. Our town. Always tryin' to grab our shit."

"Brother," came from a deep voice at the door to her hospital room.

Diesel's bulk filled the doorway, his face tight and unhappy. His eyes landed on Kiki. "You good?"

"Did you get your cut back?" Kiki asked, seeing that he had a different T-shirt over his broad chest but was still missing his usual leather vest. The one he draped over her.

"Got it."

It had to be covered in her blood. "I'll get it cleaned for you."

Diesel's eyes widened for a second then quickly narrowed as he stepped into the room. "Ain't gonna do that."

"It's the least I can do."

"Babe," Hawk said simply. Which clearly meant to let it go.

Her gaze swung to him then back to Diesel as the larger man approached the bed. "Thank you."

Diesel's chest lurched as he took in all the medical devices attached to Kiki. "Club's enforcer, babe. Gotta protect everything that belongs to the club."

Now, not only Hawk, but it was Diesel implying that she was considered a part of the club. Or more like club "property." She wasn't sure if she liked that.

"Failed," Diesel grunted.

"No," Kiki said immediately. "You found us. You saved us. You didn't fail," she assured him.

His mouth became an angry slash, reminding her exactly of Hawk's earlier. "Failed you. Failed my brother. This shit's gonna end."

"I want to see Jazz. Hawk won't take me. Will you?"

Diesel's eyes slid to his brother. Kiki didn't miss Hawk's frown and slight shake of his head. "Doctor probably won't like you movin'," Diesel finally said.

"Get a nurse with a wheelchair. I need to see her."

Diesel stared at her for a moment, looked one more time at his brother, then, with a jerk of his chin, strode from the room.

"Babe."

"I *need* to see her, Hawk."

He inhaled a deep breath, then said, "Yeah. Got you."

Diesel came back in the room not even a minute later, pushing a wheelchair with an orderly following closely on his heels, squawking at him.

"You can't just help yourself to a wheelchair, sir!"

Diesel just grunted and rolled it closer to the bed.

"You can't move her! I'm going to get a nurse."

"Do that," he grumbled.

The female orderly huffed and rushed from the room. Kiki wanted to laugh but couldn't with her broken and bound ribs, so she shot him a smile instead, even though that was painful, too, with what felt like a split bottom lip.

She didn't want to look in a mirror any time soon since she could imagine what a mess her face was. But, what she went through was nothing compared to Jazz's nightmare.

Hawk unhooked the bag from the IV pole and hooked it onto the one attached to the wheelchair. Then he pushed her hospital gown down from around her neck enough that he could peel off the pads to the heart monitor that were stuck to her chest and when the beeping went wild, he yanked the machine's plug. "Know your heart's beatin'. Don't need that shit, anyway."

Kiki tried to smirk but winced instead. She agreed. Her heart was beating and it was doing it for him, so it was beating just fine. Her eyes followed him as he reached under her to lift her. Diesel pushed him aside.

"Lemme," he grumbled to his brother.

Hawk stepped back, said "Careful," and let Diesel gently lift Kiki up and place her into the chair.

She was proud of herself when she didn't even let out a whimper as he did it.

"Got it from here, brother," Hawk said, shouldering Diesel away from the chair's handles.

D lifted his hands in surrender and stepped out of the way, then marched out the door leading the way to Jazz's room.

As Hawk pushed her into the hall, Kiki was surprised how packed the corridor was. And surprised the hospital staff hadn't herded all of the bikers and their family into a nearby waiting room. They lined both sides of the hallway from her room and beyond, all the way to Jazz's room, the direction Diesel headed, demanding people make room for Hawk and her to get past.

Jesus. It hit her then how much of a family this club truly was. Somber faces lifted a little as they saw her and Hawk heading down the narrow path.

Words of encouragement, back pats to Hawk, and thumbs up to her greeted them as they passed.

"Make a hole," Diesel barked as they rolled up to what she could only assume was Jazz's room. They made a hole.

Ace stood beside the door, eyeballing Hawk. "Son," he greeted. Then his gaze dropped to Kiki. "Should you be outta bed?"

"No, Pop, she shouldn't but she's as fuckin' stubborn as a Dougherty," Hawk answered for her.

The wrinkles around Ace's warm brown eyes crinkled further. "Yeah. Tells you somethin', son."

Hawk just grunted and pushed past his father. A pretty, older woman next to Ace laid a hand on Hawk as he passed by and she gave him a reassuring smile.

Kiki wouldn't doubt that was his mother. How she pushed children as large as Hawk and Diesel from her womb, she'll never know but the woman deserved a medal.

Kiki might have to rethink having kids with Hawk. Unless she could be guaranteed a C-section and some kind of drug like the morphine she was on now.

Her thoughts quickly fled her as Hawk pushed her into the quiet, solemn room where Jazz laid very still on a bed. She had way more machines surrounding her than Kiki had. An older couple hovered by the bed. She recognized Grizz, Jazz's grandfather, and could only assume the older woman was Mama Bear, his wife.

Mama Bear's eyes were red and puffy and Grizz kept pulling at his long, gray unkempt beard.

"She wake up yet?" Diesel asked, his voice gruff. The big man was truly affected by the small young woman laying helpless before them in the hospital bed.

"Been in an' out," Grizz answered, his voice rough, too.

"She know what happened?" Hawk asked.

Mama Bear shook her gray head. "Not sure. I'm hoping she's blissfully unaware for now. Her body needs to heal first. Then we'll worry 'bout her mind."

Kiki agreed. She tapped Hawk's hand and he brought her chair closer to the bed. Kiki reached out and stroked Jazz's still arm, then gripped her hand and held it tight. Lifting it to her cheek, she whispered, "Honey, I'm so sorry. I'm so, so sorry."

Diesel made a noise behind her and when Kiki glanced over her shoulder, he was striding quickly from the room.

Grizz's eyes followed him. He murmured, "That man's gonna rip 'em apart piece by piece with his bare hands."

"Death's too good for 'em," Mama Bear agreed with her husband.

Kiki realized now might not be the best time, but as their attorney she needed to encourage them to remain cool and let law enforcement handle justice. Not them.

It wasn't going to do anybody any good if they all ended up arrested. Or worse.

She regarded Grizz. "Were the police in here already?"

"Yeah," he grunted.

Mama Bear turned red eyes her way. "Did a rape kit. Victim's advocate was in here, too. She hasn't been coherent enough for a statement, though. I'm glad. She doesn't need to relive that horror right away."

"She's going to have to eventually," Kiki reminded Jazz's grandmother.

"They'll have your statement."

Kiki didn't want to tell her that she was knocked out during Jazz's assault. She hadn't witnessed most of it.

The squawking orderly came barreling into the room with what looked like a nurse by her side.

"What are you doing out of bed and out of your room?" The nurse shot an accusing look at Hawk. "You can't just move her like that!" The nurse was brave as she smacked at Hawk's hands and shooed him away from the wheelchair to take over. "I'm taking you back to your room," she huffed.

Kiki caught Mama Bear's gaze. "Let me know when she's awake again and wants to talk."

Mama Bear gave her a sad smile and nodded.

"Be back," Hawk grunted as the nurse rushed Kiki from the room, Hawk on her heels.

"You all shouldn't even be in this hallway," she griped as she pushed Kiki through the gauntlet of Dirty Angels and their women.

"Ain't fuckin' leavin', woman," someone said.

The nurse huffed again but froze, pulling Kiki to a stop when a high-pitched wail came from the end of the hallway near the elevators. The hair on the back of Kiki's neck stood up and Kiki noticed Hawk turn solid.

The crowd parted and Kiki had to swallow hard as she witnessed Bella, her face flushed, open her mouth and let out another haunting wail as she dropped to her knees to the hard tile floor, her hands digging into her hair.

"Jesus fuckin' Christ," Diesel shouted from behind them, then he was pushing past Hawk, Kiki and the nurse and stalking toward his cousin who seemed to be having some sort of breakdown.

A female voice shouted, "Call Axel."

Hawk's head turned sharply. "No."

"Yes," Diamond pushed forward, hands on hips. "Someone call Axel. I don't have his number, or I would."

"No one better fuckin' call Axel," Diesel barked as he rushed to Bella. "Got this."

He gathered his cousin in his arms and lifted her like she weighed as much as a feather. He smacked the *Down* button at the elevator, Bella appearing boneless and weak as he nestled her against his wide chest.

He put his mouth close to her ear and as the elevator doors whooshed open, he stepped inside, never once turning around to face the rest of them. The doors whooshed closed and they were gone.

"Maybe with D taking care of Bella, it may delay the murder and mayhem he wants to commit," said Ivy, who was wrapped tightly in Jag's arms, her face pale after seeing her sister fall apart.

"Not sure 'bout that," Jag muttered, then pressed his mouth to Ivy's temple. Ivy curved her fingers around his jaw and held tightly.

Kiki marveled at their closeness, but then her nurse was moving again, determined to get her back into her room and into her hospital bed. Just as they were making the turn into her room, the elevators binged again and Kiki hoped Bella was going to be okay. She had no idea why she would break down like that when she hadn't even made it to Jazz's room. She'd hardly made it two steps off the elevator.

She glanced up at Hawk, who hadn't left her side even as the nurse had pushed her like a madwoman down the hallway. "Is Bella going to be all right?"

Hawk's eyes fell on her, something disturbing behind his eyes. "Don't know, babe. Shit happened."

Shit happened.

What did that mean? Did he mean the same thing had happened to Bella?

Couldn't be.

Before she could ask, the nurse locked the wheels and helped the orderly lift Kiki out of the chair and place her back in the bed. She had to admit it wasn't as gentle as Diesel had been. Which, it surprised her that the big man could be that way. He seemed to be a beast through and through, so to see him affected like he was by what happened to her, to Jazz and then his reaction to Bella... it just left Kiki baffled.

As soon as the nurse had the bedcovers over her, the pads of the EKG monitor stuck back to her chest—though, Kiki couldn't figure out why in the hell she needed them—she opened her mouth to thank them, even though she was a bit miffed they had rushed her out of Jazz's room. Her mouth snapped shut as her ex-husband walked into her room.

Oh good lord.

The nurse snapped, "There's supposed to be a limit of visitors. This is getting out of hand."

"I'm her husband," Landon proclaimed and Kiki wanted to groan. He rushed to her bedside, ignoring the killer glare Hawk was shooting his way. As Hawk stepped forward to block him, Landon skirted around him and put not only the bed but the chair Hawk was sitting in earlier between them.

Smart man.

"Ex-husband," Kiki clarified.

"Sweetheart," Landon started then his eyes widened as Hawk took a menacing step toward him.

Kiki gave Hawk a look and put up a hand, hoping he'd stand down. She didn't need the man to take out his frustration with the Warriors out on Landon. Unwelcome here or not.

He shook his head. "Gotta rest, babe."

"Why are you here?" Kiki asked Landon.

"The hospital called me. I rushed over as soon as I could."

Kiki looked up at her now ex-husband, who was meticulously

dressed as always in a well-tailored suit and his hair perfect, even though he "rushed" to her side.

Kiki gave Hawk a questioning look. "How long have I been here?"

Hawk just snorted and crossed his arms over his chest, which made him seem bigger and badder than ever.

Right. Just what she thought. Landon didn't "rush" anywhere.

"Why would the hospital call you now that we're legally divorced?"

Kiki ignored the sound that Hawk made. She guessed she never mentioned it last night at the bar that it had been made official. Something he'd probably want to know.

"I'm still your emergency contact."

"I'll have that changed."

"To who?" Landon jerked his chin toward Hawk. "Him?"

Hawk took another menacing step forward.

Surprisingly, Landon ignored him. "It's because of him that you're in the hospital, Keek. You becoming tangled up with this gang caused this mess in the first place."

"Club," Kiki murmured.

"What? Club! Jesus, Kiki. You know what I'm saying is true. If you weren't messing with him, you never would've been in this situation. He almost got you killed."

Oh shit. She could feel the fury radiating from Hawk's body. The air in the room became thick with it.

"Hawk," she said softly.

"Yeah," he bit out.

"Can you excuse us for a minute?"

"Fuck no."

"Please."

"Ain't leavin' your side, babe. Not for him, not for nobody."

"Not sure what happened to you, Kiki. Not sure when you changed from appreciating class to liking a... a... thug. One with a record, too." He leaned closer to the bed and reached for her hand.

Kiki swore Hawk growled.

Landon's eyes flicked up for a second then back to her, but this time he didn't try to touch her. "I worry about you. I want you to come home with me when you get released. I'll take care of you. Make sure you get everything you need to get well."

"Landon," she began, not sure why he was offering this. Well, she knew why, he was trying to make up for his past transgression, or transgressions. For all she knew, Karin might not have been the only one. She never asked nor did she want to know. But all that was water under the bridge now.

She wasn't going home with Landon; she would never even consider it. "I'll be fine. I don't need anyone nursing me back to health. The only thing broken is my ribs. Bruises will fade, the swelling will lessen—"

"Memories won't fade," he reminded her.

"In time," she said, hoping that was true.

"Not when you see a reminder every day."

He meant Hawk. The tension in the room swirled around her and became heavy to the point it felt like a hand gripped her throat. Landon needed to go.

A noise at the open door of her room made everyone's attention land in that direction. A cop stood there, almost as tense as the other two men in the room. His hand rested loosely on the butt of his gun, which was safely tucked away in its holster, thank goodness. But it was a clear reminder of who was now the authority in the room.

"Hawk," the officer grumbled with a slight chin lift.

"Mitch," Hawk grumbled back, returning the not-quite-friendly chin lift.

"You know him?" Kiki asked.

"Used to be Z's father."

"Used to be?" Kiki repeated, confused.

"Yeah," Hawk grunted. "Now he's just a pig like the rest of 'em. Family don't gotta be blood."

"Once again," Landon cut in. "I will point out that he doesn't even know how to speak English, Kiki. Jesus."

Hawk's gaze swung from the cop back to Landon. "She understood me. 'Nough talkin'. She ain't goin' with you, so get gone."

"Kiki," Landon pleaded.

"He's right, Landon, I'm not going home with you. I appreciate you coming and caring enough to offer, but it's not going to happen."

Landon frowned. "You're making a mistake."

Kiki stared at Hawk for a heartbeat, then two as she weighed Landon's words. "I'll risk it," she finally murmured.

She noticed every tight muscle in Hawk's body loosen, his eyes soften as he looked at her, and his nostrils flare as he sucked in a breath.

Oh good lord. She was laid up in a hospital bed and all she could think about was when she would see his tattooed body naked next. Crazy.

"I'm guessing you should leave now," this cop, Mitch, directed at Landon.

Landon nodded. "Fine. Kiki, you have my number. Call me if you need *anything*." He raised his eyebrows at her. "Even if to escape."

"Jesus fuck," Hawk growled.

Landon raised his palms in surrender and weaved his way around Hawk and then Mitch as he left the room.

Kiki's eyes went from the empty doorway to Mitch, who now stood just inside the door, his gaze steady on Hawk.

"Need to ask her questions, Hawk."

"So ask."

"Need you to step out."

"Ain't doin' it."

Mitch's eyes got hard. "Not asking."

Hawk stared back at the officer, his eyes just as hard, but then after a moment he dropped them to Kiki. "You good?"

She bit back a smile at how protective he was being. "Yes, I'm sure I'll be fine with Zak's *father* who is a *cop*."

Hawk grunted, scrubbed a hand over his mohawk and then crowded the bed to lean down and press a kiss to the top of her forehead. A portion not covered in bandages. "Be right outside the door."

"I'm sure you will," she murmured.

On his way out, Hawk stopped in front of Mitch. Kiki couldn't see either of their faces, but something certainly went unsaid. Then he walked out and shut the door firmly behind him.

"So, Zak's brother *and* father are police officers. I find that interesting."

Mitch stepped closer to the bed and Kiki could see where Zak got his looks. And his hip swagger. "It was just how the chips fell."

"Like the chips off your shoulders?"

Something flashed through Mitch's eyes as he stayed silent for a moment, studying her. "Not here to talk about me or my sons. I'm here on official business."

"You need to ask me questions," Kiki stated since it was obvious as he pulled a long, thin notebook out of his back pocket and slipped a pen from the front shirt pocket of his uniform.

"Are you up for it?"

She was surprised he even bothered to ask. Being a defense attorney, she wasn't the biggest fan of law enforcement. She respected them for the most part, but in the years she'd been practicing, she'd met a few that should have never graduated from the police academy. They'd say or do anything for their charges to stick.

In the courtroom, she and the cops had a tenuous relationship since they were on the opposite sides of the room.

"I'll do what I can to help," she murmured finally.

"Before we start... Can I ask you what you're doing involved with the club?"

"It's not obvious?"

He tapped his pen against the cover of his notepad. "I've watched them all grow up. Maybe more from a distance than I should have. But I've known Hawk and Diesel since they were born. I've seen the men they've become. Not saying what they've become is good or bad, but..."

"Your son is one of them," she reminded him needlessly.

"Yes." He took a deep breath. "He is. He also did ten years at SCI Fayette. Not a proud moment for a father."

"You know he was set up, right?" Kiki knew it because when her boss handed over the files for the club, she had read through them all. Tom wasn't the one who had originally defended Zak, it was another attorney the club fired after the trial, but Tom had taken on the appeal, which they unfortunately had lost. But all the evidence Kiki could see showed that he was set up by another club. Namely the Warriors. The bad blood between the two clubs ran long, hard and deep.

She and Hawk had lay in bed one night and Hawk had talked about Z, who he was close with, and everything the former club president had endured being accused, arrested and convicted of a crime he didn't commit.

Kiki had seen all the circumstantial evidence in his file that had been suppressed during the trial and the appeal.

"That's what he says."

"I believe him. Apparently, you don't."

Mitch was good at hiding his feelings and expressions. He was like a rock. But then he was a cop, so this didn't surprise Kiki.

"Didn't say that. But let's just say I'm not happy with the direction his life took."

"Being a part of the club," she reiterated.

"Yes."

"You got out; you wanted him to stay out, too."

Mitch's eyes softened with amusement. "I'm supposed to be here asking you questions, not the other way around."

"I'm just stating facts."

The officer's eyes went from soft to hard in an instant. "Right. One of my sons makes me proud. The other one doesn't. Those are the facts."

God, that hurt Kiki's heart to hear. She hoped Zak never heard words like those come from his father's mouth. Ever. Even though he was an adult and a badass biker who had the love of a good woman, she could just imagine those words would still be devastating to hear.

She couldn't even picture her own parents judging her that way. Yes, they were "free spirits," and even though they would've loved for Kiki to be the same instead of becoming an attorney and being a part of the "establishment," they always supported her. And when they finally returned from their latest retreat, she was sure they would love Hawk, biker or not. No matter how opposite she was from her parents, they loved her just the same. She didn't realize how lucky she truly was. Until now.

"I'm sorry to hear that," Kiki murmured.

"Don't be. So, you and Hawk..."

"Hawk and I are a fact, too, Officer Jamison. And for future reference, I'm also the club's attorney. So... if you want to ask me questions regarding this kidnapping, rape and aggravated assault, please do so now. I'm getting tired."

Mitch nodded his head, flipped open his notepad, clicked the end of his pen and did what he came to do...

Asked Kiki questions that tore her wounds open all over again.

Chapter Seventeen

KIKI VISITED Jazz every day in the hospital, even after she was released. Hawk would take her in his old pickup truck so she could spend some time with her. Once Jazz was released, her parents took her home to their place in Buffalo to finish healing and get some help.

Kiki hadn't been home to her condo yet. Hawk had insisted she come back to his place, even though it was the originating point of the kidnapping. She felt empty as she stared at the spot where she had parked her Vette for the last time. Hawk had ushered her inside quickly and right up to his bed to rest.

She'd had enough of "resting" in the hospital. But his concern for her made her feel warm and fuzzy all over.

Hard to believe such a tough, badass biker had such a soft center. Not that she said that out loud. Saying something like that would definitely invoke a scowl from Hawk, since he would never admit he was a big ol' softy.

Jazz had spent five days in the hospital since, besides the nasty head wounds, she had shattered wrists, a snapped humerus, four broken fingers, cracked ribs, and countless bruises. The worst of it, besides the torn soft tissue from the sexual assault, was that they carved "SWMC" into the skin of her stomach. Kiki didn't see it, nor did Jazz volunteer to show it, and Kiki couldn't imagine having to look at those scars for the rest of her life. A constant reminder of what she went through. Hopefully, Jazz's family could find a good plastic surgeon to help minimize the scarring.

What killed Kiki the most was seeing the vibrancy and life that Jazz had extinguished in her eyes. She was now lifeless and spoke in a flat monotone, only answering questions when she was forced to, otherwise remaining quiet no matter who attempted to talk to her.

Kiki would still sit with her, hold her hand, and try to encourage conversation. Hawk would hover outside the door until Kiki had enough for the day and would leave before she started sobbing.

Seeing Jazz that way broke her heart.

Seeing Jazz that way made her not care what Diesel, Hawk and all of the club brothers had planned for those Shadow Warriors. They deserved everything that was coming to them.

The cops hadn't found them yet, and she imagined their goal was to do that before any DAMC member did.

Pierce, the club president, had even met with the president of the Dark Knights and they, too, were on the hunt.

Hawk hardly left her side. He fetched anything she needed. He changed out her bandages. If he couldn't be at the house because he had to head to the bar to handle business, he'd have one of the DAMC women there. He even had Ivy and Jewel run to her condo to pick up stuff that she had jotted down on a piece of paper, including clothes, and personal items she couldn't live without, like her brand of deodorant. She wasn't fond of her pits smelling like Old Spice.

Unfortunately, as caring as everybody acted, she was never left alone and, not being used to that, she was about to scream.

She needed alone time.

She also needed to hop back on the horse, get back to work, and, more importantly, have intimate time with Hawk. He'd hardly touched her since she'd come to his place from the hospital. He would only offer a hand to help her up or down, kiss the top of her head or change a bandage.

That was it.

She didn't need a nurse. She needed her man back.

Now, two weeks later she needed him to stop pussyfooting around and act like Hawk. Bossy, demanding, alpha and a total badass.

A sexual powerhouse.

Not to mention, she had a nagging itch that needed a good scratching.

Being that it was only seven on a Saturday morning, Hawk was still asleep. His chest rising and falling softly, one massive arm thrown over his head, the other laying across his bare, tattooed stomach. And yes, sir! She was hungry and it wasn't for food.

Unfortunately, he hadn't crawled into bed until around four in the morning, and had kept to his side of the mattress after pressing his lips to her forehead thinking she was asleep.

She hadn't been. She had a hard time sleeping unless he was beside her. He worried about her, but she worried about him, too. The Warriors could show up anytime, anywhere and they could ambush him on his way home while riding his Harley.

However, she kept those fears to herself since he was supposed to be a big, bad motherfucker—his words—and he could take care of himself.

Right.

She still worried.

She still sighed in relief when he crawled into bed in the middle of the night or early morning in one piece.

She rolled his direction and studied his profile. His face was relaxed and he was more handsome than ever when it was. No grumbling, grunting, scowling or being a bossy biker.

Just Hawk.

She scooted down the bed, her ribs only giving a slight twinge of pain. Something she could live with in order to get what she wanted.

He wasn't going to be happy that she woke him up, but he'd get over it. She was sure of that.

She slowly pulled down the sheet that was pulled half-assed over his hips, exposing all that was Hawk. Her mouth watered at the sight.

Carefully crawling between his spread thighs, she cupped him and, being soft, took all of him into her mouth.

She worked her tongue around and around the head and down his now semi-soft length. She kissed the tip, then sucked his sac deep into her mouth, working it with her tongue.

"Fuckin' Christ," came the sleepy grumble from the head of the bed.

Her eyes tipped that direction and she could see his head raised enough for him to get a bead on her actions.

"Babe."

She released him only long enough to command, "Quiet." See how *he* liked it.

His body shook with what she could guess was a chuckle and his fingers dug deep into her hair as she slipped the tip of his now fully erect cock in between her lips. Hollowing out her cheeks, she sucked him hard.

"Fuckin' Christ," he growled again, his hips rising off the mattress.

Circling the root with a couple of fingers, she squeezed hard, making the large veins pop even more. She lifted her head long enough to shoot him a naughty smile and then went to town.

His fingers dug into her scalp and she tried not to wince as he got close to one of her nearly-healed head wounds. Any pain she felt was worth it. She circled the tip of his cock with her tongue, tasting the saltiness of his precum and inhaling his musky maleness.

Her pussy clenched hard and warm wetness gathered between her thighs. She needed his mouth there, his cock there, or even his fingers. She needed to let go, but also needed to hold on at the same time.

"Babe."

Kiki smiled around his cock at his strangled voice. She didn't stop, though.

"Babe," he said again, this time it sounded like a warning. "Babe, gonna blow if you don't stop."

His cock slipped from her mouth, shiny and wet, and she smiled up at him. "That's the point."

He shook his head. "You're not ready, babe."

She knew what he meant, he'd been indicating that for the last few days. Not in so many words, but by his actions. He was worried she hadn't healed enough, mentally and physically.

"I'm ready, honey."

His eyes held hers. "No."

"Yes. Don't you want me?"

His eyes narrowed. "That ain't even a question."

"Then give it to me."

"Babe."

"Hawk, I asked the doctor, we can do this."

"You did what?"

She nodded as she slowly slid up his body, making sure her nipples brushed along his skin. She straddled one of his thick thighs and pressed her pussy to him. Hard.

He tensed.

"He said it was fine."

"For fuck's sake," he muttered.

She lowered her voice and pretended to sound like a biker, "Gotta break the seal sometime."

Hawk snorted, shook his head, hooked her under her arms and hauled her up over him. She settled her knees on both sides of his waist, and planted her palms on his chest.

"So fuckin' hot, babe."

"Yes, even with my beautiful green and yellow bruises?" Her face, her ribs, her arms still showed signs of discoloration.

"Don't care 'bout that."

She tilted her hips, rubbing her damp folds on his lower belly. "Then let's do it."

"Babe, you're killin' me. Don't wanna hurt you."

"You're not. Just don't squeeze my ribs, that's all. I'll be on top and ride you."

His eyes darkened. He wanted it badly, too. But she could see the worry mixed in with his desire. "Fuck," he muttered.

She lifted a *wait-a-minute* finger and then leaned over to the nightstand, snagging her reading glasses. As she slipped them on, she pouted and tossed her head until her long hair settled over her shoulders and breasts.

"Fuckin' goddamn," he muttered again. "Ain't playin' fair, babe."

She smiled. "Nothing's fair in love and war."

His eyes flashed at her words. "Want you underneath me so bad. But will take you on top if I gotta."

She chuckled at what sounded like him "suffering" because he wouldn't be the one in control. "You're going to stop resisting?"

"Fuck, babe. Can't fight you. So, gonna lay back an' let you ride me like a rodeo queen."

"Yee haw," she whispered.

He slapped her ass and shouted, "Yee fuckin' haw!"

With a laugh, she rose up, grabbed his shaft and sank down on him. Then both of them were no longer laughing. She sighed and he grunted, his fingers digging into her hips as she rose and fell on him at a slow pace.

"Been too long," he grumbled.

"Yes," she hissed.

"So fuckin' tight."

"Yes," she hissed again, arching her back, grinding her hips, grabbing both of her nipples between her fingers to twist and pull them. She cried out, throwing her head back.

"Eyes to me," he grunted.

Kiki dropped her chin and held his gaze, still tweaking her nipples. Her mouth parted and little puffs of breath escaped as she slid up and down his long length.

"Belong right where you are, babe."

"Yes."

"On my dick, in my bed, in my house."

"Yes, honey," she breathed.

He slid his arms around her and grabbed two handfuls of her ass, trying to control the pace. He wanted her to speed up.

She was in no rush. She'd waited too long to get him back inside her. She wasn't going to have it end too soon.

"Gotta go faster, babe."

"No, Hawk. I'm good." She could tell by the expression on his face he wasn't. She rocked her hips back and forth and he ground his teeth hard enough she could see it.

"Faster, babe."

"Uh-uh."

"Fuckin' Christ," he barked, squeezing his eyes closed and blowing out a breath.

"Eyes on me, honey," Kiki echoed.

He rocked his head back and forth. "Ain't gonna last."

"Eyes on me," she repeated. And when his eyes popped open, she released one of her nipples and found her clit with her fingers. She pressed, circled and tweaked until her walls closed in around him, squeezing tight.

"Babe," he said like a warning.

"Yes, honey?" she asked, as his hips rose and she lowered. He was hitting the perfect spot deep inside her.

"Drippin' down my balls."

"Do you like that?"

"Fuckin' love it."

"How much do you love it?"

"Not as much as you."

Kiki stilled, she planted her hands on his chest again and leaned forward. "Say again?"

"Get so wet, love you drippin' down my balls."

Kiki's breath rushed out of her. She must have misheard him. That was all. She pushed it out of her mind and began to move again. "Make me come, Hawk."

His thumb pressed to her clit and with his words, "Babe, gonna make you come then gonna blow my load deep inside you," she came, her walls contracting around him.

"Fuck," he grunted, his hips shooting off the bed and as he pulsated, spilling himself deep inside her, she came once again, the ripples more intense this time. She cried out his name and he threw his head back, watching her ride the last wave.

"Fuckin' beautiful, babe."

"Me or the sex?"

"Both."

"Good answer." She leaned over and pressed her mouth to his. He took her gently, sweeping his tongue over her lips and into her mouth. He deepened the kiss, cupping her cheek.

Finally, she broke it off and pressed her forehead to his. "Next time I'm going to be under you."

"Yeah."

She smiled. "Now that proves I'm almost completely healed, I need to go home and get back to work, too."

Hawk was silent for a moment, then said, "You're home."

She pushed up to a seated position, his cock still planted deep inside her. "My condo."

He frowned. "Break your lease."

She pulled off her glasses, folded them carefully and handed them to him to set aside on the nightstand. Which he did. "I don't have a lease. I own it."

"Outright?"

"Well, the mortgage company and I own it."

He reached up and grabbed a lock of her hair, winding it around his finger. "Okay, then. Sell or rent it."

"Why?"

He tugged on the lock. "You're not leavin'."

"Hawk."

"Babe."

It was a stand-off. One Hawk clearly thought he was going to win. "I'm not commuting into the office every day from here."

He softened enough to slip out of her, but when she went to shift off him he held her in place with his hands. "Quit your job."

"What?" Was he serious?

"Quit your fuckin' job."

Oh good lord, he *was* serious. "And do what? That's just crazy!"

His powerful shoulders lifted and fell as he shrugged. "Start your own practice."

"Where? Here? In Shadow Valley?"

"Yeah, babe. Twenty minutes to the 'burgh if you need to get there."

"On a good day. Starting a new practice isn't so easy, you know."

"Will help you get clients."

Her brows shot up her forehead. "Oh great."

His lips twitched. "You can defend all the people asshole Axel arrests. Be a thorn in his side."

"That's not nice."

"Family fucked Z over, so don't give a shit."

"Yes, I got that, but this has nothing to do with Z or Axel or their family... Honey, I make good money where I'm at."

"Bar makes good money."

She sighed impatiently. "I make *really* good money. A local practice isn't going to bring that kind of money home. And, don't forget, I need a new car."

"With your kind of scratch, Jag'll make you a really sweet custom ride."

She made a noise. "I don't need an old Impala that has a suspension lift and hydraulics with switches on the dashboard. Decked out with fuzzy dice and spinners."

Hawk's eyes crinkled at the corners and his lips twitched. "We're bikers, babe, not gangbangers. This is Shadow Valley, not the barrio."

"I know," she huffed, unable to hide her smile.

"You ain't gettin' any of that shit."

"Good."

"Jag got good taste."

"Like Ivy."

"Like Ivy," Hawk agreed. "Fuckin' master at customs." As an afterthought, he added, "And redheads."

"It'll be easier for me to head to the dealer and pick out something new. With a warranty. And no shag carpet on the dash."

Hawk snorted. "Gonna return that Jesus bobble head, then."

"Well, hold off on that. I could see that glued to the dashboard of my new Vette."

"Even I would spank your ass for shit like that."

"Hmm. That sounds like a challenge."

"Still healin' those cracked ribs. No spankin' yet."

"I'll have to just get off on the anticipation."

He grunted. "Yeah, do that." He wiggled his fingers. "My palm's itchin' right now."

"But seriously, Hawk. I need to get back..." Her words faded off.

"Back to what? Your life?"

"Yes. To work, to my place. I need to get back on track."

"That track include me?"

She leaned over and brushed her lips over his. "Yes, honey, it does."

He grinned. "Then you're gettin' rid of your place an' movin' in here."

She arched a brow at him. "Just like that?"

"Yep. Just like that."

"Are you going to make me your ol' lady?"

He blinked. Then something crossed his face. She had no idea what. "Want that?"

"What does it all entail?"

Hawk barked out a laugh. "Jesus."

"I have to know what I'm getting into."

"Right," he muttered.

"If it means you plan on being a dictator and bossing me around... let me clarify that, *trying* to boss me around, I'm not sure I'm agreeable to that."

"The only *dick* you're getting is mine deep inside your cunt."

"Sweet and so romantic."

He shrugged again while pushing to sit up, Kiki still straddling his lap. He shifted until he was leaning against the headboard.

Kiki had a feeling he was starting to take this conversation much more seriously. She curled her hand around the back of his neck as he spread his fingers along her hips. "Tell me what you want from me," she whispered.

"Just you, babe."

She shook her head. "It's not that simple. I know that. You know that."

His nostrils flared. "Right. Want you to be my ol' lady."

"Then tell me what that entails."

HAWK REGARDED the woman sitting naked in his lap. She had a freshly fucked look, one that showed she was satisfied, her hair long and wild as it fell over her shoulders and tits, her eyes soft but curious with their line of conversation.

He was stepping into dangerous territory because he truly did want Kiki to become his ol' lady. Though, as much as he wanted that, as much as he tried to imagine it the last couple of weeks, he wasn't sure, once again, if it would work. Whether her tying herself down with someone like him, a biker, would be enough for her.

As much as he wished it would be, truth was that he couldn't be sure that it would.

And that scared the fuck out of him. Not as much as what happened a couple weeks ago scared the fuck out of him. But it was a close second.

He thought he lost her then. He didn't want to lose her now.

But he couldn't get out of his head any of the words her ex-husband said. That night in the restaurant and again that day in Kiki's hospital room.

He hated to admit it, but the guy had a clue.

"We'll make it what you wanna make it."

Kiki drew a finger over his chest. "Now *I* know and *you* know that's not how it works. You belong to a club with some rules. Some ancient, misogynistic rules, albeit. But, no matter what, you follow those rules, you live that life. And, honey, you're the VP, for crissakes. You aren't going to give that up nor would I ask you to. So," she leaned forward, her lips a hair's breadth from his, "tell me what being your ol' lady entails."

"You'd be mine," he answered simply.

"I'm already yours," she answered back, which made something in his chest tighten.

"Yeah, but like *mine*."

"Okay, got that part. I'm okay with that."

She wasn't getting it. Then suddenly she was. Her mouth became an *O*. "You mean I'd be your property."

Jesus fuck, he didn't want to admit that to her.

"You'd *own* me."

Goddamn.

"Or at least, according to your brothers you would."

Where was she going with this?

"Does Ace own your mom?"

He blinked.

"Does Jag own Ivy?"

He opened his mouth, but she wasn't done.

"Does Zak own Sophie?"

He shut his mouth.

"Because what I've witnessed with *them* has been nothing but deep love and respect."

Jesus.

"Now, Grizz can be a bit grumpy with his wife."

"Yeah," he finally grunted.

"But it's easy to see that he loves her to death, too."

That was true. Both Grizz and Mama Bear griped at each other, but they'd been together forever and would be until the day they died. And Grizz would continue to be the thorn in Mama Bear's side even in the afterlife, if there was one.

Hawk grinned.

"So, if that's what being an ol' lady entails, then it doesn't look horrible to me."

Hawk's grin widened. "Babe," he started.

Apparently, she still wasn't finished.

"I love you, Hawk."

Jesus. His chest squeezed and he struggled to breathe. As much as he wanted to accept those words from her, to take them just as they were, he was still worried that she had no idea what she was getting into. He didn't want her to decide she made a mistake down the road. When he was so far gone, he'd never recover if she decided his life wasn't for her. He needed her to be sure. So he needed to make sure that she was sure. That her decisions were solid. As much as he wanted her to move in and become his ol' lady, he also didn't want her to make a mistake by falling too fast and too hard. Because he'd already done that.

"You sure, babe?"

"Sure about what?"

"Loving me."

"Why wouldn't I be sure?"

"Not good enough for you. You deserve better."

"Oh, okay. Well, that settles that."

"Babe, seriously, know you got a good life. Wanna give you a good life, too, but it ain't gonna be what you had with that... that... *Landon*." He hated that name. Just like he hated the fact that that douchebag had been there before him.

"Thank fuck!"

His jaw dropped at her exclamation. He wasn't sure he liked her cursing like that. He must be rubbing off on her. Which might not be a good thing. He liked having a classy piece of ass in his bed...

As long as that ass was attached to Kiki.

"If you start nailing our teenage neighbor we're going to have a problem." She lowered her voice. "Hawk, honestly, my life felt empty. It's now full because of you. Because *you* are in it. Your *family* is in it. And by family, I don't just mean your blood relatives."

He shook his head. "Afraid you're gonna wake up one day an' realize your mistake."

"I didn't know you had a crystal ball."

"Ain't stupid."

She sighed and cupped his cheek, brushing a thumb over his jaw that needed a shave. "No, you aren't. Not at all. So, let's try this again, big man... I love you."

"Yeah."

"Yeah?" she squeaked.

"Fuck yeah."

"Oh good lord," she whispered and rolled her eyes to the ceiling. "Hawk…"

"Yeah, babe?"

She sighed dramatically. He laughed and then twisted until he had her on her back and he was above her on his hands and knees, face to face.

"Say it again," he demanded, pinning her gaze with his.

"What?" she teased, a small smile pulling at her lips.

"Know what," he grumbled.

"I love you?"

"Without the question mark."

"*Ah*. Let me try it again." She cupped his cheek. "I love you."

"Babe."

"Yeah?"

He curled his fingers around the back of her neck and pressed his lips to hers, whispering, "Me, too."

Epilogue

"GOTTA STOP WITH THAT LIPSTICK, BABE," Hawk griped as he approached Kiki sitting at the private bar at church. He scrubbed at his lips with his thumb.

She swatted a dismissing hand his direction. "What am I going to wear, then?"

"Nothin'."

"I can't wear *nothin*'!"

Hawk's mouth twisted as his ol' lady mocked him. Since she had been fully healed for a while now, nothing stopped him from taking her over his knee. "Brothers are bustin' my ass. Come into church my mouth the same color as yours."

"So?"

He cocked an eyebrow in her direction. "Whataya mean, so?"

"Who cares?"

He ducked behind the bar and grabbed a couple shot glasses. "Me. Can't go into a meetin' wearin' lipstick like a fuckin' bitch."

Kiki snickered.

"Ain't funny, babe."

She lifted a hand, *pretending* to control herself. Even her faking was a fail. "I'm trying to picture it."

He shook his head as he poured them both a whiskey. "Don't have to. They don't tell me first, just snap pics with their fuckin' phones then laugh their asses off. Got plenty of evidence out there." He came around the bar and slid in between her and the next stool.

"Out where?"

"There. There!" He waved an impatient hand over his head. "Interspace."

A squeak came from his woman. He was glad she was finding all of this amusing.

"You mean cyberspace?"

"What-fuckin'-ever."

Kiki's snicker turned into a full-blown laugh. "Poor baby."

"Yeah. Gotta do somethin' to make up for my hurt feelin's."

"Do I now?"

"Yep."

"What do you suggest?"

"Gettin' on your knees might give you an idea."

"Ah, so you want lipstick on your cock instead."

"Better place for it."

Kiki bit her bottom lip. She planted a hand on Hawk's chest and leaned into him. "Maybe I won't kiss you goodbye when I leave for my office in the morning."

"Ain't a good solution."

"No? How about I just apply my lipstick after I get into my car?"

"Yeah," he grunted, sliding a hand under the fall of her hair and down her back. "But don't do it while you're drivin'."

Watching her smile up at him made him think about what a lucky fucker he was.

"Understood."

Hawk hooked a hand around her hip and pulled her even closer. "How'd it go today?"

Her smile flattened. He hated that he was the one to make that happen.

"Tom wasn't happy."

"To be expected," he muttered.

"I'm not so thrilled myself."

He sighed. "Babe."

"It's just that it's going to be a long road ahead with me opening a new office and trying to find clients."

"Gonna be fine."

"Tom actually suggested I open a satellite office in the Valley and put his name on the letterhead."

"Fuck that."

She nudged him in the chest with her shoulder. "I'd figured that would be your response to his suggestion."

"All that money goes in your pocket, not his."

"And the club's reserves, too."

"Right. Part of bein' my ol' lady." He'd thought she'd be bitter about that part, but surprisingly she wasn't. All the businesses paid a percentage into the club coffers and in return they all reaped the benefits.

"Maybe whenever Jazz comes home, she can help me around the office."

"That'd be good."

"So, you're not saying it, but I've been waiting. I guess everything went okay in there?" She tipped her head toward the closed door of the meeting room.

"Took two seconds for that vote... *Once* I wiped your lipstick off my fuckin' mouth."

"At least they know you're *gettin' some*." Then she grunted loudly.

He forced back his laughter. "Ain't nobody in that room that ain't gettin' some, babe."

"Yes, I suspect you're all very virile."

"Whatever that means. But don't you worry 'bout anybody gettin' some 'cept me. Got me?"

She patted him on the stomach and took a sip of her whiskey. He guessed that was her answer.

He looked around the common area. "Speakin' of gettin' some... D'ya see where D went?"

Kiki rolled her lips in and then her eyes slid toward the bathrooms.

"Fuck," he muttered.

"That's about right," Kiki answered and raised her shot glass to her lips, emptying it.

It was early, he couldn't imagine what piece D had up against the wall in the women's room.

The door to the back parking lot whipped open and Jewel blew in, her head spinning back and forth, searching for someone. Hawk frowned as the prospects who were playing pool and drinking beer all hesitated to watch her rock and roll across the floor, heading their direction.

"Where's my brother?" she asked in a rush.

Since Hawk was one of the last ones to leave the room after the meeting, he tipped his chin down to his woman and lifted a brow.

Kiki shrugged. "I saw him and Ivy leave as soon as your meeting broke up."

Jewel scrunched her face up. "Great," she muttered.

"Whataya need, Jewelee?" Hawk asked.

"Nothin'."

"Bullshit," Hawk grunted.

"Have to talk to D, then."

"For what?" Hawk prodded.

She bit her bottom lip as she eyeballed him. "Might have a bead where that shit-for-brains Squirrel is hanging out."

Hawk's spine stiffened at the mention of the prospect D kicked out of the club awhile back for disrespecting Ivy. The one who ended up as a prospect for the Warriors. The one who was going to die a slow, painful death. He also didn't miss Kiki's sharp inhale.

"He here?" Jewel asked, still searching the room. "If not, I'll text him."

"Ain't gonna answer right now," Hawk said, then downed his double shot of Jack. He held his breath until it settled warmly in his gut.

"Why? Wasn't he at the meeting? Is he..." Her head swung slowly toward the restrooms. "You're fucking kidding me," she grumbled, narrowing her eyes.

She made to head that direction and Hawk grabbed her by the arm. He shook his head. "No," he said sharply.

"Fucking beast," she mumbled under her breath.

He didn't know why she started calling his brother that, but Hawk didn't like it and neither did D. "Jewelee, quit it," he warned.

"Why? He can't keep his damn dick in his pants."

That was nothing new, so why was it bothering her now? He narrowed his eyes at Jewel. "Why do you care?"

"I don't," she said way too quickly, which obviously was a lie.

"Right."

She jerked her arm and snapped, "Let go of me, Hawk."

"Gonna behave?"

"Yep. Just going to wait."

"Right."

Jewel raised a hand. "I swear."

"Wanna go home an' fuck my ol' lady, an' now I gotta sit here an' babysit you."

"You can go." She slid her eyes to Kiki. "Congrats, I guess."

Kiki gave her a smile. "Thanks, I guess."

Jewel peeled his fingers off her arm one by one. "I'll just go sit at the other end of the bar and wait. Promise."

Hawk grunted. "Swear, Jewelee, you walk in that bathroom, I'll tan your hide myself."

She frowned at him. "Fine. Going to sit right," she lifted her chin, "down there."

"You do that. Not a fuckin' inch further."

With a huff, Jewel stomped over to the last stool at the end of the bar nearest the bathrooms and settled her ass on it, crossing her arms over her chest.

"Fuckin' bullshit," Hawk grumbled to Kiki. "Wanna get under that tight skirt of yours."

She lifted her shot glass. "Honey, why don't you get me another drink while we wait."

He leaned over the bar and snagged the bottle of Jack. Cracking open the top, he poured them each another double.

"Drink now, 'cause when you're pregnant with my kid, you ain't drinkin'."

Kiki turned wide eyes up to him. "Are we planning that sometime soon?"

"You'll be the first to know."

She smiled and shook her head. "Well, thanks for that. Are you planning on putting a ring on my finger first?"

"Bein' my ol' lady's the same shit."

"So, we got married while you were in that meeting room making me your *ol' lady*?" she asked. Her heavy sarcasm smacked him right in the face.

"Need a ring to plant my seed in your belly, then yeah, I'll get you a ring."

She sighed. "Once again, super romantic. Especially if that was a proposal."

"Need flowers with that ring, I'll stop at the guy who sits at the corner of main an' third."

"The guy with the wilted roses?" Kiki laughed, reaching up to cup his cheek.

He turned his face into her palm and kissed it. "Need that shit?" he asked.

"Just need you."

"Just need you, too, babe." His eyes left hers and landed on the other side of the room. "Fuck," he muttered.

Hawk watched as a young, blonde, big-titted female came out of the alcove where the restrooms were, pulling down her miniskirt as she walked away in *way-too-high* heels. Hawk had seen her around church but didn't know her name. And with Kiki in his bed and heart, he didn't need to.

Two seconds later his brother followed, still buckling his belt, not paying attention to the hellcat that was about to launch a whole bunch of hurt on him when he least suspected it.

"Fucking beast!" Jewel said, loud enough that almost everyone in the large room heard her and became quiet.

"Jesus fuck," Hawk mumbled under his breath.

Diesel's head shot up, his eyes fell on Jewel and his face twisted into a mask of surprised annoyance. Without a word, he took two long strides to her, snagged her by the upper arm, yanked her off the stool and dragged her across the room as she bitched at him the whole way. His brother bound up the stairs two at a time, but not before tossing Jewel over his shoulder.

"Umm," Kiki murmured next to him. "Should we help her?"

Hawk turned his attention to his woman. "Nope."

"She going to be okay?"

"She is. Not sure about D, though."

"Oh."

Hawk shot her a grin. "Yeah, babe. That 'bout sums it up. Let's go home." The word "home" warmed his gut since his home now included Kiki permanently in it.

The only thing better would be to go home and find Jazz sitting on the couch, wearing her earbuds, eating nachos, kicking her feet up on the coffee table and giving them a big smile as they walked in the door.

Hawk didn't think that would happen any time soon. Or ever again.

As he wrapped his arm around Kiki and steered her toward the back door, he realized how lucky his woman had been.

She had proven how strong she was and he was proud of how well she'd dealt with the shit she'd been handed. She'd recovered better and faster than he could have ever guessed.

Now he was anxious to get home, strip her out of her *hot-as-fuck* work clothes, make her slide on her sexy glasses, let down her hair and watch her count every tattoo on his body. He'd make sure she'd miss one or two in her search and make her start all over again.

He grinned, dropped his hand down to her ass and squeezed.

He was one lucky fucker.

Sign up for Jeanne's newsletter to learn about her upcoming

Jeanne St. James

**releases, sales and more! http://www.jeannestjames.com/
newslettersignup**

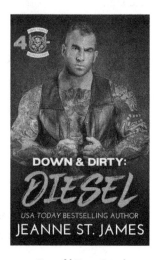

Down & Dirty: Diesel

*Welcome to Shadow Valley where the Dirty Angels MC rules. Get ready
to get Down & Dirty because this is Diesel's story...*

She calls him "The Beast."

Diesel, the MC's Sergeant at Arms and enforcer, is tasked with not
only keeping the club's property and its members safe, but also taking
care of "business" when needed. His motto, "live free, die free," means
he sees most women as nags and clingers and he wants none of that.
The last thing he needs is to have one sitting on the back of his bike
and trying to dictate his life.

Unlike the other DAMC women, Jewel wants to be an ol' lady. Being
born and raised within the club, her goal is to earn her place on back of
a brother's bike. But not just anyone's. No, she had to pick the biggest,

218

most pig-headed and quick-tempered of the bunch. The one she nick-named "The Beast," because that's how he acts both in and out of bed. She's wanted Diesel for so long she's not about to give up the fight to become his. She's bound and determined to win this battle one way or another.

Diesel fights his desire for Jewel until a rival MC threatens what he realizes is his, and no one gets away with that. No one.

Turn the page for a sneak peak of book four in the Dirty Angels MC series, *Down & Dirty: Diesel*

Down & Dirty: Diesel

Chapter One

DIESEL GROANED and rolled to the left, hitting a soft, naked body. The woman dropped to the floor with a squeal.

Shit.

He rolled to the right and hit another soft, naked body. That one fell to the floor with a yelp.

Fuck.

He kept rolling and knocked the third one out of his bed, too.

Jesus fuckin' Christ.

His bed at church was way too small for four people. What the fuck had he been thinking?

Fuck him, he hadn't.

A rustle of bodies in the dark, groans, grumblings and typical female bitching rose up.

"One of you bitches hit the light."

The room stilled and got quiet.

"Now!" he barked.

He heard scrambling, cursing and squeals from stubbed toes. Then the bare bulb in the broken light fixture over his bed blinded him.

A few seconds later, he sat up in the middle of his mattress while his gaze bounced from one of Dawg's new girls to the next. Three in total stood at the end of his bed blinking back at him like a bunch of brainless twats.

"Don't fuckin' just stand there, get dressed an' get gone."

"D..."

"No lip. Go."

The women quickly sorted through the piles of clothes and shoes on the floor, picking up pieces and handing them to their rightful owner. Occasionally they would sneak a peek at him and he'd growl back at them.

"Faster," he urged in a tone that encouraged no back talk.

Finally, when they were at least partially dressed, he pushed himself out of bed with a grunt, went to the door, opened it, and yelled, "Out!"

One by one they filed past him, still zipping, pulling and wiggling parts into place.

"Call me."

"It was fun."

"Anytime."

Fuck that. He slammed the door shut.

He fucked up royally by bringing them up to his room. He rarely did that. And he never fell asleep with anyone in his bed, either. *Ever*.

They got ideas if you did.

They were always looking for a way to dig their claws into you and drag your ass down. He'd never let that happen.

"Live free. Die free," was his motto right behind the club's "Down & Dirty 'til Dead."

He lumbered into his bathroom, scratching his balls. He took a piss, which luckily didn't burn, then checked for crabs.

He was the first one of the brothers to fuck those bitches, that's why he picked them. He wouldn't touch them again. Too risky.

He left the small bathroom and stepped over his own clothes, which were strewn all over the floor, to grab his cell phone from the nightstand. He pushed the power button to see the time.

4:33 AM.

Fuck, no wonder church sounded as quiet as a real church. The party was over. Everyone was passed out, asleep, had died or just simply left.

He picked up the box of condoms off the top of the scarred night-stand and peered inside.

Empty.

He glanced at the floor.

Damn.

He needed to get one of the sweet butts up there to pick up all the used condoms and discarded wrappers. She could do his laundry while she was at it. Because he'd let that go a little too long. He had more dirty clothes on the floor than he did clean shit in his dresser.

He was proud of himself, though. At almost thirty-three years old, he could still bang three women and last for hours. His endurance was legendary.

Yeah, in his own mind. He grunted.

Even so, he still had it. But he was getting too old for this shit.

These nameless, faceless fucks weren't satisfying him anymore. Yeah, they scratched an itch. But that was it. He saw what Z had with Sophie, Jag with Ivy, and now his brother, Hawk, with Kiki.

Hell, even what his father, Ace, had with his mother. Thirty-five years of marriage and they were still going strong. And they hadn't tried to kill each other yet, either.

What the fuck was he thinking? Was he getting soft like them?

Hell no.

Live free. Die free.

Fuck, it was supposed to be "Live free, ride free." *What-fucking-ever.*

He glanced at his phone again and realized he had a message.

Shit.

He hit the voicemail icon and put the phone to his ear. His blood ran cold when Jewel's voice came through the speaker.

"D... Fuck! Why aren't you answering? Damn it! This is the fifth time I'm calling. I need you to come get me. *Please.*"

Her voice didn't sound normal. That was not Jewel's typical smartass self. No, she sounded like she was in some sort of trouble.

Again.

And here she was calling the club's Sergeant at Arms, the enforcer, who was so busy fucking three cunts that he missed her calls.

Fuck!

Nothing had better have happened to her or he'd never forgive himself. He needed to find her and needed to do it now.

He hit the Send button on his phone and pressed it to his ear. She answered on the first ring.

"D." Her voice was breathless and low.

A prickle ran up his spine. "Where the fuck you at?"

"In the 'burgh. Come get me?" She was whispering.

"Why the fuck you whisperin'? What's goin' on?"

"I just need out of here."

"Where?"

"I'm at a... house."

His jaw got tight and a muscle ticked. "With who?"

"Nobody."

Fuckin' *nobody*. Bullshit. "This nobody drive your ass there?"

"Forget it, D... I'll call my brother."

"Address," he muttered.

"What?"

"Fuckin' address," he barked louder.

She gave it to him.

As he listened, he felt his blood start to boil. She was not in a good section of the city. And she was alone.

"Gonna beat your ass."

"I—"

He hit End. After finding his jeans, he yanked them up, threw on the nearest T-shirt, shrugged on his cut and tucked his phone into his back pocket. He sat on the edge of the bed after finding a half-decent clean pair of socks that didn't have any holes in them, tugged them on, then shoved his feet into his boots and zipped them up.

As he pushed to his feet and scrubbed a hand over the stubble on his chin, he realized he hadn't had a chance to wash the pussy off him.

Too fucking bad. If it bothered her, she could find another way home.

With a curse, he locked up his room and headed out.

———————

Jewel paced the dark sidewalk back and forth, pausing to listen carefully every few minutes.

Nothing.

It would soon be dawn and she should've been out of here a long time ago. In truth, she shouldn't have come here at all.

But she had been bored. She didn't want to go to the party at church last night and Kelsea convinced her the party she was headed to would be fun.

Little did she know, her club sister had a motive for coming to this party in the city. She'd been hanging with some questionable people lately. And she'd hooked up with a guy that was a DAMC hang-around. Plus, she said with the two of them there, they could keep an ear open for any activity of the Shadow Warriors. Maybe hear where that asshole former prospect Squirrel and his buddy Black Jack were hiding out.

As Jewel had mingled with a much younger crowd than her, her first clue she shouldn't have agreed to come was that she suddenly found herself deserted there alone. And most of the party attendees ended up either drunk, high on drugs, or both.

Not her scene. She gave up that kind of partying years ago. Not that she was old. At twenty-eight she still liked to party. But being at a house in a questionable part of the city with no vehicle, and surrounded by a bunch of wasted twenty-one and -two-year-olds had her really rethinking her choices.

So, here she was outside a rowhome waiting for Diesel to come "save" her.

He would be pissed but that was nothing new for the club enforcer. Still, as the club's Sergeant at Arms, it was his duty to protect and take care of her.

Or that's what she wanted to believe. She wasn't so sure Diesel would agree. Maybe on the protect part. But that's where he'd insist it ended.

He was too busy being a walking, talking—no, that wasn't right —*grunting* testosterone-filled beast, to worry about taking care of anyone but himself. And by "taking care of" she meant sticking his dick in every conscious vagina he could find.

Every vagina but hers.

"Hey, baby."

Jewel jumped as a male voice she didn't recognize drifted her direction. She looked around but couldn't see anybody or even any movement. The hair on the back of her neck stood up.

D, hurry up.

"You out here by yourself? You need a friend?"

The voice came closer and Jewel's heart began to race. She squinted, trying to get a bead on who the voice belonged to.

"No. I'm good. My man's coming to pick me up."

"He stood you up, baby. I'm here for you, though."

She patted at her jeans' pockets hoping a knife or some sort of weapon would magically appear.

She was going to kill Kelsea.

"Just so you know, he's really jealous. He'll kick your ass for just talking to me."

A shadow moved between two of the cars that were parked along the curb.

"Is that right?"

"Yeah."

"Then we should go somewhere he can't find us."

Holy fucking shit!

Why didn't she ever take a self-defense course? The only thing she knew how to do was kick a guy in the gonads, scratch his eyes out... or call Diesel.

Fuck my life.

She looked down at her fashionable high-heeled boots. She couldn't run in those things. She could hardly even walk in them.

They were strictly for looking good and making her legs look hellishly long.

Which they did. But that wasn't going to help her out right now.

The shadow moved again and Jewel bit back a scream. She couldn't act afraid, she had to act fearless.

Right.

"Whoever you are, get gone!" she yelled, bracing her feet wide apart.

"Really, baby, you don't want me to do that. We can have some fun."

"Not looking for fun," she said firmly, hoping she sounded like the tough biker bitch she was.

Riiiiight.

"I am."

"My man's a mean biker, he'll kick your ass." Silence. Which made the skin on the back of her neck prickle. "He's huge, too. Killed a man."

Oh, Jesus. If someone told her that, *she'd* be the one rolling her eyes.

Jewel let out a yelp when the male voice came way too close to her ear and a hand wrapped around her bicep. "Well, we won't tell him."

"The fuck I won't!" she yelled desperately. The guy wore a baseball hat and it was too dark to see his features. She yanked at her arm, but he wouldn't let go.

No shit.

"Got a place we can go."

"I'm fine where I'm at," she assured him, trying to keep her voice steady since she was starting to unravel. This shit was getting serious. She yanked at her arm again. "Let me go!"

Suddenly, she was yanked so hard that she found herself off balance and tumbled backwards, landing on her ass. All the oxygen escaped her lungs in a *whoosh*.

"Get up, bitch." The guy pulled at her.

She pulled back. "Fuck you."

He pulled her harder. "Get the fuck up!"

"No!"

She needed to get a good kick in with her high-heeled boots right in his dick. Then he'd leave her alone. Once he was down, she'd sink one of those heels right into his eye socket.

That'd teach him to fuck with her.

She yelped again as he grabbed her hair and began to drag her over the ground.

Her arms started flying as she tried to whack any part of his body she could make contact with. Which wasn't much.

Jesus. She really needed to learn self-defense.

Then she heard the roar of the straight exhaust pipes and relief flowed through her. When the single headlight came at them at a high rate of speed, the relief quickly fled. She was going to get run over.

She squeezed her eyes shut as the sled came to a sliding stop inches from them, the man was off the motorcycle and the guy who was trying to drag her away was no longer moving.

Face meet fist.

He was now flat out on his back, groaning. Even in the dark, Jewel knew Diesel was furious. She could feel the waves of controlled rage rolling off him. Good thing it wasn't directed at her.

"What the fuck you doin'?" D bellowed, grabbing her by the arm and hauling her to her feet.

"Me?" she squeaked.

"Yeah, fuckin' you!" In the glow of the headlight, she didn't miss him checking her out head to toe. "What the fuck you wearin'? Jesus fuckin' Christ."

Jewel yanked her short skirt down, since in the tussle it had ridden up to her crotch. Good thing she had thrown on some panties before she left her apartment.

"You gotta be fuckin' kiddin' me. Your fuckin' ass in a bad section of town, wearing that fuckin' bullshit?"

Jesus. She had thought she'd looked nice. Hot, even.

Diesel stalked back over to the man on the ground, who was still groaning, holding onto his face, but trying to get to his knees.

D pointed his finger her direction but was talking to the guy. Well, not actually talking, more like bellowing in a scary fashion. "You see this bitch again, run the other direction, got me? Not walk. Run. Otherwise, huntin' your ass down. Got me?"

The man put up his hand in surrender, then pushed shakily to his feet.

"Now, get gone!" D yelled so loudly even Jewel winced.

The man quickly stumbled away and once he was out of sight, D's head swung in her direction.

Uh oh.

"Jesus fuckin' Christ. How many times do I gotta bail your ass out of a jam, woman? How many?" He stalked over to her, grabbed her upper arm firmly and steered her toward his bike.

She yanked at her arm. "I should've called Jag."

He didn't release her until they stood next to his Harley. "Yeah, right. Do that next time. Sick of this shit."

Grumble. Grumble. Grumble. Jewel frowned. The man was nothing but a Debbie Downer.

"How long you been out here?

She shrugged. "A while."

"Ever think of callin' a taxi?"

"My wallet was in..." *Shit.*

He eyeballed her. "In?"

"The car," she finished reluctantly.

"Whose car?"

Her mouth twisted.

With a curse, he mounted his bike. "Get on my sled. Discussin' this somewhere other than here."

"D, I don't think I can straddle the bike in my skirt."

"Take it off."

Her eyes bugged out. "What?"

"Take. It. Off."

"I'm only wearing a thong," she whispered.

He dropped his head and stared at his boot for a second, then two, then for more than thirty seconds.

Finally, with a tight jaw, he shrugged his cut off his shoulders, ripped his T-shirt over his head and without even looking at her, held it out. "Put it on. Take that shit off, then burn it. Don't want to see you in that again."

There was no way she was burning her skirt. It was cute and she looked good in it. She just wouldn't wear it to church. Or the garage. Or in front of Diesel.

With a sigh, she plucked the oversized tee from his fingers, yanked it over her head and then, after unzipping it, she shimmied out of her skirt. His T-shirt was so big she felt like she was wearing a muu-muu. It covered her practically to her knees.

She wrinkled her nose. And it smelled funky. She couldn't quite place it.

"You done?"

"Yeah," she answered.

"Then why we still sittin' here?"

After a slight hesitation, she climbed on behind him, grabbing onto his thick waist over his leather vest, which he had shrugged back on over his bare torso.

Well, his anger would have to keep him warm on the ride back, she thought. At least she had his shirt covering her formerly bare legs since the nights were starting to cool down as they approached the end of summer.

"Gotta hold tighter than that, woman. Otherwise, your ass is gonna be on the pavement."

With a sigh, Jewel wrapped her arms as much as she could around his waist and pressed her cheek to his back. She jerked her head back. She finally recognized the smell. "You and your shirt smell like pussy."

"Yep. Shit you get when you call me in the middle of the night."

"It's morning."

"Like I said, middle of the fuckin' night." He kicked his starter and the bike roared to life, his straight pipes rumbling through the city streets, echoing off the row homes.

Get *Down & Dirty: Diesel* here:
mybook.to/DAMC-Diesel

If You Enjoyed This Book

Thank you for reading Down & Dirty: Hawk. If you enjoyed Hawk and Kiki's story, please consider leaving a review at your favorite retailer and/or Goodreads to let other readers know. Reviews are always appreciated and just a few words can help an independent author like me tremendously!

Bear's Family Tree

		ZAK Jamison DAMC (President)
	MITCH Jamison Blue Avengers MC	AXEL Jamison Blue Avengers MC
BEAR Jamison DAMC Founder		JAYDE Jamison
		JEWEL Jamison
	ROCKY Jamison DAMC	DIAMOND Jamison
		JAG Jamison DAMC (Road Captain)

Doc's Family Tree

		DIESEL Dougherty DAMC (Enforcer)
	ACE Dougherty DAMC (Treasurer)	HAWK Dougherty DAMC (Vice President)
DOC Dougherty DAMC Founder		DEX Dougherty DAMC (Secretary)
	ALLIE Dougherty	IVY Doughtery
		ISABELLA McBride
	ANNIE Dougherty	KELSEA Dougherty

Also by Jeanne St. James

Find my complete reading order here:
https://www.jeannestjames.com/reading-order

Blood & Bones: Blood Fury MC®

A twelve-book motorcycle club series

Motorcycle Club Crossovers:

Crossing the Line: A DAMC/Blue Avengers MC Crossover

Magnum: A Dark Knights MC/Dirty Angels MC Crossover

Crash: A Dirty Angels MC/Blood Fury MC Crossover

Beyond the Badge: Blue Avengers MC™

A six-book law enforcement/motorcycle club series

COMING SOON!

Double D Ranch (An MMF Ménage Series)

Dirty Angels MC®: The Next Generation

WRITING AS J.J. MASTERS:

The Royal Alpha Series

A five-book gay mpreg shifter series

About the Author

JEANNE ST. JAMES is a USA Today and international bestselling romance author who loves an alpha male (or two). She writes steamy contemporary M/F and M/M romance, as well as M/M/F ménages, and has published over 63 books (so far) in five languages. She also writes M/M paranormal romance under the name: J.J. Masters.

Want to read a sample of her work? Download a sampler book here: BookHip.com/MTQQKK

To keep up with her busy release schedule check her website at www.-jeannestjames.com or sign up for her newsletter: http://www.jeannest james.com/newslettersignup

www.jeannestjames.com
jeanne@jeannestjames.com

Newsletter: http://www.jeannestjames.com/newslettersignup
Jeanne's Down & Dirty Book Crew: https://www.facebook.com/groups/JeannesReviewCrew/
TikTok: https://www.tiktok.com/@jeannestjames

facebook.com/JeanneStJamesAuthor

amazon.com/author/jeannestjames

instagram.com/JeanneStJames

bookbub.com/authors/jeanne-st-james

goodreads.com/JeanneStJames

pinterest.com/JeanneStJames

Get a FREE Sampler Book

This book contains the first chapter of a variety of my books. This will give you a taste of the type of books I write and if you enjoy the first chapter, I hope you'll be interested in reading the rest of the book.

Each book I list in the sampler will include the description of the book, the genre, and the first chapter, along with links to find out more. I hope you find a book you will enjoy curling up with!

Get it here: BookHip.com/MTQQKK

Printed in the USA
CPSIA information can be obtained
at www.ICGtesting.com
LVHW072144170923
758470LV00033B/284

9 781954 684690